EDGE OF NIGHT

SHADOW SECURITY BOOK TWO

RAMONA GRAY

EK PUBLISHING INC.

EDGE OF NIGHT

Will fear determine her fate?

The moment the kind and beautiful Daisy Martin applies at Shadow Security, lion shifter, Cooper Brooks, wants to make her his mate.

Except she's terrified of shifters.

Daisy will never be his mate, but Cooper's lion refuses to accept defeat. With his human and lion sides at odds, Cooper creeps toward madness.

Wanting a normal life, Daisy accepts the job for the money and her last-ditch effort to overcome her trauma. She doesn't have to be friends with them, she just needs to overcome her fear.

But she never expects her boss, a large, tattooed, and certified badass lion shifter, to have such a soft and protective side. With patience and persistence, Cooper shreds her fears one by one, and when she realizes that only she can save him from insanity, their connection grows.

But when she's caught between a dangerous cheetah

shifter and his intended victim, Daisy confronts her biggest fear.

With Cooper's help, can she conquer the shifter and her past?

———————

CHAPTER 1

"Are you fucking kidding me?" Cooper's voice echoed in the empty room. He didn't give in to his desire to simply slam his fist on his laptop, but it was a hard-won battle.

His lion barely moved within him. Normally if Cooper was pissed, his lion was automatically pissed too. But ever since he'd been shot three days ago trying to save his best friend, his lion had been… weird. Cooper wanted to chalk it up to the whole being shot thing, but he'd been shot before and it had barely affected his lion at all.

Using his left hand, he scratched clumsily at the beard on his throat. It was years since he'd gone longer than a couple days without shaving and his skin was already irritated and red. But it was bad enough that Wes would be helping him shower tonight, he wouldn't ask him to shave him too.

He stopped scratching his irritated skin and switched to gingerly massaging his arm above the sling. After three days, he was ready to toss the sling and give using his right hand a go. It was bullshit trying to do everything with his left hand and he was over it.

He stared at his laptop, the automatic update that had started and cost him an entire two hours worth of work making his temper rise again. When the fuck would he ever remember to save the document he was working on? Daisy had reminded him numerous times to stop every twenty minutes or so and save his work, but did he? Of course he fucking didn't.

Not even the mention of the receptionist at Cooper's security firm stirred his lion. The beginnings of panic unfurled in his belly. Deep down he knew exactly what his lion's apathy was about, but he had no idea what to do about it.

He couldn't demand his lion stop believing that Daisy was his mate, just like he couldn't demand Daisy to stop being terrified of him and his lion.

She's afraid of all shifters, not just us, his lion growled.

At least that had stirred his lion out of his funk a little. It was right. Daisy wasn't just afraid of Cooper - she was terrified of all shifters. Which made her decision to interview for a job at a security firm where she would be the only human just that much weirder.

Why would a human afraid of shifters want to work with them?

He had no idea and in the three months that Daisy had worked for him, he still hadn't figured it out.

You should never have hired her.

Fuck, wasn't that the truth. He one hundred percent agreed with his inner voice, but his lion... for one of the few times in Cooper's life, his lion had surged forward in the interview and taken control, hiring the tiny auburn-haired human before Cooper could regain control.

From the moment Daisy had walked into his office for the receptionist interview, so terrified she could barely speak, his lion had claimed her as his mate. Cooper had denied it for the last three months, but after what happened a few days ago, he couldn't deny it anymore.

Doesn't matter. We scared her. Our mate is afraid of us and she'll never come near us again.

His lion's whimper made goosebumps break out on his skin and a wave of depression washed over him.

It was true. He'd lost control and almost shifted in front of Daisy and that was enough for him to lose her forever.

She was never ours.

His lion whimpered again at his inner voice. Normally it would have been angry and lashing out, and the whimpering and depression was setting Cooper's nerves on edge.

We'll go into the office tomorrow so you can see her, okay? he said to his lion.

It was too soon to go into the office. His arm was still throbbing and aching. Trying to work on the report from home today had exhausted him, but his lion going insane wasn't exactly an option.

When his lion made a listless growl in response, Cooper's unease intensified.

"Snap out of it!" he growled to the empty room. "Stop being such a fucking baby about it. She's not our goddamn mate."

Shit. Now his lion was giving him the silent treatment. In frustration, Cooper slammed his hand on the desk, making the picture to the left of the laptop fall off the desk. It hit the hardwood, the telltale sounds of glass breaking made him pinch the bridge of his nose and close his eyes in defeat.

He pushed back from the desk, grabbed the small trash can under it, and walked to the front of the desk. He squatted and flipped the frame over. Jagged pieces of glass littered the floor and he picked them up with his left hand, tossing them into the trash can.

Jesus, he was having a fuck of a day and if –

The front doorbell rang, making him jerk and then hiss with pain when the piece of glass he was reaching for sliced his finger. Blood dripped out of his finger, and he growled at the sharp pain.

"Are you fucking kidding me?" he muttered. "Jesus Christ, Wes, you have a goddamn key. Let yourself in."

Shit, the blood was really flowing now. Holding his hand over the garbage can to try and minimize the mess, he made another low growl when the doorbell rang again.

"Use your key!" he shouted as he stood and grabbed some tissues off the desk. He used the fingers of his right hand to wrap the tissue around his left fingers, muttering a curse when even that small movement made his injured shoulder throb. Leaving the mess of glass and blood on the floor, he left the office. He needed to get the goddamn first-aid kit before he got blood all over his fucking office.

The doorbell rang a third time as he was headed toward the bathroom. With an irritated snarl, he turned around and stomped toward the front door. He flipped the lock, ignoring the pain in his finger and the blood smeared on the lock, and turned the handle, yanking the door open.

"For fuck's sake, Wes, why aren't you using your…"

His breath caught in his throat. His lion sat up and busted out an excited roar before purring so loudly, Cooper could barely hear the traffic going by on the street.

He stared silently at the small auburn-haired woman standing on his front porch with the scent of her fear rolling off of her in heavy waves.

Cooper swallowed hard. "Daisy? What are you doing here?"

OKAY, SO VOLUNTEERING TO CHECK ON COOPER TONIGHT after Wes got sidetracked at a job, was the worst mistake of her life. Her very short life, if the anger in Cooper's eyes was any indication.

Daisy told herself to flee, told herself to haul ass back to her car, but, like always when she was confronted with an angry shifter, she was immediately paralyzed with fear.

"Daisy? What are you doing here?"

The anger in Cooper's gaze had already faded. He sniffed the air, his face twisted like he'd eaten a lemon, and he took a step back. The added space gave her the confidence to breathe again. She sucked in a breath, hoping she didn't look like she was about two minutes away from wetting her pants.

"It's okay, Daisy," Cooper said in that low and cautious voice he often used with her. The one that said, *this chick be straight up crazy.*

"It's okay," he repeated. "I won't hurt you."

"I... I know," she said even though that was a bold-faced lie. The way her entire body was trembling made it more than obvious she was lying.

"Is there a problem at the office?" Cooper said.

He did that a lot. Changed the subject from her obvious fear, pretended like he couldn't smell her terror or see the way she was on the verge of bolting if only she could get her frozen legs to carry her.

She didn't mind. In fact, she appreciated it. Cooper ignoring her debilitating fear often made it ease a little, which she supposed was strange if she really thought about it, but any port in a storm, right?

"No. Wes got stuck with a client and I offered to check on you tonight and, uh, help you with stuff."

That stuff included helping Cooper shower. Wes had been totally blunt about that, and she had pretended on the phone when he called into the office like it was no big deal. Had pretended like seeing her boss naked for a second time in less than a week was absolutely normal. She didn't relish the idea of seeing Cooper naked, but he had saved her from that horrible jaguar shifter, and she owed him.

Please, girl, like you don't want another glimpse of that hard, tattooed body and giant dick of his.

Her face got hot and her neck got itchy and her fear disappeared under a wave of embarrassment. She'd only gotten a glimpse of Cooper's penis before he'd covered up, but it'd been more than enough for her to see exactly how large he was.

And you gave him a glimpse of how tiny your tits were.

More heat flooded her face and she resisted the urge to fan herself. Cooper had been bleeding badly from the shoulder and she needed something to stem the blood before he bled out. She'd had to take off her shirt, giving him a view of her boobs in their boring beige bra in the process.

"Wes had to work late?" Cooper was still blocking the doorway with his big body, confusion on his face, and blood dripping from his hand, and ... wait, blood?

"You're bleeding," she said.

He glanced at his hand. "Yeah, I cut myself on some glass."

"It's bleeding a lot," she said. "Do you need stitches?"

"Nah, I'll put a Band-aid on it."

If the blood dripping onto the front porch from the soaked tissue wrapped around his finger was any indication, it needed a lot more than a Band-aid.

"I can help you," she said.

"That's okay," he said. "I appreciate you stopping by, but my arm is better. I can handle things."

Stupidly, she felt a little hurt by his obvious desire for her

6

to leave. Cooper had always been nice to her. In fact, he was probably the best boss she'd ever had, and he'd never once made her feel stupid about her fear of him and everyone else in the office.

Also, he's, like, a great kisser. Right?

She skittered away from that thought immediately. She wouldn't – couldn't – think about kissing Cooper. Not when half an hour after kissing her, he'd almost shifted in a parking lot and scared the bejeezus out of her.

He hadn't meant to scare her, she *knew* that, but it didn't negate the fact that she'd been terrified when he'd started swelling and growing hair and threatening to kill the jaguar.

"Do you?" she said. "It's only been three days and you're right handed. How are you going to cook dinner?"

"I'll order in," he said.

"How will you fix that?" She pointed to his finger.

"It'll be fine," he said. "Talk to you later, Daisy."

"I want to help you," she said. "Please let me."

Weird laughter was bubbling up in her chest. Was she actually begging to be allowed into the – literal and figurative – lion's den?

The pupils of his eyes turned to slits as he went inward and spoke to his lion. Just seeing his pupils go from round to slit, the startling blue of his eyes beginning to turn yellow, brought fresh fear to her belly.

She made herself breathe her way through it, repeated, *he'll never hurt you*, a half dozen times in her head while Cooper talked to his lion.

"I don't want to frighten you," he said. His eyes were back to normal and a heavy layer of guilt covered his face.

It was one of the few times he'd directly mentioned her fear and she hated the shame she felt about being so afraid. "I appreciate that, but, uh, I'm good."

She wasn't good, not by a long shot, but she needed to do this. Not only because she felt the need to repay Cooper for saving her, but because it would be good for her. Being alone with a shifter in his house was a major step toward conquering her fear.

"I appreciate the offer, but I don't think it's a good idea," Cooper said.

"I know you don't, but I'll feel terrible if my boss bleeds to death on the night I said I would check in on him. Pretty sure Wes would fire me if that happened."

His face relaxed the tiniest bit. "It would be Grayson who did the firing. He's next in line for running the office."

She smiled at him and it almost felt natural. "Let me come in and help you with your hand, okay? If it's, uh, too much for me, I'll leave and let you fend for yourself. Deal?"

His pupils turned to slits for about ten seconds before they flipped to normal and he nodded. "Deal."

This is a very bad idea.

Now that it was actually going to happen, her inner voice had completely changed her tune.

Please don't go in there, Daisy. Please. We can't be alone with him.

We've been alone with him before, she said to inner Daisy.

Not like this. Not in his house where he could trap us and scare us and-and hurt us. No one will hear us scream. Is that what you want? To die like Josh did, in a puddle of our own piss and blood? Please, don't do this. He's not good. No shifter is. We're going to die.

He won't hurt us.

"No, I won't. Ever." Cooper said.

Shit! She'd spoken the words out loud... what was wrong with her?

She swallowed hard. "I know."

Cooper studied her for a few seconds before backing into the house until he was standing at the far end of the hallway. Light spilled out from the open doorway to his right, accentuating the way his shaggy blond hair stuck up from his head at odd angles. The poor guy really did need to shower. She took a deep breath and stepped across the threshold, shutting the door behind her.

Trapped!

His nostrils flaring, Cooper took another step back. He looked uncomfortable and nervous, and she suddenly hated herself for making such a nice man feel bad.

He's not nice! He's a shifter!

She let the anger at being such a chickenshit fill her up a little, pushing out some of the fear until she felt a semblance of normal. "Where's your first-aid kit?"

"In the bathroom upstairs," he said.

"Go sit down at the table before you pass out from blood loss," she said. "I'll grab the kit."

"Sure." He disappeared into the open doorway and she made herself take the first few steps. It got easier with each step and she glanced into the room to her right as she passed by. She could see the broken glass gleaming in the sunlight on the floor in front of the desk as well as some splashes of drying blood.

She passed the kitchen, satisfied when she saw Cooper sitting at the table like she'd asked, and climbed the stairs at the end of the hallway.

"First door on the right," Cooper called. "The kit's under the sink."

She stepped into the mid-size bathroom and squatted next to the cabinet. She grabbed the kit tucked neatly next to the pipes and then stood and checked her reflection in the mirror.

Her face was a little red, but she didn't have a look of terror in her eyes, so she called it a win and left the bathroom, standing at the top of the staircase for a moment.

She was alone in the house of a powerful shifter who could kill her with a flick of his fingers.

No big deal.

She could do this.

CHAPTER 2

Daisy's inner voice had apparently given up on trying to convince her that she was going to die. It was weirdly silent, and that was freaking her out a little. She stepped into the kitchen and set the kit on the table before opening it.

She rummaged through it and pulled out a non-stick bandage, medical tape, a couple packets of antiseptic wipes, and a package of steri-strips.

Cooper sat perfectly still at the table, his admittedly very pretty blue eyes watching her as she laid out the supplies in a neat row.

Ignoring the herd of rhinos stampeding through her stomach, she said, "Ready?"

He nodded and held out his hand. She unwrapped the tissue from around his finger. She winced when it stuck to the cut, but Cooper didn't flinch. It had started to clot, and she studied the slice in his finger before glancing up at him.

"I think you actually might need stitches."

"Just put some steri-strips on it. It'll be fine," he said.

She wanted to argue but what if that upset him and he got angry with her?

She ripped open an antiseptic wipe and carefully cleaned up the blood all around the cut before using a second one to get the smears she missed with the first one.

His hands were warm and rough feeling. The hands of a guy who worked in construction instead of an office.

As if he'd read her mind, he said, "I've been helping Boone restore his house."

"That's nice of you." She mentally cheered at how normal she sounded.

She pushed together the edges of the cut, glancing up at Cooper when he hissed out a breath.

"Sorry," he said, like it was his fault she was hurting him.

"I'm almost done. Hang in there." She applied the steri-strips, then placed the non-stick bandage on top of it and taped it into place.

"Thank you, Daisy."

"You're welcome."

He scratched at the red and irritated skin on his neck with his left hand.

"Be careful," she said. "You don't want your finger to start bleeding again."

"Yeah," he said before scratching again anyway. "I'm not used to being unshaven, so my skin is bugging me."

She cleaned up the wrappers and the bloody wipes, putting them in the garbage can at the far end of the kitchen. Cooper's kitchen was nice, maybe a little on the messy side, but the guy was down an arm at the moment. She wouldn't be putting the dishes in the dishwasher either if she'd been shot in the shoulder.

"If you tell me where the broom and dustpan are, I'll clean up the glass in your office," she said.

"You don't have to do that. I'll clean it up later," Cooper said.

She pointed to his bandaged finger. "Maybe you shouldn't risk it. You keep this up and Wes won't only have to make you dinner, he'll be spoon feeding you too."

A grin crossed Cooper's face and her breath caught in her throat. Not from fear this time – oh no, this was something else. Something that felt a little like lust. Which was absolutely ridiculous because as good of a kisser as Cooper was, she would never want any shifter in a sexual way. Ever. The day he'd kissed her, when she'd felt the same tingling in her lower belly and in her nipples that she felt now, that wasn't lust either. That was just a... weird type of fear.

"Broom and dustpan are in the front closet. Thank you."

"You're welcome. I'll be right back."

She grabbed the broom and dustpan as well as a large garbage bag from the closet. She placed the broken picture frame on the desk and quickly cleaned up the glass and dried blood. When the floor was spotless and glass free, she tied the garbage bag and set it on the floor before glancing at the doorway.

It was empty and she picked up the picture frame and studied it. It was a picture of Cooper, Grayson, Boone, and Wes, as well as a man she didn't recognize. They were standing in a row in some hot and dusty desert. Their arms were slung around each other's shoulders, their military fatigues were dirty, and the dog tags around their necks glinted in the hot sun.

She knew they'd been in the military together. Knew that Cooper had left and then started Shadow Security, knew that one by one the others had left the military and joined him. But she didn't know who the fifth man was, the one standing next to Boone with laughing brown eyes and a recklessness to him that radiated out from just the picture.

She turned her gaze back to Cooper, studying each feature

of his face before tracing it with her finger. He looked every bit the leader in the photo that he was, and a shiver went down her back. For all his kindness toward her, for how attuned he seemed to be to her fear, she couldn't forget that he was a killer. All the shifters were. It was in their nature.

Grayson, a tiger shifter who worked at the firm and was Cooper's best friend, had just, in fact, killed a human.

Because he went after the woman Grayson loved. You can't blame him for that. The human was crazy and would have killed Grayson's mate. Remember when Cooper gave you that amazing kiss, and then called you his mate and almost killed that jaguar? Same thing.

Her inner voice was back and, like she did a lot as of late, was vacillating between trying to convince Daisy that Cooper was gonna kill her and reminding her that Cooper was a really great kisser.

It was enough to drive a person crazy.

She set the photo frame down and picked up the garbage bag, carrying it back to the kitchen and placing it in the garbage can.

"Thank you, Daisy. I appreciate you cleaning that up," Cooper said.

"It's no problem. Do you mind if I grab some water?"

"Not at all. There's bottled water in the fridge."

She grabbed two bottles of water and opened the first one, handing it to Cooper who said, "Thank you."

He tilted his head back to drink, and she winced at how red and irritated his throat was. She drank some water and capped the bottle before clearing her throat. "So, do you want to start with dinner or a shower?"

THE WATER EXPLODED FROM COOPER'S MOUTH WITH THE force of a geyser. He gasped for air and unfortunately sucked more water into his lungs. He coughed and choked as Daisy patted his back. He hacked out another harsh bout of coughing that sent fire radiating from his shoulder down his arm. He groaned and grabbed at his arm through the sling as he coughed and coughed again.

Daisy's small hand touched his right forearm, touched and then pressed firmly, stabilizing his arm against his chest as he coughed. It helped a surprising amount. He covered his mouth with his left hand and coughed up the remaining water in his lungs.

He drew in a ragged, whistling breath and Daisy used her other hand to rub his back. "You okay?"

"Yeah," he croaked. He wasn't. His shoulder was throbbing and burning. He glanced at the pain meds sitting on the counter. He hadn't taken any today because they made his lion side slow and uncoordinated, and his human side say stupid shit.

Last night, Boone had stopped in after work with pizza. He'd taken one look at Cooper's pale and sweaty face and made him take a couple pills. Half an hour later, Cooper was babbling about his secret love for romantic comedies and exactly why they were the perfect movies before he'd revealed his stash of over a hundred romantic comedies downloaded on his laptop. The last thing he remembered before the meds knocked him out was making Boone lay in bed with him and watch *When Harry met Sally* on his laptop.

Maybe that's why Wes sent Daisy in his place? Boone probably told him all about your goddamn romantic comedy love.

He scratched at his throat. Boone would fucking ride his ass forever about the romantic comedy shit.

His lion had started purring the second Daisy rubbed his back and, too busy thinking about romantic comedies and how much his shoulder hurt, he hadn't even tried to hold it in. He realized that the kitchen practically vibrated with the sound of his purring.

He swallowed the sound, ignoring his lion's growl of disapproval, and cleared his throat. "Sorry."

"Is your arm okay?" Daisy stopped rubbing his back and stepped away. His lion whined in protest.

"Yeah," he lied.

She studied him before glancing at the pain meds sitting on the counter. "When can you have your pills again?"

"Anytime," he said. "I haven't taken any yet today."

An adorable scowl crossed her adorable face. "You shouldn't do that, Cooper. I know you're tough but there's a reason you were given pain meds."

She thinks we're tough!

His idiot lion was strutting and purring and asking him to shift so he could mark her. He almost laughed out loud. The idea of shifting in front of Daisy was so ridiculous, it bordered on insanity. She would freak the fuck out if she ever saw him in his lion form.

That hurt his lion's feelings and the damn thing made a pathetic whimper before retreating. He wanted to soothe it but talking to his lion was a mistake around Daisy – a mistake he'd already made twice in the last half hour. It made her nervous when he spoke to his lion, and he usually tried hard not to do it in front of her.

"So, do you want to eat first, or do you want to shower first?" Daisy said.

"I don't need to shower," he said.

"Wes said you did."

"Wes was wrong."

"You don't smell like he was wrong," Daisy said.

He flushed, and the scent of her embarrassment washed over him. "I'm sorry. That was rude. But Wes did mention that you haven't been able to shower since you left the hospital and that's over three days. You must want a shower."

"I do," he admitted.

"Okay, well, let me help you."

His lion sat up, purring and preening and acting like he thought Daisy might take one look at his naked body and fuck him in the shower.

His cock stirred in his track pants and he gritted his teeth. Yeah, the shower thing was definitely not happening. If Daisy touched him, started bathing his naked body like Florence fucking Nightingale, he would immediately spring a fucking woody. She'd take one look at his erection and run screaming – right after she told him she quit, that was.

"No," he said.

The look of exasperation on her face was kind of cute. Especially since it was usually fear. It reminded him of how she'd looked when he made her stay in his truck while he tried to save Grayson and Ryan from that insane jaguar bitch who was holding them hostage. Daisy had been pissed that he wouldn't let her help.

Maybe the key to her getting over her fear of him was to constantly piss her off?

Yeah, smart plan, Einstein.

"It's no big deal," she said.

"Maybe to you," he said. "But I've never let an employee see me naked and I'm not starting now."

"I've already seen you naked," she said.

His blush burned brighter. She'd ignored his instructions to stay in the truck and had shown up while he was lying naked and bleeding on the floor.

His gaze dropped to her perfect tits. She'd whipped off her shirt and used it to stem the blood flowing from his shoulder. He could still remember how pale and silky soft her skin had looked. How absolutely perfect her breasts had looked even in the ugly beige bra she was wearing.

He made himself look away from her chest before he really did spring a woody. "Only briefly and only because you didn't do what I told you to do."

She scowled at him again. "You're only the boss of me during work hours."

"It was during work hours," he said.

She blew out her breath in another exasperated sigh. "You were shot and needed my help."

"It was dangerous, and you could have been hurt."

"So you keep saying. Except here I am, perfectly fine, and here you are, in a sling and needing help to shower."

He wanted to scowl at her but secretly he was enjoying this feisty side of Daisy. It was a welcome change from her usual fear.

"I'm sorry," he said, "but I'm not comfortable with you helping me shower."

"Okay, that's fair." She traced the tips of her fingers over the long scar that ran along her forearm. She did that whenever she was thinking, and he found it utterly enchanting.

Of course, he found everything Daisy did enchanting.

"You really only need help with getting your sling and shirt on and off, right?" she said. "Like, if you had to, you could wash your hair and body with your left hand. It would be awkward but doable."

"Yeah," he said.

"Okay, well, I'll help you with that stuff, turn the shower on for you, make sure you can reach the soap and shampoo and then leave you to it. Deal?"

He scratched at his throat. "Deal."

"Okay. Are you good with the shower first and then I'll cook you dinner?"

"Sure." He stood and acutely aware of how good she smelled, he left the kitchen. She followed him upstairs to his bedroom.

He cleared his throat. "Uh, it's kind of messy."

"That's okay," she said. "I won't judge."

He pushed open the door with his left hand, wishing he'd at least picked up his clothes off the floor. His bedroom wasn't a pigsty, but he did have quite the pile of dirty clothes and he hadn't made his bed.

"This is nice," she said.

Her fear was back. He could smell it covering her like a wet blanket. He automatically moved away from her. Being alone with him in his bedroom would obviously terrify her. Why was he so fucking stupid? He should have used the guest bathroom instead of the one off his bedroom.

"We can use the other bathroom," he said. "I'll need to grab my shampoo and some soap from this bathroom."

She was standing near the door, her arms folded across her torso and her fingers tracing the scar on her forearm. She took a deep breath and gave him an approximation of a smile. "Don't be silly. This one is fine."

He studied her for a few seconds, and she made a 'go on' motion with her hand. He headed into the bathroom, honestly surprised when she joined him. He didn't think she'd be able to stand in the small room with him, and a trickle of pride went through him at how brave she was being.

Our mate isn't brave yet, but we'll take care of her until she is.

He ignored his lion. Daisy wasn't their mate, no matter how much his lion thought she was.

He scratched again at his throat and Daisy said, "Did you want me to set up your shaving supplies for you first?"

"No," he said. "Shaving with my left hand isn't a good idea." Although he was seriously considering giving it a try. The itching was driving him crazy.

"I can shave you," Daisy said.

He jerked in surprise and his sudden movement made her cringe and back away. The smell of her fear thickened, and he decided now was the perfect time to put his newfound knowledge to use. He'd annoy her into forgetting her fear.

"No offense," he said, "but women can't shave a man properly. You'll either not get a close enough shave or you'll shave off the skin. I like it exactly where it is – covering my throat."

The scent of her fear turned to astonishment and then, he grinned inwardly, to annoyance.

"Cooper Brooks that is the most sexist thing you've ever said."

He shrugged. "Men are better at shaving than women. Well, maybe not legs, but definitely faces."

She gave him a huffy look. "Oh, that's it. Sit down on the toilet. You're getting a shave whether you like it or not."

When he didn't move, she stepped closer and poked him lightly in the chest. "Sit your butt down."

"Yes, ma'am," he said.

He closed the lid with his left hand and sat on the toilet, watching as she picked up the shaving cream and squirted a healthy dollop into her hand. When she moved toward him, he opened his legs. His lion purred like an idiot when Daisy stepped between them without hesitating.

She smoothed a layer of shaving cream over his face and then his neck. She didn't caress the cream onto him so much as she slapped it onto him, but his lion didn't care. It was purring and trilling, and it was taking all of Cooper's willpower to hold the sounds in.

She rinsed her hands and then filled the sink with hot water before wrapping a towel around his shoulders. She was still annoyed with him, he didn't need her scent to tell him that, but she was infinitely careful when she placed the towel around his injured shoulder.

He inhaled her sweet scent, the smell of vanilla nearly making him dizzy with desire. He studied her mouth as she reached for the razor. Thanks to the kisses they'd shared, he now knew the vanilla scent came from her lip gloss. He was dying for another taste.

He was starting to get a stiffy and he immediately thought about how it would feel if she accidentally cut his throat open. He leaned back when she brought the razor toward his face.

"Have you done this before?" he said.

"I haven't shaved a face, but how hard can it be?" she said.

"More difficult than legs," he said.

Her annoyance flared deeper. "I shave my girly bits for God's sake, I think I can handle your face."

Her face flamed red the moment she said it and she stared at him in horror. "Oh my God, I can't believe I said that."

He couldn't believe he was purring and purring embarrassingly loud. He blamed it on the fact that he'd had to switch to using every ounce of his willpower not to stare at Daisy's pussy. Okay, so he knew she shaved. No big deal. Plenty of women shaved.

Sure. But does she shave everything? Or is there a small patch of perfect curls for you to kiss? You should ask her.

Imagining the look of horror and disgust on Daisy's face when he asked if he could kiss her pussy was enough to stop the purring. The silence seemed very loud as he and Daisy stared at each other. God, she had such pretty green eyes.

"I'm sorry," she said.

He made a 'no big deal' motion with his left hand before changing the subject. "Just promise that you won't slice my throat open."

"I promise," she said.

He tilted his head up, silently giving her the go ahead. She took a deep breath and drew the razor over his throat with slow and steady pressure before rinsing it in the sink.

"No blood," she said.

"I might live through this after all," he said teasingly.

She crinkled her nose at him, and he started purring again when she used her free hand to gently push his head to the right.

"I'm sorry," he said.

"It's fine," she said. "I don't mind. It's kind of… nice."

That made his lion purr louder and he gave up on trying to swallow the sound. It made his head ache to hold in the purring if he was completely honest.

"My lion is, um, very happy," he said. "He doesn't like the itchy skin."

It wasn't a complete lie. Being itchy and uncomfortable did annoy his lion.

"It's really not a problem," she said.

He kept his eyes on Daisy's sweet face as she carefully and methodically shaved his throat before moving on to his face. He loved the look of concentration on her face, and the way she bit down on her bottom lip as she shaved him. Intent on her job, her fear had completely dissipated, even if she was kissing distance from him.

He deliberately stopped looking at her mouth. If he didn't, he'd definitely get an erection. He closed his eyes and kept them closed while Daisy finished shaving his face. To his surprise and relief, she didn't so much as nick his skin.

He opened his eyes after she'd rinsed his face to find her giving him a smug look that made him grin.

"You survived," she said.

"I did. It feels a lot better already. Thank you."

"You're welcome." She hesitated. "Listen, I was thinking you should let me wash your hair for you. You've got a hand-held shower head. If you sit on the edge of the tub and tilt your head back, I can use it to wash your hair."

He didn't reply and she pointed to his bandaged left hand. "It'll be easier on your finger if all you have to do is wash your, um, body."

"Yeah, okay," he said. Partly because she was right and partly because it meant Daisy being close to him for a little longer.

"Good. Sit on the edge of the tub." The pleased scent drifting from her skin made his lion happy for the first time since Cooper had kissed Daisy's perfect lips.

When he was sitting on the edge of the tub, she said, "We'll take the sling and your shirt off first, so they don't get wet. All right?"

He nodded and Daisy carefully eased the sling off his arm. His shoulder was throbbing, and he'd wished he'd taken some pain meds before he tried this whole shower thing. Of course, if he'd done that, he probably would slip in the shower and break his fucking left arm or some bullshit like that.

"Ready?" Daisy had the hem of his shirt in her hands and at his nod, she helped him take his shirt off his left arm before they started on his right. He gritted his teeth as she eased the shirt over his right arm. She went slow and was about a thousand times gentler than Boone had been last night.

He appreciated Wes and Boone and Grayson taking turns helping him each night, but he'd die a happy man if it was Daisy at his house every night helping him.

"You okay?" Daisy was eyeing him with concern.

"Yeah." He took a deep breath, the sweet scent of his mate soothing his restless lion.

She was staring at his chest, at the array of tattoos that covered his arms and upper body. "You have a lot of tattoos."

"Do you hate tattoos?" Jesus, he sounded like an idiot.

"No, not at all. I don't have any, but I've thought about getting one. Yours, um, look really good. Maybe I'll get the name of your tattoo artist."

"Sure," he said. He had no intention of giving her Gerald's name. The guy was an excellent tattooist, but he was also a total horndog when it came to the ladies. Cooper wasn't letting Daisy get anywhere near him.

Daisy moved to his side and grabbed the handheld before turning it on. When the water was warm, she smiled at him. "Head back."

He tilted his head back, appreciating the way she cupped the back of his head and helped support it as she wet his hair.

"Keep your head back."

He did what she asked as she grabbed the shampoo and poured some into his hair. Using her left hand to support his head again, she used her right to massage the shampoo in. At the touch of her fingers against his scalp, he could no more stop the purring than he could stop breathing.

It rumbled out of his chest, embarrassingly loud in the small bathroom, and he muttered an apology before purring even louder.

"I told you – I don't mind," she said.

She scratched at his scalp and he made a low moan of pleasure. "Shit, that feels good."

She didn't reply, but she used her nails to scratch all across his scalp, working the shampoo through his hair. The hair washing was over way too soon, he and his lion could have sat there all night while Daisy rubbed his scalp.

She rinsed the shampoo away and then used her right hand to squeeze some of the water out of his hair. "You have really thick hair," she said. "Do all shifters have hair this thick?"

"Nah," he said. "I have an uncle who went bald by thirty. He tried to hide it with a toupee but then he'd forget he was wearing it and shift. We have so many pictures of him in his lion form with this ridiculous fake rug sitting on top of his head."

She laughed and his lion purred happily. *We made our mate laugh. She loves us. Claim her as ours before another takes her.*

Jesus, his lion was a right idiot lately.

She stepped away and dried her hands on the towel on the towel rack. He smiled at her. "Thank you."

"You're welcome." She unwrapped the bandage on his left hand, leaving the steri-strips in place. "I'll put a new bandage on once you're done showering."

She eyed his track pants. "You're good to take your, um, pants off?"

"Yes," he said quickly. "I can handle it from here."

"I'll be downstairs if you need me," she said.

"Okay."

Her gaze dropped to his naked chest and his lion went bonkers when it smelled the faint scent of Daisy's lust.

Afraid he'd do something insane like start kissing her, he said, "Okay, well, you should go downstairs now."

Her face flushed red, embarrassment replaced the lust, and his lion snarled angrily at him. Without saying anything,

Daisy left the bathroom. Cooper ran his left hand through his freshly washed hair as his lion snarled and growled.

Ignoring his lion's anger, Cooper took a deep breath. Daisy's lust didn't mean she wasn't afraid of him anymore. It was just her body's biological reaction, and it probably upset her to have that type of reaction to him.

She didn't want him, and she never would.

CHAPTER 3

By the time Cooper returned downstairs, she'd used the microwave to thaw the mystery meat she found in the freezer and had the two cans of vegetable soup she'd discovered in a cupboard heating up in a pot on the stove.

"You're cooking?" Cooper said.

She glanced at him. "Yes?"

"With what? I have no food."

She laughed. "I found what turned out to be sausage in the freezer and a couple cans of soup in the cupboard."

She turned down the burner under the pan of cooking sausages and stirred the soup before walking toward him. He was wearing a clean pair of track pants and he carried a fresh t-shirt and his sling in his left hand.

"Feel better?" she asked.

He nodded but she could see the weariness in his face and the pain lines around his eyes. Without speaking, she helped him into his t-shirt, blushing a little when her fingers grazed his bare chest. God, he really did have a beautiful chest. Wide and muscular and covered with a thin layer of blonde hair. She'd never actually seen a six pack on a man in real life.

His whole body was lean but powerful and the strength she sensed lurking below all that warm rough skin was... terrifying.

No, intoxicating.

She helped him into the sling, making sure it was in the right position. "Does that feel okay?"

"Yes, thanks."

"Sit down. Dinner will be ready in a few minutes."

She returned to the stove, stirring the soup and turning the sausages. She hunted through the cupboards and found bowls and glasses. She cleared a spot on the table and laid out silverware and filled the glasses with water.

She read the instructions on the bottle of pain pills before opening it and shaking out two on the table in front of him next to his glass of water. "Take some meds, Cooper."

"They make me tired and slow," he said.

"Were you planning on going somewhere after dinner?" she said.

He smiled a little. "No, but -"

"Take them," she said. "It's obvious you're in pain."

To her surprise, he took the pills with a swallow of water. Satisfied, she shut off the burners and quickly sliced up the sausage before adding it to the bowls. She poured soup into the bowls and carried them to the table.

She sat next to Cooper, mentally giving herself a high five at not taking the chair furthest from him and picked up her spoon. "Eat up."

As Cooper clumsily picked up the spoon with his left hand, she winced. "Shoot. I'm so sorry. Soup wasn't the best option for -"

"It's fine," he said. "I still can't believe you actually found food in my kitchen to cook."

He spooned some soup into his mouth, doing a surprisingly good job of it even with his non-dominant hand. "Holy fuck. This is delicious."

She flushed, more pleased by his praise than she was willing to admit.

"Seriously. When did canned soup start being so flavourful?" he said.

"Well, I added some spices to it. You might not have food, but you do have seasonings," she said.

"It's amazing." He was spooning soup into his mouth like he hadn't eaten in days. Considering the lack of food in his house, that could have been a possibility. They ate in silence. She filled Cooper's empty bowl with the remaining soup, and he ate the second bowl only slightly slower.

When they were finished, he sat back and wiped his mouth with his napkin. "If this is how you cook with just canned soup and mystery sausage, I'd love to taste what you can do with actual groceries."

She set the empty bowls in the sink and filled them with water. "If you'd like, I can pick up some groceries tomorrow and stop by after work to make you dinner."

"Oh, uh, I wasn't…" Cooper cleared his throat. "I didn't mean to make it sound like you had to cook me dinner again. Grayson said he would come by tomorrow night so…"

"Oh, right, of course," she said.

He cleared his throat again. "But if you wanted to come over tomorrow night, I would appreciate it. I'm worried about Grayson doing too much with his injuries. He says he's fine, but he came this close to having his spinal cord severed."

"I don't mind," she said. "I like cooking."

What are you doing? You want to give him another opportunity to hurt you? To maybe kill you?

She ignored her inner voice and turned to face Cooper.

"I'll talk to Grayson tomorrow at the office, let him know that I'll stop by after work."

"Thank you, Daisy," he said.

"Anything in particular you don't like for food?"

"I'll eat anything." He reached for his wallet that was sitting on the table. "Here, use my credit card to buy the groceries."

She stared at the plastic card he was holding out. "You're giving me your credit card?"

"Yes?" He stared at her in confusion. "I don't expect you to buy my food."

"I know, but…"

"But, what?"

"You shouldn't hand your credit card over like this. I could go on a shopping spree or something."

He laughed before wincing and rubbing at his arm above the sling. "I trust you."

She took the card from him and tucked it into her purse. "What's your food budget?"

"I don't have one," he said. "Buy whatever you want."

God, what she would give to have an unlimited food budget. She wasn't starving but her food budget was as low as it could go without starving herself. She missed being able to walk into a grocery store and not have to count every penny as she shopped.

Your own damn fault. You should never have trusted Jeff.

Lord, wasn't that the truth.

An awkward silence descended. Cooper was still rubbing his arm and the pain lines had deepened around his eyes. She chewed at her bottom lip. She'd had an ulterior motive for stopping by tonight, but he looked like he was in a lot of pain. Maybe this wasn't the right time.

You've put it off for long enough. You need to apologize. Hell, you're lucky he hasn't fired your ass.

"So, um, part of the reason I told Wes I would come by tonight is because I owe you an apology."

"For what?"

"For," her face was turning red, but she continued, "saying you were my boyfriend when we met with Lori's crazy father at the coffee shop."

He didn't reply. Staring grimly at the kitchen table, she said, "I shouldn't have done that because I know your cover story was that you were the editor of the website, but he, uh, he…"

"He scared you," Cooper said quietly.

The kindness in his voice gave her the courage to look at him. "Yes. Very much. He started saying really rude comments and he kept touching me -"

"He touched you?"

"Yes, and I felt like I couldn't get away from him and… Cooper?"

Her heart kicked it up a notch and she gripped the back of the chair in front of her.

"Yeah?" His voice was a rough growl and she swallowed hard.

"Your eyes are glowing," she whispered.

He closed his eyes and she watched in fascination as the fur that was sprouting on his face slowly receded. She realized that she wasn't even afraid. Maybe it was because she was certain his obvious anger was for Corbin, the gross jaguar shifter who she'd tried to grill for information.

She took a deep breath. Pretending to be a journalist for a fake website to get information from Corbin seemed exciting at first, until Cooper got stuck in traffic and she had to talk to the shifter by herself. Her fear had been out of control and the moment Cooper joined them in the parking lot of the coffee shop, she'd glued herself to his side.

Better the devil you knew than the one you didn't, right?

Only, Cooper hadn't felt like the devil. No, he'd felt like home and safety and everything she wanted. Before she knew it, she was clinging to him like an octopus and calling him her boyfriend and, she cringed inwardly, kissing him without his permission.

"Sorry," Cooper said. His eyes were back to their normal blue.

"Th-that's okay," she said. "Anyway, I'm very sorry for forcing you to pretend you were my boyfriend and for kissing you without your permission."

Something that almost might have been a strangled laugh slipped out of Cooper's mouth. She flushed again, feeling like an idiot. "Thank you for not firing me for inappropriateness."

"I would never fire you, Daisy. You're the best admin person we've ever had in the office."

She smiled at him. "You're only saying that because I help you with your computer."

"No," he said. His pupils had gone weirdly large, and his big body was weaving back and forth the tiniest bit. "No, I said it because you're amazing. You're really good at your job, and you're so pretty, and I liked kissing you. I liked kissing you a lot."

She stared at him and when he smiled at her, that weird little tingle happened in her crotch again. Christ, when Cooper smiled like that, even she had to admit he was gorgeous.

Please, like you don't think he's gorgeous one hundred percent of the time.

"I crocheted you a scarf," Cooper suddenly said. "I

crocheted it for you because you're so pretty but I'm too embarrassed to give it to you."

"Cooper are you – oh God, the pain meds have made you high."

"Have they?" He blinked at her like a coked-out owl. Holding in her urge to giggle, she stepped toward him, touching his arm a bit tentatively.

"You should probably go to bed, Cooper."

"Sure, okay." He suddenly grabbed her hand. "Shit, do me a favour? Don't tell Daisy that I crochet. I don't want her to know because it's not a manly hobby."

"There's nothing wrong with crocheting," Daisy said.

"I'm really good at it. I made the guys dishcloths for Christmas and I'm making Wes a granny square blanket for his birthday. It's gonna be epic."

He grinned at her, and she tugged on his arm. "C'mon, Cooper. Time for bed."

"Sure, okay. I crocheted you a scarf." He studied her hair. "I found a colour that matches your beautiful hair. Do you like scarves?"

"I do," she said. "Thank you for crocheting me a scarf. Stand up now."

"Okay." He stood up and she grabbed at his waist when he swayed on his feet.

Shit, if he couldn't walk to the bedroom on his own, she'd have to call Wes or Boone. There was no way she could help support him.

"Cooper, can you walk on your own? Or should I call Wes?"

"I can walk," he said. "It's no problem. Hey, guess what?"

"What?" She walked behind him with her arms held out as if she might actually be able to stop him from falling.

"My arm doesn't hurt at all." He stopped on the first stair,

33

his body weaving again.

"That's good. Hold the handrail, please."

"I'm holding it," he said, sounding so much like a stubborn little kid that she giggled.

He glanced over his shoulder at her. "I like your laugh."

"Thank you. Pay attention to the stairs."

"Why? What are they gonna do?"

She rolled her eyes and patted his lower back. "Hold the handrail and go up the stairs, Cooper."

"You're a bossy little thing, aren't you?" he said but he did what she said.

Holding her breath, she followed him up the stairs, only releasing it when he was safely in the hallway. He weaved his way into the bedroom and collapsed on his bed with a loud sigh. "God, I'm tired."

She tucked the covers around him and he reached for her hand, his thumb stroking along hers in a gentle caress. "Thank you for taking care of me tonight, Daisy."

"You're welcome."

He yawned, his eyes slipping shut for a few seconds before they popped open. "Can I tell you a secret?"

"Sure."

"I liked kissing you."

She flushed red, butterflies fluttering around in her belly. He was studying her mouth and a tinge of guilt went through her when he said, "I feel bad that I liked it because it scared you to kiss me."

"It didn't scare me," she said.

He studied her, his eyes glassy and his pupils huge. Confident he wouldn't remember any of this in the morning, she said, "Kissing you was really nice. It actually helped me to be less afraid."

His eyelids closed and he started purring loudly. "Anytime you want to try kissing me again to help with the fear, you let me know. My lips are your lips, hot stuff."

She laughed and he blinked at her before pursing his lips. "Want to try again right now?"

"Not while you're high on pain pills," she said.

He scowled in a way that was cute instead of scary. "I'm perfectly lucid."

"Are you, though?" she said.

"No," he said in a woe is me voice that made her laugh again.

"I mean it," he said earnestly before yawning again. "Anytime you want to kiss me, let me know. I'm really good at kissing, you can ask our receptionist at work. I've kissed her."

"All right." She patted his chest. "Go to sleep, Cooper. I'll see you tomorrow okay."

"Okay. Bye, Daisy."

"Bye, Cooper." She sat on the side of the bed, waiting until his breathing turned deep and even and his face relaxed. When she was certain he was asleep, she left his room and returned to the kitchen. It was only eight and she set to work cleaning the kitchen.

As terrified as she'd been to come to Cooper's house, now she was actually enjoying being here. It was a nice house – a thousand times better than her rathole of an apartment – and she had no one to go home to.

As she loaded the dishwasher, she couldn't help but grin. Never in a million years did she ever think she would be alone in a shifter's house and cleaning his kitchen. Not only that, but she hadn't felt a trickle of fear since just before she'd helped Cooper in the shower.

"Progress," she told the empty kitchen. "I'm making excellent progress."

CHAPTER 4

P *lease, I miss our mate.*

"She's not our mate," Cooper told his lion for what had to be the millionth time.

His lion growled and whimpered. Cooper grabbed his head as his skull throbbed and ached. It felt like a herd of buffalo was stampeding through his brain and had felt that way for most of the week.

It was the discord between him and his lion. His refusal to give his lion what it wanted was driving the beast mad and giving Cooper a horrific headache in the process. He never thought that going insane would be this painful.

Panic ate at his insides. His lion was going mad and Cooper had no idea what to do about it. His lion's pacing and prowling and whining for Daisy was a constant chorus in his brain. It blotted out his ability to do anything else.

He couldn't think past the headache, couldn't think past the madness that he could taste and smell and see on his lion. He'd seen a cougar shifter go mad once. Had seen what happened when the human side and the shifter side no longer lived in harmony.

He rubbed at his aching temples. The cougar shifter had blown his brains out in front of him and Grayson. Cooper would forever live with the memory of the blood and brain matter splattered on the wall.

He shuddered all over. That couldn't happen to him, it *wouldn't* happen to him. He just needed to keep doing what he'd been doing all week – reminding his lion that she wasn't his mate and avoiding Daisy. Which, frankly, was a real challenge this week. Normally, Daisy was remarkably self-sufficient, but she'd come by his office multiple times a day this entire week asking questions he was pretty sure she already knew the answer to. It made it almost impossible for him to think clearly or act normally. He had to constantly stop his lion from trying to rub up against her and mark her.

I miss her.

He soothed his lion as he paced back and forth in his office. He missed Daisy too. Of course he did. He'd sat alone in his house every night this week, sitting on his couch and staring at the chair where Daisy had sat. He couldn't even distract himself with TV. Not when he'd gotten used to watching TV with Daisy. It was ridiculous, but his goddamn lion had convinced itself that Daisy making him dinner every night and then watching TV with him for a couple of hours meant she thought of him as her mate.

It didn't mean that. They had barely even talked after that first night for God's sake. He'd wanted to talk to her, wanted to find out everything he could about her, but afraid to do anything that might scare her, he'd tried to follow her lead. And she hadn't seemed inclined to talk that much.

He rubbed his right shoulder. It was aching slightly, but he'd only had to wear the sling for a week. The rumours about shifters having instant healing powers weren't true, but they did seem to heal a little faster than humans did. The doctor had given him a clean bill of health on Friday and he couldn't get rid of the sling fast enough.

He continued to pace. He should have kept the sling. Daisy had shown up at his place Friday night after work, just like she'd been doing all week, but as soon as she'd seen him without his sling, she hadn't stayed.

His lion whined loudly, its mournful cry making Cooper clench his teeth as his guts churned.

She didn't stay because we scare her. That's why she's not our mate, he told his lion. *She's afraid of us and she always will be.*

Stop lying!

His lion's angry roar made Cooper flinch.

Stop lying about our mate! She isn't afraid of us anymore!

"She isn't as afraid of us," Cooper said to his empty office. "And only because we were extra careful not to move too quickly or stand too close. But she's still afraid. I'm sorry, but it's the truth. We need to find another mate."

His lion growled but the sudden apathy in it made Cooper extremely nervous.

He sat down at his desk and opened the bottom drawer, staring at the half-started granny square lying in the drawer. Normally crocheting soothed both him and his lion, but he had no desire for the hobby that used to make him happy.

He had no desire for anything but Daisy. He rubbed absently at his right shoulder again. He'd been careful to wait until Daisy left each night before taking pain pills. Especially after what happened that first night. He still couldn't remember exactly what he'd said to her after they'd kicked in. He had a bad feeling that he'd confessed to not only his love of crocheting, but his love of kissing her too.

He closed his eyes, trying his hardest to remember exactly

what he'd said to Daisy, but the whining restlessness of his lion made it impossible.

There was a knock on his office door before it opened. He stared blankly at Grayson. The tiger shifter was his best friend and trying to keep his impending insanity from Gray was becoming more and more difficult. Grayson wanted to come by last night to watch the football game with him, but Cooper had refused. He couldn't act normal for that long. It was too exhausting to even try.

"Hey, what's up?" he said.

Grayson frowned. "You wanted to meet with me about the Henson file."

"Did I?"

"Yeah. It's in the calendar," Grayson said.

"Right." He rubbed at his forehead. "Can we reschedule?"

"Coop, are you okay?" Grayson said.

"Fine. Just a headache."

"It is only a headache or is it -"

"I said I'm fine!" He growled at Grayson as fur sprouted on his cheeks. "Mind your own fucking business for once."

Shame immediately flooded through him. He forced his angry lion to retreat and said, "Gray, I'm sorry. I didn't mean -"

"It's okay," Grayson said. Cooper hated the cautious way he was staring at him. "What are your plans for tonight? Why don't you come over to our house and have dinner with us? Ryan's making ribs and -"

"Nah, I can't. I've got plans," Cooper said. That was a lie. Unless sitting at home and trying to ignore his lion's growing insanity counted as plans.

"Cooper -"

"Can you go, Grayson? I have some work I need to finish. Talk to Daisy about rescheduling our meeting, okay?"

Grayson hesitated before nodding. "Yeah, okay."

He left Cooper's office, closing the door behind him. Cooper leaned back in his chair, closing his eyes as his lion paced ceaselessly within him.

DAISY HESITATED OUTSIDE OF COOPER'S OFFICE. SHE RESTED her hand on the doorknob before pulling it back. God, what was she doing? More importantly, why was she doing it? This weird compulsion to come up with every excuse in the book to see him was, at best, going to be super noticeable by the others in the office if it wasn't already, and at worst, get her fired for being incompetent at her job.

Asking a million questions she already knew the answers to might get her close to Cooper, might feed her sudden craving to be near him, but it would also land her in serious trouble if she didn't knock it off. She lived paycheque to paycheque. If she got fired and didn't find another job immediately...

She shuddered, thinking about the homeless people that lived in a tent city situation only a few blocks from her apartment building. Her apartment might be crappy and scary and possibly on the verge of collapse from mold and water damage, but it was better than being completely homeless.

More importantly, her inner voice whispered, *why are you so determined to be around someone who scares the living hell out of you?*

Cooper would never hurt me.

Her inner voice scoffed so loudly she was surprised Cooper didn't hear it through his office door. *Are you really that naïve? After everything you've been through, you still believe that a shifter might be good? That Cooper wouldn't hurt you the first chance he got?*

If I didn't, I wouldn't have taken this job to try and get over my fear, would I have? she snapped back.

You're playing a dangerous game. One that's gonna get you killed. Cooper and Wes and Grayson and all the other shifters in this office are dangerous. It's like you want *to be murdered by shifters.*

Her heart pounding, she moved away from Cooper's door, her limbs jerking along like a marionette whose strings were tangled tight. She didn't have a death wish, she just needed to get over her fear of shifters. She couldn't keep living life this way. That was why she was trying to spend more time with Cooper. That was why she volunteered to cook him dinner every night last week while he was recovering. It was taking much longer than she thought to conquer her fear. By spending extra time with her boss, she was moving along her own self-therapy.

Or you're really fucking horny and want to get laid.

Inner Daisy almost recoiled in horror at that errant thought. Becoming friends with a shifter was one thing, but sleeping with one? No fucking way.

Oh yeah? Then why do you keep thinking about the kisses you shared? And what about that weird sex dream you had about him two nights ago?

Her cheeks turned scarlet and she hurried down the hallway, almost half convinced that just by thinking about her sex dream in the office, Cooper would somehow find out. She'd woken from the dream both horny and terrified, and certain she was losing her damn mind.

She needed to step back from Cooper and find a different shifter to try and be friends with. One she wasn't possibly, maybe, sexually attracted to, which was really freaking her out because she never once imagined she'd be attracted to a shifter.

Although, maybe sleeping with a shifter was the way to get over her fear. Like, a total immersion/exposure thing. It would be kind of hard to be terrified of Cooper if he'd given her multiple orgasms, right? She thought about his big hands, about the way it had felt when he'd cupped her face and kissed her. God, he was a good kisser. Sure, it had been a little scary kissing him, but when he'd touched her tongue with his, it had...

Enough! You're not sleeping with him. Stay away from him. Something weird is going on with him lately. He's acting strange.

She wanted to pretend her inner voice was wrong, but... well, it wasn't. Cooper *was* acting weird lately. There was something off about him. He'd seemed mostly normal when he returned to work on Monday, if not a little distant, but with each day that passed, he got... weirder. The other day, she'd sworn he was talking to himself as he stood at the copier. And as much as she was suddenly trying to see more of him, she couldn't shake off the nagging feeling that he was trying to avoid her. Not that he'd spent all that much time with her before, but he'd always been nice to her and often asked her to help him with his ongoing computer issues. And she'd thought that after spending every evening with him last week, their tentative friendship would continue at the office.

How wrong she'd been.

He hadn't asked her even once to help fix his computer this week, and she was pretty sure she saw Lusa helping him yesterday. Hurt weaved its way into her stomach and she berated herself immediately. What did she care if Cooper didn't want to spend time with her anymore? He was her boss and that was it.

Thinking she should try and be friends with him, or even more crazy – have sex with him – was insanity on her part.

"Cooper's getting worse."

Boone's low voice stopped her in her tracks. She crept forward a few steps and leaned against the wall outside of the boardroom. The door was partially open, and she strained to hear. Listening in on private conversations wasn't something she normally did, but she couldn't seem to get her feet to keep moving. Her suspicions about Cooper were true, and she needed to know what was wrong.

Maybe she could help him.

"He's okay." Grayson's voice was only slighter louder than Boone's.

"He isn't, man. I know you want to think he is, but he's not," Boone said.

"He's stressed out right now. He needs a few days off to -"

"It's more than that, Gray."

This time it was Wes speaking and his voice was so close to the half-open door, that Daisy held her breath. Shit, he would smell her soon. She knew he would. Still, she couldn't move. She had to know.

"His lion is going mad," Wes said. "If we don't do something soon, it'll be too late."

"What are we supposed to do?" Gray said. The worry in his voice made Daisy's stomach churn. "We can't make her have sex with him."

"No, but maybe we could talk to her," Boone said. "Tell her about the mate thing and what it's doing to Cooper."

"Are you serious?" Grayson said. "How do you think that conversation will go? Hmm? You think we can walk up to her and just say, 'Oh, hey, Daisy. We know you're terrified of shifters, but Coop's lion believes you're his mate and if you don't have sex with him, he's going to descend into madness and never recover.' Yeah, that will go over real well, Boone."

The breath Daisy had been holding leaked out of her lungs in irregular and patchy sips. Cooper thought she was his mate?

Duh, he called you his mate that day at the coffee shop.

Yeah, because he was playing a part. One you forced him to play because you were being your usual terrified self. He called you his mate because you introduced him as your boyfriend, remember?

"Maybe we can think of a more polite way to say it," Boone said.

"Oh my God, Boone, there is no polite way to tell our goddamn receptionist that if she doesn't fuck the boss, he's going to go mad and we'll have to put him down like a rabid dog," Gray said.

"Calm down, Gray," Wes said.

"Don't tell me to calm down. This is my best friend we're talking about, Wes. He's going crazy and there isn't anything we can do about it. We'll never convince Daisy to fuck Cooper."

"Maybe if we fired Daisy…" Boone said hesitantly.

"We can't," Wes said. "The only thing that's stopped him from going insane already is being around Daisy at work. He's gotten so much worse so quickly because she was spending more time with him when his arm was still in that sling. Daisy went to his place every night and cooked him dinner. His lion got used to it and now that he's recovered and she's not at his house every day, his lion's losing his grip on reality."

"This fucking mate thing is such bullshit," Boone snarled. "Cooper is the strongest guy I know and he's going to be

45

taken down because a woman doesn't love him. It's not fucking fair."

"We have to do something," Grayson said. "You guys are right, he's getting worse. I didn't want to admit it, but he is. I wanted to go over to his place last night and he wouldn't let me. He's getting twitchy and weird and -"

"He spends most of his time talking to his lion," Boone said grimly. "His pupils are almost always slits now. We have to talk to Daisy."

"We do," Wes said. "Which one of us is doing it?"

"Not me," Boone said. "You think I want a sexual harassment charge on my permanent record? Because you know Daisy is going to file one against the guy who tries to convince her to fuck her boss."

"I'll talk to her," Grayson said.

"Take Ryan with you," Wes said. "Maybe hearing it from another human female will help. Maybe you don't have to mention the sex thing. If he isn't too far gone yet, just getting Daisy to spend one-on-one time with him again would help. It would soothe his lion enough to keep it from going mad, right?"

"That's a good idea," Grayson said. "But even if we could convince her to spend time with him, that eventually won't be enough. You know how our cats are. His lion will keep pushing for more and Cooper knows Daisy is terrified of him. He won't attempt anything sexual with her. He'd rather go mad than scare her like that."

"It's the only and best idea we have at the moment," Wes said. "We get her to spend some alone time with him again and that'll buy us some time until we can figure out what to do."

"Maybe we could introduce him to someone else," Boone said. "Another woman who will make him forget about wanting to fuck Daisy. Maybe, if he gets laid by anyone, that will help?"

"Maybe," Wes said.

A weird sensation burned in her belly. After a moment, she placed it. Holy shit...was she jealous? She heard Cooper's office door open and immediately darted down the hallway to reception. She sat down at her desk, her heart thumping like a rabbit and her mouth dry. She was right. Something *was* wrong with Cooper. He was going insane and she could help him. She swallowed down her jagged laughter.

If she wanted to save Cooper from madness, all she had to do was fuck him.

CHAPTER 5

"I'm sorry, did you just say you need to have sex with a shifter? And not just a shifter, but your goddamn boss?" Megan stared at Daisy, the shock on her face evident even on Daisy's phone screen.

"I didn't say I would have sex with him, I said having sex with him might be the only way to stop him from going insane," Daisy said.

"I'm sorry, who are you and what have you done with my best friend?" Megan said. "I knew you moving all the way to fucking California was a mistake, but I didn't realize it would be this epic of a mistake."

"It isn't a mistake. Look, Cooper's been really good to me, okay? He's a nice guy and I feel bad that he's going insane because he thinks I'm his mate. I mean, I didn't even know that could happen to a shifter."

"Yeah, because you avoid them at all costs and for good reason." Megan plopped down on a bench. Behind her, Daisy could see children playing in a park. "Honey, maybe it's time you found another job."

"What? Are you kidding me? I took this job to help me

get over my fear of shifters and it's working. I'm almost friends with Lusa now and I spent time alone with Cooper all last week. For the first time since I was a kid, I'm not afraid of shifters."

"No, you're not afraid of certain shifters. I'm glad you're making progress, but that doesn't mean you're over your fear of shifters. You told me last night that you're still afraid of the other shifters in the office."

"Yeah, but Cooper is the biggest of them and I'm not afraid of him."

"Because he's nice to you and you like the way he kisses, and you had a sex dream about him."

Daisy blushed furiously and looked around even though she was in her car with the windows rolled up. "I should never have told you about that stupid dream. Besides, it was barely a sex dream. All we did was kiss in the dream."

"But you were naked and so was he… that makes it a sex dream, Daze."

Daisy didn't reply and Megan held her phone a little closer to her face. "Honey, you can't seriously be considering sleeping with him, are you? I support your mission to get over your fear of shifters but having sex with one isn't a good idea. The trauma you went through, the stuff you've seen, it doesn't just disappear."

"You think I don't know that?" Daisy said. "I'm the one who was in therapy for years, remember? It was my therapist's idea to immerse myself in the shifter world, to try and become friends with them."

"Yeah, friends, not lovers," Megan said. "Look, I get it. I went to Shadow Security's website and creeped on Cooper's profile and his Facebook page. He's hot and I get why you'd might want to bang him. But, at the end of the day, he's a shifter and your boss. Even if you could get over your fear of him, sleeping with him is a quick way to get fired."

"But they said he was going insane," Daisy said.

"I'm not trying to sound cold-hearted, but how is that your problem?" Megan said. "You haven't done anything to make him think you're his mate. That's on him. You're not even friends with the guy."

She held up her hand before Daisy could protest. "I know, I know, you were at his house every night last week making him dinner and hanging out with him. But you said you didn't even talk to him. Right?"

"Well, I didn't know what to say and he didn't really talk, and I didn't want to upset him or make him -"

She stopped abruptly but it was too late. Megan stared at her in sympathy. "Or make him angry."

"I'm not afraid of him," Daisy said.

"Not being afraid of him and not *wanting* to be afraid of him are two different things, Daze," Megan said gently.

"He's a good guy and he saved me from that crazy jaguar shifter."

"Yep, he did," Megan said, "and if I ever get the chance to meet him, I'm gonna let him know how awesome he is for coming to your rescue. But that doesn't mean you have to fuck him as some kind of thank you for helping you."

"I know that," Daisy said. "but they said spending time with him would help so maybe I just hang out with him again. What's the harm in that?"

"Plenty of harm, especially if what they said about his lion pushing for more is true. Maybe he'll stay sane being just friends, but what if it isn't enough? What if he does push you for sex? You haven't slept with a shifter before, but I have. They like sex, okay? They like sex a lot. Let's say you did get over your fear enough to have sex with your boss and stop him from going insane." Megan made a face. "Jesus, even saying that makes me sound crazy. Anyway, say you could do it, what happens if he wants sex again? You gonna keep banging him just for funsies? That isn't your style, babe."

"Just because Jeff thought I was a cold fish in bed doesn't mean it's true," Daisy said. "I told you that I tried with him but he -"

"Honey, I know. He's a lying sack of shit. I'm just saying that he's also the only guy you've slept with and since he didn't make that great of an impression sex wise, your lady boner seems to be in permanent stasis."

Daisy laughed. "You're so gross, Megan."

"I know. But it's true. You're the least interested in sex of any of my friends. I'm not trying to hurt your feelings, but you are."

"I just don't see what the big deal is. I can get myself off faster and better," Daisy said.

"Yeah, because Jeff the con artist sucked in bed," Megan said. "Get the right guy touching your crumpet and you're going to hornytown…trust me."

"Did you just call my vagina a crumpet?" Daisy said.

"Would you prefer me to call it your pink taco?" Megan said.

"Oh my God, I hate you," Daisy said with a laugh.

"No, you love me. Look, you need this job. If you get fired, you'll be homeless. Although, from what you've told me about your apartment, that might be an improvement."

Shame made her cheeks hot. They must have been bright red because Megan squinted at the screen. "It's not your fault, Daze. You're only in an assload of debt because Jeff conned you into thinking he would actually get an inheritance. You wouldn't be in money trouble if it wasn't for him."

"Yeah, I know," Daisy said. "Doesn't mean I don't feel stupid about trusting him."

"You were with him for three years. You were supposed to trust him. I hate what he did to you and I hate even more that you had to move across the goddamn country because of him."

"I didn't have to move. I wanted to," Daisy said. "I needed a fresh start."

"Fine, but don't pretend he's not ten pounds of shit crammed into a five pound bag, because he fucking is. Anyway, my point is, you have a good job that you need. Sleeping with your boss puts that in jeopardy."

"I know, you're right," Daisy said. "But I'm worried about him. And if he goes insane, I'd lose my job anyway."

"You don't know that for sure," Megan said. "Besides, didn't the other guys in the firm say they had a plan to get him to sleep with someone else?"

"Yeah," Daisy said as her gut twisted.

"So, there you go. Problem solved."

"Maybe," she said. "Listen, I'd better go. My lunch hour is almost over, and I want to grab a coffee before I head back to the office. Love you, Megan. Thanks for listening to me babble on your lunch hour."

"Anytime, babe. I love you and I miss you so much."

"I miss you too. I'll text you later."

She ended the video call and stared blankly at the office building for a couple of minutes before shoving her phone into her purse and sliding out of the car. She locked the door and headed across the street toward the Starbucks.

Everything Megan said was true. Thinking she could even get over her fear of shifters to try and sleep with Cooper was stupid.

No harm in trying. He's a great kisser.

She opened the door and stepped inside the busy coffee shop. There was a huge difference between kissing a guy and having sex with him and she'd be a fool to forget that.

"YOU'RE OKAY. YOU'RE FINE. YOU'RE SAFE." DAISY DIDN'T know if muttering that mantra repeatedly helped or not, but it did stop her from bursting into tears.

Pain etched across her knuckles and she stared at the cup of coffee. Her hand was trembling so much that hot liquid spilled out even with the lid on it.

Numb with terror, she set the coffee on her desk and wiped her hand with a tissue. She stared at the mail that was sitting next to her computer before sorting through it.

Her hands were still too shaky, and she pressed her lips together when the pile of mail dropped on the floor. She crouched and tried to gather it up as her breath sawed in and out of her lungs and her heart tried to trample its way through her ribcage.

"You're okay," she said again. "She didn't hurt you. You're okay."

There was a piece of registered mail for Cooper. She staggered her way down the hallway toward his office. Her trembling legs would barely support her, and she clung to the wall as she walked. She kept seeing the shifter's fangs as they pushed past the perfectly painted lips, kept seeing the way her manicured nails had thickened and lengthened into razor sharp claws.

Claws that could hurt, claws that could tear, claws that could slice open Daisy's jugular and spray the walls with her blood.

A low moan escaped her throat and she clamped her hand

over her mouth before knocking on Cooper's door. At his gruff 'come in,' she opened the door and stumbled into his office.

He was sitting on the small leather couch in his office, his head back and his eyes closed.

"Cooper?"

He stiffened, his nostrils flaring delicately. He lifted his head and opened his eyes as she forced her trembling legs to cross the room to the couch. She held out the piece of mail, ashamed at how obviously shaky she was. "You have a piece of registered mail."

"What happened? Why are you so afraid?" He sat up straight on the couch and ignored the mail she was holding out.

"Nothing," she whispered. "I'm okay."

"You're not. Tell me what happened," he said.

Her lower lip trembled, and she wanted to die of shame when she started to cry. But there was no holding back the tears or the fear. "I went for a coffee and I bumped her and spilled her coffee, and I said I was sorry, but she was so mad, and she scared me. She scared me so much and I c-c-couldn't get away and-and-and…"

"Baby, it's okay," Cooper said. His big warm hand gripped her wrist and when he gave it a gentle tug, she didn't even stop to think. She dropped the mail and practically fell into his lap, wrapping her arms around his shoulders and burying her face in his thick neck.

"It's all right, Daisy." Cooper's hands rubbed her back in slow circles. "You're safe. I won't let anyone hurt you."

She sat in his lap and clung to him like a frightened little kid. She was embarrassed by her behaviour, but the irrational fear didn't care how stupid she looked. She hadn't been this badly frightened by a shifter since she was a kid. She both hated and was filled with a bone-aching weariness that the progress she thought she had made was nothing but a lie.

"Will you purr for me?" she blurted.

Oh my God, what was wrong with her? She was making a total fool of herself.

Cooper started to purr, and she rested one hand on his chest, feeling the vibrations under her palm as he purred. God, she loved that sound. It was weirdly comforting to her.

She didn't know how long she sat on Cooper's lap listening to him purr and breathing in his scent, but it was long enough for her shaking to stop and for the tears to dry up. She took a deep shuddering breath, twitching when she heard the phone ring.

She tried to slide off Cooper's lap and his arms tightened around her as his purring cut out. "Stay with me."

"The phone is ringing," she said.

"It can go to voicemail."

"It's my job to answer it."

"I'll tell the boss that I gave you permission not to answer it."

She smiled before relaxing in his lap again. Sitting on your boss's lap and crying was the biggest career ending move ever, but she couldn't bring herself to care. Sitting on Cooper's lap had taken the fear away. She'd sit on his lap forever if it meant never being that afraid again.

"Will you tell me what happened?" Cooper's hand was rubbing her back again.

She didn't want to tell him, it was such a small thing, but how could she not tell him? She had sat in his lap and cried on his shoulder, she owed him an explanation for… shit, his shoulder!

She sat up straight, staring horrified at his right shoulder. "Oh my God, have I hurt you? Did I reinjure your shoulder?"

He shook his head, one big hand still rubbing her lower back, the other resting on her thigh. "No, it's fine."

"Are you sure?"

"Yes."

"I messed up your shirt," she said. His collar was wet, and she could see some smears of makeup on the fabric. Thank God she wore waterproof mascara. "I'll pay to have it cleaned."

"I don't care about my shirt. Tell me who frightened you," Cooper said.

She didn't even have the urge to flinch when he reached up and wiped the tear streaks from her face with his thumb. "Tell me, baby."

"I went to Starbucks at the end of my lunch to get a coffee. I was leaving but I was looking at my phone and not paying attention. I bumped into this woman pretty hard and I spilled her coffee a little. Some of it splashed on her shirt."

She was starting to shake again, and she was grateful when Cooper rubbed her back and purred to her. It helped calm her. "I apologized and said I would buy her a new coffee, but she was so mad. She started yelling at me about being clumsy and staring at my phone instead of watching where I was going."

She took a deep breath, staring intently at Cooper's face. "I didn't even know she was a shifter at first. I thought she was human but then she kept yelling at me, and she was getting angrier and her eyes they- they switched to yellow. Her pupils narrowed, and I could see her fangs."

Her throat was dry. She didn't know how Cooper knew it, but he grabbed his glass of water sitting on the small end table next to the couch and handed it to her. She took a large swallow, easing the dryness. "Thank you."

"You're welcome." He took the glass from her trembling hand and set it back on the table. "What happened then?"

"She called me a stupid human bitch and started ranting about how all humans were idiots. Her fingernails were... they were turning into claws... and I wanted to run but she had me trapped against the wall and I couldn't – I couldn't get away."

Her breath hitched in her throat and Cooper tugged her against his chest again. "It's okay, baby. You're safe."

She rested her forehead against his throat, the rumbling of his purring a soothing balm. "This guy finally stepped in – I don't know if he was human or a shifter – and told her she needed to calm down. She started yelling at him, and I squeezed past them and ran out of the shop. I thought she was going to slice my throat open. She was so mad."

"I'm sorry, baby. I wish that hadn't happened to you." Cooper rubbed her back.

"I looked like an idiot," she said. "I was starting to cry, and I know I was shaking, and my face was red and -"

"You were afraid, and she was the asshole who looked like an idiot," Cooper said. "It was a simple mistake, nothing to lose her shit over."

"I hate that I'm so afraid," she whispered. "I hate that I can't go out in public without being frightened. I stare at every person around me and wonder if they're human or shifter. I hate that I'm always looking for exits in every room I'm in. I hate that any shifter I meet immediately knows I'm afraid of them. I look like such a fool all the time, but I don't know how to stop being afraid that the shifter might hurt me."

She waited for him to ask her why she so afraid, waited for him to ask the question that she wouldn't answer. Would he get upset with her? Would he get angry?

To her surprise, Cooper said, "I might be able to help you be less afraid when you're out in public."

She sat up and stared at him. "What do you mean? How?"

Looking a little uncomfortable, Cooper said, "I could mark you."

CHAPTER 6

C ooper's lion purred so loudly the minute he suggested they mark their mate, that even if Daisy had said anything, he wouldn't have heard her.

His lion was already surging forward, trying to force Cooper to shift so he could mark Daisy properly. Cooper pushed him back. *Stop it! You can't mark her. It'll scare her. I'll mark her.*

You won't do it right. His lion was acting like a pouty cub.

Daisy sat as still as a mouse on his lap, staring at his eyes, and he muttered a curse to himself. Fuck, he'd spoken to his lion again in front of her. He hadn't meant to do that.

"It's okay," he said quickly. "I won't hurt you."

"I know. What do you mean by mark?"

"It's a thing that shifters can do. We can, uh, rub up against a human and mark them with our scent. It lets other shifters know that the human belongs to them and they'll stay away from the human."

"Seriously?" She was staring wide-eyed at him. A little of her colour had returned to her face and he breathed a sigh of relief. She'd been so pale and the scent of her fear so overwhelming when she walked into his office, he'd been worried she would faint.

"Yes." He rubbed her back again. He shouldn't have, but he couldn't help it. Daisy being so close to him, allowing him to comfort her as if he were her mate had done more for his lion's sanity in the last five minutes than any of his calming techniques over the last five days.

For the first time since Monday night, his headache had receded, and he could actually think straight. His lion purred to Daisy, the sound making her smile. Cooper knew it wasn't his imagination that the purring made Daisy happy. She had literally just asked him to purr and he could smell how much she liked it.

"Do shifters mark humans a lot?" she asked.

"Usually only when the human is their mate," he said. "But we can mark a human that isn't our mate."

"But if you do mark me, the shifters will think I'm your mate?"

"Yes, and they won't go near you," he said.

"How do you know that for sure?"

"Because they can tell by my scent that I'm a lion shifter and a powerful one. They wouldn't dare touch my mate. They know I'll kill them if they do."

"Is that why you told Corbin at the coffee shop that I was your mate?"

He looked away. "Yes. It was the quickest and easiest way to keep you safe."

"Cooper?"

He made himself look at her. "Yeah?"

"Would you really kill another shifter for hurting me – I mean, hurting your mate?"

"Yes." He probably should have lied to her. It wasn't exactly helping him convince her not to be afraid of him.

"How do shifters not just go to prison for murder all the time?" she said.

He laughed. "Because we rarely have to kill another shifter for hurting our mates. Our scent on our mate keeps them away."

"Grayson had to," she whispered.

"He did," Cooper said. "But the human was going to kill his mate. Grayson only killed him to save his mate and that's why the police cleared him of any wrong-doing."

"I know," she said. "Is this a guy shifter thing only?"

"No. Female shifters will mark their mates as well."

She tugged on the hem of her skirt. She was no longer afraid, but she hadn't made any effort to get off his lap, and he wasn't about to suggest that she move. He would be perfectly happy to have Daisy sit in his lap all goddamn day.

"Do you have to, um, be in your lion form to mark me?" The scent of her fear returned, and his lion whined its displeasure. Cooper hated that she was afraid of his lion but there wasn't anything he could do about it.

Yeah, well it'll be difficult for her to be your mate if you can never shift around her.

His lion snarled at his inner voice, but it wasn't wrong.

"Cooper?" Daisy said.

"No," he said. "I can mark you in my human form. It won't be as strong and it won't last as long, but it will work to keep you safe. You would just, um, have to let me mark you every day as opposed to every few days in my lion form."

"Okay," she said. "Go ahead and mark me."

"You're sure?" he said.

His lion growled at him, but Cooper wanted to make sure Daisy knew what she was asking for. "I'll have to get close to you."

She stared at his chest. "I'm literally sitting on your lap, Cooper. I think you being close to me to mark is a non-issue at this point. Speaking of which, I want you to know I don't make it a habit of sitting in my boss's lap."

He grinned at her. "I don't make it a habit of asking my employees to sit in my lap, so I guess this is a new experience for both of us."

She smiled at him before it faded a little. "Seriously though, I'm sorry I was so frightened and acting like a big baby."

"It's fine," he said. "I'm glad you came into my office. I like helping you, Daisy."

"Thank you," she said. "I really appreciate your help."

"It's no problem. Are you ready?"

She nodded and leaving one hand on her firm thigh, he cupped the back of her neck. He could still smell the faint scent of her fear and he hesitated. "Are you sure this is what you want, baby?"

"Yes," she said in a low voice.

She closed her eyes, and he studied the beautiful face of his mate before leaning in. He gently tugged her head back and rubbed his face across her throat. She gasped and her hands gripped his arm. He squeezed her thigh lightly in response before rubbing her throat again. God, she smelled so good.

He started purring and he rubbed his face all over her throat before sliding it along her exposed collarbone. She gasped again and the smell of her lust made his lion growl happily. He brushed his mouth against the hollow of her throat and her nails dug into his forearm.

"You okay, baby?"

"Yeah," she whispered. Her breathing had quickened, and

he could see the outline of her nipples through her bra and shirt. "Yes, I-I'm good."

"Good. Just a bit more, all right?"

"Okay." Her voice was a low moan and the need in it was giving him a semi. Fuck, he needed to get her off his lap before she felt how hard he was getting for her. Instead, he marked her again. Her throat and upper chest were bright red and, unable to resist, he pressed a light kiss against her throat.

"Your skin is red now. I'm sorry."

"That's okay, I... ohhh..." she trailed off, her back arching when he licked the hollow of her throat.

He rubbed just below her jaw line, the feel and smell of her soft skin driving him wild with need. He had a full on erection now that pressed against her hip, but she wasn't pulling away.

Her nails dug into his forearm again and she bit at her bottom lip. "Is it, um, working?"

"Yes," he growled before marking her throat again. "You smell like me now, baby. You're my mate and no shifter will touch you. I promise."

"Cooper, I..."

His lion surged forward and took control. "You're my mate, little human. Say it."

She blinked at him. "I... I'm your mate?"

His lion roared with happiness and Cooper rubbed her thigh before kissing her collarbone. "Come home with me tonight, my mate. I'll take you to my bed and put my cub in your belly."

Her eyes widened and the lust faded in them. "Um, what did you say?"

Shit! Cooper pushed his lion back. Jesus, how the fuck was he going to explain this to Daisy?

"Daisy, I -"

"Hey, Coop? Have you seen Daisy? She's not at her desk and...hello, what's this?"

Cooper groaned inwardly as Daisy squeaked and scrambled off his lap. She stared at Boone who was leaning against the doorjamb and grinning at them both.

"Sorry, didn't mean to interrupt your...whatever this is." He studied Daisy's red throat and Daisy's cheeks immediately flushed.

"Sorry, I'm – uh, I'll be back at my desk in a few minutes, Boone."

Without looking at Cooper, Daisy headed for the door.

"Move," Cooper said to Boone.

The tiger shifter stepped into the office, giving Daisy plenty of space to pass him by. He sniffed the air as she passed him and turned to stare at Cooper as Daisy practically ran out of his office.

"So... you gonna explain why Daisy was sitting on your lap and why she smells like you now, or can I start making wild and incredibly inaccurate guesses?" Boone said with a grin.

"Out," Cooper said. "Out of my office, Boone."

Boone laughed and started toward the door. "Talk to you later, boss."

"MORNING, COOP." GRAYSON WALKED INTO HIS OFFICE without knocking and sank into the leather chair across from Cooper's desk.

Cooper closed the calendar app on his computer. "Morning."

"You look better today."

Cooper scowled at his best friend. "What's that supposed to mean?"

"It means you looked like shit yesterday."

"I had a headache and my lion was having a bad day. He feels better."

"Because Daisy sat in your lap yesterday?" Grayson said.

"Fucking Boone," Cooper muttered. "I'm gonna fire him."

Grayson laughed. "No, you won't. Besides, I didn't need Boone to tell me. Daisy stinks like you so bad. The entire reception area has a distinct eau de Cooper smell. Does she know you marked her?"

"Yes," he said.

Grayson glanced at the open doorway and lowered his voice. "Buddy, did you have sex with Daisy yesterday?"

He jerked and nearly spilled the cup of coffee he'd been reaching for. "What? Why would you say that? What the fuck did Boone tell you?"

"All Boone said was that he walked in on Daisy sitting on your lap. But your scent is super strong on her and that only happens if you're in your lion form when you mark or if you're fucking the human while you mark them. I know you didn't shift into your lion form to mark her – Daisy would have quit on the spot if you'd shifted – so did you fuck her?"

"No, of course not. The marking was strong because..."

Grayson stared knowingly at him. "Because you *want* to fuck her."

When Cooper stayed silent, Grayson sighed. "Coop, it's me. Grayson. Talk to me, okay? I know you better than anyone and you thinking you can hide your attraction to Daisy from me, or hide that your lion thinks she's your mate, is ridiculous."

Cooper gulped down some coffee, grimacing at the cold

bitterness. "My lion won't listen when I tell him that Daisy isn't our mate. I don't know what to do about it. Before Daisy sat on my lap yesterday, before she let me mark her, I was…"

"Feeling off-balance?" Grayson suggested.

Cooper grimaced. As much as he appreciated what Grayson was doing, there was no point in sugar coating it. "I was going mad."

He could see his own fear reflected in Grayson's eyes for a few seconds before Grayson said, "It won't happen. We'll make sure it doesn't happen, buddy."

"How?" he said hoarsely. "My lion believes Daisy is his mate. He's believed it for three months now and I can't convince him otherwise. It was really nice of Daisy to help me out last week, but I shouldn't have let her do that. It's made everything so much worse."

His voice sounded plaintive and weak. He slammed his fist on his desk, wincing when pain radiated from his shoulder. He rubbed his shoulder and said, "Having her in my house, making my dinner, helping me shave and shower -"

"She helped you shower?" Grayson stared in surprise at him.

"Yeah. She was afraid, I could smell it on her, but she helped me shave and washed my hair three times that week. After a few days, she wasn't afraid at all being in my house. It made my lion happy. Hell, it made *me* happy. It made my lion think there was a possibility she could be our mate. You know?"

"Fuck," Grayson said.

"Yeah. But then as soon as my sling was off, she stopped coming over. I think having one arm in the sling helped her believe that I couldn't hurt her. I don't know. Anyway, I avoided her this week, told my lion repeatedly that she wasn't our mate, and that's when my lion really started losing it." He rubbed at his shoulder again before glancing at Grayson. "His depression and his sorrow are terrible, Gray. Like… I can't even explain how awful it is. And then you get this horrible headache and…"

He took a deep breath and drank another swallow of cold coffee. "Yesterday after lunch, Daisy came into my office and her fear was obvious. She was terrified. Even more afraid than she was the day of her interview."

"Jesus," Grayson said. "What happened to her?"

"Some female shifter scared her in the coffee shop. Daisy accidentally spilled her coffee and she started yelling at her and dropping her fangs and her claws. Daisy felt trapped and…"

His lion roared angrily at even just the thought of his mate being afraid. Cooper soothed him as Grayson waited patiently.

"She came into my office. I could smell her fear and when I asked her what was wrong, she started crying. I had to comfort her, *needed* to comfort her, and she let me. She let me hold her on my lap. She asked me to purr and her fear dissipated, and my goddamn lion was going batshit crazy with happiness."

He stared blankly at his computer monitor. "My headache disappeared almost immediately."

"That's good," Grayson said.

"After she told me what happened, I told her I could mark her, and that it would keep other shifters away from her." He turned his gaze to Grayson. "I offered to mark her because I wanted to help her, Gray, I swear. But there was a part of me that…"

"Wanted to mark her because you think she's your mate."

"Yeah. I'm such an asshole."

"Our cats like to mark our mates, Coop. You can't help that."

"It's not just my lion though. I wanted it too."

"Look, it helps Daisy feel safe and it will definitely keep shifters away from her, so I don't think you need to beat yourself up over the reasoning for doing it. Is she going to let you mark her every day? Because your scent won't last long on her if you're not having sex with her on a regular basis or letting your lion mark her."

"That was the plan," Cooper said. "But then I fucked that up."

"How?"

"I," he laughed bitterly, "got excited by marking her and she was a little turned on by it too. I could smell her lust. It wasn't as strong as when I kissed her, but it was there. I – my lion took control and kind of made Daisy say she was my mate and then…"

"Then?" There was no judgement on Grayson's face, but Cooper still squirmed at telling him the next part.

He said it fast, getting his shame out into the open like a festering sore that needed draining. "I asked her to come home with me so I could take her to my bed and put a cub in her belly."

"Shit." Grayson said. "That's bad, man."

"I know! You think I don't know that?" Cooper said. "Before I could try and think of an explanation for what I'd said, Boone walked in on us and Daisy left. I haven't talked to her since. I don't think she's actively avoiding me – I know phones have been busy all morning and I'd asked her to type some reports for me – but she's not gonna let me mark her again."

He glanced up at Cooper. "Right?"

"Definitely not," Grayson said. "Fuck, we're lucky she didn't quit on the spot."

"Don't fucking soften the blow or anything," Cooper said.

Grayson grimaced. "Sorry, but you basically asked the receptionist to let you breed her yesterday. You can't tell me you're not a little surprised that she showed up to work this morning."

Cooper groaned and sat back in his chair, scrubbing his hand across his face. "Fuck me. I'm so fucked."

"No, you're not fucked, which is part of the problem. But we might have a solution."

"We? Who is we?"

Grayson waved his hand in the air. "You know, we... the guys and... Ryan."

"Are you fucking kidding me?" Cooper glared at him. "You told your mate about this?"

"She might be able to help," Grayson said.

"How? How exactly is your human mate supposed to convince my lion not to think of Daisy as my mate? And how long have you, Wes, and Boone been talking about me behind my fucking back?"

"Cool it, buddy. We weren't talking about you behind your back. We were discussing how worried we are about you and what we could do to help."

Cooper nodded grudgingly. "Yeah, okay." Truthfully, he was incredibly grateful to his friends for trying to help him. He should probably actually verbalize that to Gray and the others, but he was pretty certain they already knew.

"Anyway, our original plan was for me and Ryan to talk to Daisy about spending more one-on-one time with you for a while. Just to soothe your lion. We know it's not a solid solution and that Daisy spending time with you could make things worse, but we were worried about your sanity so..."

"I'm okay," Cooper said.

Which was easy to say right now because he *was* okay. His lion was still on a high from yesterday and Cooper didn't have the courage or the strength to remind him that Daisy would never let them mark her again or ever consider being their mate. He needed to, his lion was already itching to mark Daisy again, but Cooper wanted even a few more hours of peace.

"You're not okay, but we're going to help you," Grayson said. "Ryan and I will talk to Daisy this weekend about spending some time with you. We won't give her exact details about what's happening, just tell her that -"

"What? There's nothing you can tell her that won't make her run screaming or quit her job. And then I'll be really fucked. If I can't see her every day, I – Gray, I have to see her."

"I know, buddy. Ryan and I won't screw this up, I promise. Ryan's good at helping people to relax and feel comfortable with her, and she's already planning what she's going to say to Daisy. We have your back, Coop."

"Say you can convince Daisy to spend alone time with me again. Then what? My lion wants me to mate with her and if I don't, he's going to lose his mind and then I'll…" Cooper swallowed hard, the image of the cougar's brains splattered on the wall impossible to forget.

"No, you won't," Grayson said. "I won't let that happen. Ryan has a friend. Her best friend actually. Her name is Shay and she's willing to meet with you and see if you could maybe have a mutually beneficial relationship."

Cooper stared at him. "What the fuck does that mean?"

"It means, you guys have dinner together. If there's an attraction for both of you, then you scratch her itch and she'll scratch yours."

The air petered out from Cooper's lungs and it took almost thirty seconds for him to remember to suck in more air. "You're fucking kidding me."

"I'm not," Grayson said. "Meet with Shay. She's smart and attractive and funny as hell. I think you'll like her. Meaningless sex with Shay on a regular basis might help with your Daisy problem."

"It doesn't work that way," Cooper said.

"How do you know? You haven't even tried. Maybe spending platonic time with Daisy and having sex with Shay will help keep your lion happy and the two of you in harmony. We only need to keep him happy and content while we find you a new mate. Hell, maybe Shay and you will hit it off and be more than friends with benefits. She's a pretty cool human."

"Daisy is my mate," Cooper said.

"Your lion believes that right now, but you know as well as I do that we can change our minds. Divorce rate among shifters is just as high as it is with humans."

"I don't think it'll work," Cooper said.

"We have to try."

Cooper hesitated and then nodded. "Yeah, okay."

"Great. I'll give Shay your number and she'll text you to set up dinner."

Cooper scrubbed his hand through his hair. "Thanks, man. I appreciate everything you're doing for me. I hate that I'm so weak and -"

"You're not weak," Grayson said. "You're one of the strongest guys I know. It's this mate thing… it's fucking bullshit, but we can't change the way our cats think. But it doesn't mean you're weak."

Grayson checked his watch and then stood. "You still

want me to sit in with you and Wes for the eleven o'clock client meeting?"

"Yeah. The client still isn't certain if all he wants is a security system installed or if he wants some private security for his daughter as well. If he wants private security, it'll be you and Wes."

"All right. See you in half an hour."

He turned to leave, and Cooper said, "Gray?"

"Yeah?"

"Thank you. For everything."

Grayson smiled at him. "You'd do the same for me."

CHAPTER 7

Daisy paused outside of Cooper's office with the papers in her hand. She'd finished typing the reports Cooper had asked her to type, and normally she'd email them to him and let him print them out.

So why did she print them? Why was she making it a point to deliver them to his office?

Because you want to see him. You're suddenly obsessed with a shifter and if that isn't the very definition of fucking irony, I don't know what is.

Inner Daisy was right about the weird obsession, and it was totally messing with her head, but that hadn't stopped her from printing the reports.

Nor would it stop her from letting Cooper mark her again today.

So he can talk about knocking you up again?

She stared down at her flat abdomen. She wanted kids but she wasn't planning on having them this year. And definitely not with an enormous lion shifter who also happened to be her boss.

That giant penis of his could probably blast a bucketful of swimmers up the old pink taco, right? You'd be pregnant with a baby lion probably after the first try.

She flushed bright red, a spat of giggles bursting from her mouth. Oh my God, it was like Megan was living in her damn head.

It wasn't completely lost on her that she was thinking about sex with a shifter and having his baby without breaking into tears or a cold sweat, but she decided to think of that as progress as well and keep going. I mean, it wasn't like she was *actually* considering having sex with Cooper, right?

The idea of a full immersion/exposure thing to shifters by banging one wasn't really a viable idea, she knew that, but it stuck in the back of her brain like a piece of flypaper she couldn't peel off.

Which was stupid because she knew for a fact that there was no way she could have sex with a shifter. The idea of getting naked in front of them, of being vulnerable and intimate with them was laughably ridiculous. She didn't even like it when shifters touched her.

You don't mind when Cooper touches you.

She swallowed hard, the memory of yesterday making her face feel hot and her stomach clench with something that was remarkably close to pleasure. She hadn't minded when Cooper marked her. Hadn't minded it at all, in fact, and –

Girl, please. Who are you trying to fool? It made you hot. You were so turned on by it, your panties were wet. Don't even try and tell me it's not partially the reason why you're coming back for more today. You liked when Cooper touched you and kissed your throat and called you his mate.

She ran her fingers along the scar on her forearm. Okay, so maybe she did like it, but she was a woman with certain biological needs and Cooper was a good looking guy. She would never get the courage to sleep with him or anything, but being touched by him was very pleasant. And as far as not minding being called his mate – the reason behind that was more than obvious.

She'd grown up without a family, without anyone to feel connected to or loved by. She'd glommed on to Megan the first day of high school and that was the first meaningful relationship of her life. It was no surprise that being told by a hot guy that she was his mate was a little... enticing. Even if he was a shifter. Everyone wanted to be loved by someone, right?

Loved?

She rubbed harder at the scar on her arm. Okay, maybe she was being a bit presumptuous but Cooper calling her his mate did kind of give the impression that he loved her. Which that in itself was weird because he knew nothing about her, and they'd only known each other three months. She'd spent most of those three months trying not to burst into tears of fright or wet her pants from fear when she was around him.

But he'd been so gentle and kind to her every day at work and he'd never once shown anger toward her, even when she made a mistake. He constantly thanked her for helping him with his computer, he respected her physical space, he paid her a good wage, and he'd pretended to be her boyfriend without hesitating when she'd been on the verge of a panic attack.

Also – don't forget how good of a kisser he is.

Her brain had a one-track mind. But, lord, was he ever. Like, the kind of kissing that you can't seem to forget. The kind of kissing where you really, really want to try it again, just to see if it was as good as you remembered.

She glanced at her watch. Shit, their eleven o'clock client would be here in fifteen minutes, and if she wanted to have Cooper mark her again, this was his only free spot all day.

Now was not the time to be daydreaming about Cooper's kissing abilities.

She knocked on the door and opened it when Cooper called 'come in'. He was sitting on the edge of his desk, studying the open client folder in his hand. The office had casual Fridays, and like her, he was wearing a pair of jeans. They were a bit worn and clung to his thick thighs. The dark blue t-shirt he was wearing highlighted the leanness of his stomach and the heavy muscles in his upper arms.

Her back was starting to sweat, and she swallowed hard. Cooper really was a handsome guy. The thick blond hair, tanned skin, and blue eyes gave him a distinct surfer vibe even though she was pretty certain he'd never been on a surfboard in his life.

He glanced up, his eyes widening a little, before he stood. "Hey, what's up?"

"Hi. I have those reports you wanted." She closed the door behind her and walked toward him.

She could almost smell his surprise. She never closed the door of his office, ever, but she didn't want Boone or someone else walking in on them like yesterday.

Especially before you can get to the good stuff, like kissing.

She held out the reports and he took them, glancing briefly at them before setting them on the desk behind him. "Thanks."

"You're welcome."

There was awkward silence and she took a deep breath. She needed to ask Cooper to mark her again. She was going grocery shopping tonight. How nice would it be to not worry about shifters potentially hurting her?

"So, I wondered if -"

"Is there something else -"

They both stopped and she laughed nervously. "Sorry, what did you say?"

"You first," Cooper said.

"I was wondering if you would mark me again?"

Surprise washed over his face. "You want me to mark you right now?"

Embarrassed, she said, "It's, um, your only availability all day."

He didn't say anything. Her cheeks burned as she started to back up. "I'm sorry, I thought you said it would have to be every day, so I thought, uh… I should go."

"Daisy, wait." Cooper's fingers curved around her wrist. "I'll mark you now."

"I… are you sure? I feel like maybe I'm overstepping or -"

"No, it's good. I just thought that after yesterday and what I …" he stopped, his own cheeks reddening. "Never mind. I'm happy to mark you again."

"Okay, thank you, that's great. I really appreciate it. I have to go grocery shopping tonight and normally it's really stressful because I don't know for certain who's a shifter or who isn't. I mean, I'm pretty good at guessing because you guys are often bigger than humans, but not all shifters are giant sized, and sometimes there are just larger humans, and…"

She made herself stop talking. Shit, would she ever learn not to babble when she was nervous?

"Anyway," she said, "I really appreciate this. I'm hoping it'll help me be less afraid at the stores if shifters think I, um, belong to a lion and avoid me."

"They will." He was still holding her wrist and his thumb rubbed her pulse point. "You won't have to be afraid. I promise any shifter at the store will avoid you."

"Okay, that's great." She sounded a little weak but not with fear… no, she wasn't afraid at all. More… turned on. Which was super embarrassing because all he was doing was holding her wrist. But the way his thumb was rubbing across her skin made her feel too warm, and that warmth was traveling straight to her damn crotch.

He sat down on the edge of his desk again. She automatically stepped between his open legs without needing even a hint of encouragement. His inner thighs were warm against her legs and when he slid his arm around her waist and cupped her hip, she didn't protest.

His other hand slid under her hair to grip the nape of her neck. The rough calluses on his palm brushed against her skin and sent goosebumps skittering to life. His hand on her neck was comforting rather than confining, and she let her head fall back when he tugged lightly.

He dipped his head and she told herself not to touch him but at the first brush of his lightly stubbled face against her throat, one hand clamped down on his thick upper arm and the other clutched at the front of his t-shirt.

She pressed her lips shut against the moan that wanted out, but it escaped anyway when he rubbed the other side of her throat. When he nuzzled the hollow of her throat, her back arched and she leaned in even closer. He was so warm and solid and… safe.

And sexy. Christ, don't forget the sexy part.

How could she forget? It was impossible to forget with the way his mouth kept brushing against the sensitive skin of her throat. Impossible with the way his thumb was rubbing her hipbone and his hand was kneading the back of her neck.

God his warm skin felt so good against her. When he lifted his head, someone said, "more" in a breathy and pleading tone.

"Your skin is red, baby. It's too sensitive for more." This time Cooper slid his thumb back and forth over the pulse point at her throat.

"I don't care. I want more." She wasn't ready to step away. Wasn't ready to go back to her desk where she'd be away from Cooper.

She squeezed his bicep. "Please, Cooper."

He groaned made butterflies dance in her stomach. "Whatever you want, my mate."

He rubbed his face across her throat and then along her collarbone. She arched into him. Her clothes suddenly felt too constrictive, her nipples chafed against her sensible bra, and she wished that she was naked. Naked and in Cooper's bed while he marked every part of her, while he kissed and tasted and –

"I can smell how wet you are for me, little mate." Cooper's mouth was pressed against her ear and when he nipped at her earlobe, she moaned and leaned forward until her breasts touched his chest.

Immediately, Cooper's big hand slid down to her ass and cupped one cheek, squeezing it firmly before he kissed below her ear. His hand threaded through her hair and he nuzzled her throat. "I love how soft your hair is, how good you smell, how quickly you respond to my touch."

Oh God, this was so wrong. She absolutely should not be in her boss's office letting him squeeze her ass and – oh! – lick her throat. She needed to tell him to stop. Needed to remember that she needed this job desperately and if –

His warm breath washed over her mouth and she forgot about all the reasons she shouldn't kiss Cooper. Her lips parted and she made a sound of encouragement in the back of her throat.

"Does my mate want to be kissed?" Cooper's low voice was almost a growl and it was sexy as hell.

"Yes." She tried to press her mouth against his, moaning in frustration when his fingers tightened in her hair and held her immobile.

He licked her bottom lip, a quick flick of his tongue that set her entire body on fire.

"Cooper, please," she whispered.

He licked her top lip this time and she dug her fingers into his chest and pressed her abdomen against his delicious hardness. "Cooper, kiss me."

He purred and her delight at the sound was eclipsed by the feel of his firm lips against hers. He was already sliding his tongue between her parted lips, angling his mouth over hers so he could take the kiss deep.

Kissing him was as intoxicating as the last time, but even better because this time they weren't in a coffee shop parking lot and there was no gross jaguar shifter watching them. This time he wasn't kissing her because he was playing the part of her boyfriend. He was kissing her because he wanted her and, right or wrong, she wanted him too.

His tongue brushed against hers and his purring grew louder when she returned his kiss. Their tongues touched and tasted and explored. When his big hand cupped her breast, she gasped into his mouth.

He pulled back, studying her swollen lips, his thumb rubbing almost idly over her hardening nipple. "Do you want me to stop, little mate?"

"No," she whispered. "No, I want more."

He smiled at her and her stomach muscles clenched in a delicious spasm of pleasure. His groan when she rubbed against his erection made her feel powerful. She kissed him again, pushing her tongue into his mouth and moaning when he sucked hard on it. She slid her hands under his shirt, suddenly desperate to touch his warm skin.

She traced the muscles of his abdomen before running her fingers over the wiry hair on his broad chest. Her finger brushed against one flat nipple and he growled into her mouth. She froze and pulled her head back, her eyes widening and a tingle of fear going down her back.

Cooper's eyes were bright yellow, his pupils narrowed to slits, and – more fear slithered up and down her spine – she could see the tips of his fangs between his parted lips.

She pulled away immediately, backing up on trembling legs.

"Please don't hurt me." She cringed at how afraid and weak she sounded.

Cooper's eyes had already faded to blue and at the look of regret and shame on his face, her fear faded like a photo left in the sun.

"I'm so sorry," he rasped. "Daisy, I won't hurt you. I promise."

"I know," she said. She straightened her shirt, terribly aware of how much her nipples were protruding against the thin fabric. "I'm sorry, I shouldn't have kissed you. You're my boss and it was really inappropriate and I… I'm very sorry."

"It was my fault," he said. "You don't need to apologize."

She backed toward the door, fumbling for the handle as she tried to will her racing heart into a slower beat. "No, I asked you to kiss me. The marking, it makes me a little…"

Sweet Jesus, she was not about to tell her boss that his marking made her horny.

She cleared her throat and sucked in a deep lungful of air. "I'm sorry. Thank you for marking me again. I appreciate it. But I'll also understand if you want me to resign and -"

"What?" He stood with what almost looked like panic in his eyes. "Jesus, no, Daisy. I do not want you to quit. You're not quitting, I won't let you. Do you understand?"

He took a deep breath. "Fuck. I mean, obviously you can do whatever you want, but you don't have to quit. I won't do that again. I promise."

"Me too," she said. "I have to get back to my desk now. Uh, bye."

"Bye, Daisy."

She stepped out of his office and thanking God there wasn't anyone in the hallway, she ran back to the desk and sank into her chair. She stared blankly at her computer screen before touching her swollen mouth.

Holy fuck, she'd made out with Cooper in his office and she'd... she'd liked it.

CHAPTER 8

"You still want me in the meeting?" Wes stuck his head into Cooper's office. His nostrils flared and while the expression on his face didn't change, Cooper knew he could smell his and Daisy's mutual lust.

He cleared his throat, thankful it was Wes and not Boone. He loved Boone, but the guy didn't know when to keep his mouth shut. Wes, on the other hand, barely said two words on a good day.

"Yeah. The client should be here any minute. I'll meet you and Grayson in the boardroom, I'm gonna grab a coffee."

"Sure." Wes left and Cooper took a deep breath. Jesus, he needed to concentrate on his upcoming meeting and not how fucking great Daisy's ass felt in his hands. If he didn't stop thinking about her sweet moans and how good she tasted, his fucking erection would never go away.

He adjusted his dick before heading toward the kitchen. He really did want a coffee, he told himself. He wasn't going to the kitchen because he'd have to go through reception and it would give him the opportunity to smell Daisy's lust again. Nope that wasn't it at all. He had some fucking self-control.

The so-called self-control didn't stop him from inhaling or slowing down as he stepped into the reception area. He glanced at Daisy. She was staring studiously at her computer screen, but her cheeks were bright red and even under the overpowering scent of him that covered her, he could smell her lingering arousal.

His lion purred happily. Daisy being covered in his scent had calmed the beast for the first time in months and Cooper was feeling almost giddy about it.

The door to the office opened and a male human stepped inside, followed by a teenager. He was tall and dark haired, wearing a business suit that Cooper suspected cost more than his entire wardrobe combined, and he radiated confidence. The teenager with him wore skinny jeans and a t-shirt. Her dark hair hung halfway down her back and she wore thick makeup. She gave Cooper a look of bored disinterest as she shifted her backpack on her shoulder.

"Have a seat and finish your math homework, Anna," the man said.

She rolled her eyes but walked over to one of the chairs and sunk into it. She pulled a binder out of her backpack and stared morosely at it as the man in the suit walked up to Cooper.

Cooper held out his hand. "Mr. Landon?"

"Yes." The man shook his hand.

"Cooper Brooks, we spoke on the phone. It's nice to meet you."

"You as well. Call me David. This is my daughter Anna."

"Hello, Anna," Cooper said.

Anna made a little wave without taking her gaze off her binder.

Cooper turned to Daisy who had stood up behind the receptionist desk. "This is our admin person Daisy."

"Hello," Daisy said. "Cooper, I'll bring water to the boardroom."

"Thank you, Daisy." Cooper turned to David. "We're meeting with my associates in the boardroom if you'd like to follow me."

"Sure." David followed Cooper to the boardroom. Wes and Grayson were already in the room and they stood, shaking hands with David as Cooper made introductions. He nodded his thanks to Daisy when she brought glasses and a pitcher of water into the boardroom and set them on the table before she left.

"So," Cooper settled into his chair, "why don't you give us a little background on why you're looking at personal security options."

David took a sip of water before pulling at the knot on his tie and loosening it a little. "Eight years ago, my wife and I divorced. She moved to Colorado shortly after the divorce, taking our daughter Anna with her. We have joint custody, so Anna spends some holidays with me, and I fly her out once a month for the weekend."

He leaned back in his chair, tapping his fingers idly on the table. "Last year, Anna got a part time job in retail. She met a cheetah shifter who also worked at the store and became romantically involved with him. He is not a good man."

"In what way?" Cooper said.

"He's twenty-two years old. Anna is sixteen."

"Jesus Christ," Grayson said. "What's the age of consent in Colorado?"

"Seventeen," David said. "Only, Colorado has a Romeo and Juliet law."

"What is that?" Cooper said.

"It's a close-in-age exception," Wes said. "A minor who is

at least fifteen can have consensual sex with a person within ten years of their age."

"Are you kidding?" Grayson said.

"No," David said. "Anna's mother is a lawyer and Anna is… well, let's say she's very clever and will probably follow in her mother's footsteps when it comes to a career. When Maria threatened to have Xander arrested for statutory rape, Anna immediately brought up the Romeo and Juliet law. She had," David closed his eyes for a second, "done her research before she slept with him."

Cooper studied his notes in front of him. "You said you were looking for a security system for your home to keep your daughter safe. Anna is living with you now?"

"Yes." David pinched the bridge of his nose. "About four months ago, Anna confessed to her mother that she had broken up with Xander, but he was refusing to accept it and was, in fact, scaring her. He was insistent that Anna and he would be married, and he wanted her to quit school and move in with him. Maria went to the police who spoke with Xander but because he hadn't technically broken any laws, they couldn't arrest him. When Xander kept showing up at Anna's school, Maria had a temporary restraining order put out against him. It was only for a couple of weeks and once it ended, he went right back to stalking her."

David's face had paled and when he reached for his water glass, there was the slightest tremor in his hand. "He sent her flowers and gifts and constantly texted her. Maria got Anna a new phone number but somehow Xander found out her new number and continued to text her. He sends her messages through all of her social media. Anna had to basically stop using social media of any kind which made her a bit of an outcast with her peers."

He set his water glass down on the table. "Maria had a

new permanent restraining order put out against him. We thought that might help but," he took a deep breath, "one evening while Maria was at a client function and Anna was home alone, Xander broke into the house."

"Jesus," Cooper said.

"He told Anna that she was leaving with him and made her pack a bag. As they were walking to his car, Anna managed to escape and run to the neighbour's house. They called the police but by the time they arrived, Xander was gone. When they went to his house, his roommate said that Xander had sold most of his stuff earlier in the month and told him that he and Anna were getting married and moving to Montana. Xander had loaded his car with what was left of his personal things and moved out that morning."

"I take it the police didn't find him?" Grayson said.

"No." David tapped at the table again. "He has a warrant out for violating the restraining order and for attempted kidnapping, but he's so far avoided being arrested. The police suspect that he has several different aliases. We hoped that with the warrants out, that might be the end of his obsession with her. But not even two weeks later, he was sending gifts to Anna again, contacting her through social media to say she belonged with him and he'd forgiven her for running away from him."

David pushed his chair back and stood. He paced the small room, staring blankly out the row of windows on the far wall. "Maria and I decided it would be in Anna's best interest to move to California and live with me. She didn't want to, all of her friends are in Colorado, but we didn't give her a choice. She's been living with me for two months. It hasn't been easy. She misses her mom and her friends, she's sad and feeling lonely, and on top of that she's having some trouble with her schoolwork, but there's been no contact from Xander. Until last week."

He paused by the windows, glancing at Cooper and the others before turning his gaze back to the street. "Flowers arrived at the house for Anna. No name attached to them. A day later, an envelope with a letter from Xander showed up on the front porch."

"Do you still have the letter?" Cooper said.

"The police have it," David said. "I contacted them immediately. They've let the Colorado state police know that Xander is probably here in California and they advised me to get a restraining order as well, which I did, but…"

"There isn't much else they can do," Wes said.

David huffed out an angry laugh. "Not really. It's ridiculous. One of the officers assigned to the case actually gave me your name, Mr. Brooks. He said you were one of the best for providing home security systems and personal security as well."

He returned to his seat, sitting down and rubbing at his forehead. Cooper could smell his weariness and his fear. "I am afraid for my child, Mr. Brooks. This shifter is crazy, and I believe he'll stop at nothing to have Anna."

"Based on what you've told us," Cooper said, "I'd recommend not only the security system installed, but a private security detail for Anna as well whenever she leaves your home."

David nodded. "Whatever you think is best. I just want to keep my Anna safe. She's what matters. Nothing else."

"WOULD YOU LIKE SOME WATER OR JUICE?" DAISY SMILED AT Anna.

The teenager shrugged. "Yeah, sure, I'll take a glass of water if you don't mind."

"I don't." She walked to the kitchen and returned with a glass of water as Anna muttered a curse and tossed her binder on the chair next to her.

She picked at the eraser on her pencil as Daisy handed the glass of water to her. "Here you go."

"Thank you." Anna sipped at the water.

As Daisy turned to go, she said, "You like working here?"

"I do," Daisy said. "It's a good place to work."

"They're all shifters, huh? Are you one too?"

"No, I'm human." Daisy hesitated. "Are you, um, a shifter?"

"Nah. Human." Anna picked at her pencil eraser again. "I'm Anna."

"Daisy. It's nice to meet you."

"You too."

Daisy turned to leave, and Anna said, "How long have you worked here?"

Smiling, Daisy sat in the chair next to her. "About three months."

"You from California?"

"No. I grew up in Connecticut. How about you?"

"I was born here but when my mom and dad got divorced, I moved to Colorado with her. Still came back to California every month though to see my dad and I spend, like, every other holiday with him."

"That's good that you could see him on a regular basis."

"Yeah. My parents had what they refer to as an amicable divorce. They're friends but it still kind of sucks they don't love each other anymore. Your parents still together?"

"I grew up in foster care," Daisy said.

"Shitty." Anna picked up her binder, flipping it open to

where Daisy could see an equation written out. Anna poked at the page with the tip of her pencil. "I hate math. I wanna be a lawyer like my mom and she says math is important, but I don't see how it's that important. It's not like I'm going to be doing equations in front of a judge or something."

She glanced up at Daisy, a shy conspiratorial glance with a hint of anxiety that Daisy recognized well. "I'm failing math. My dad's gonna have a shit fit when he finds out. He knows I'm having trouble, but I haven't, like, showed him my grades or anything."

She drew across the equation with an angry slash of her pencil. "It doesn't make sense to me, you know? I've been working on this same stupid equation for days. It's a PD day for teachers today but if I don't have my math homework done by Monday, I'm screwed. But I can't even get past the first dumb equation."

She made doodles in the side margin, big looping flowers and smiley faces. "My dad said he would help me, but I get more confused when he tries to explain it to me."

"Well, I'm pretty good at math, maybe I can help?" Daisy said.

Anna glanced at her. "Yeah? You'd do that?"

"Sure," Daisy said. "Show me the first question."

"It was good to meet you, David." Cooper led the human back out to reception. "As I mentioned, Lusa will be in charge of installing the security system. We'll be at your place Monday at nine to take a look at your house, go over options, and discuss which system will work best for you."

"Thank you," David said.

"You're welcome. I know we went over how the personal

security detail works already, but if you have any questions, don't hesitate to contact the office. Wes will be taking the weekend shift. Please remember to email your daughter's weekend schedule to the office this afternoon so that Wes can contact you with any questions he may have ahead of time."

"There won't be much this weekend. I'm home all weekend and Anna is behind on some math homework and will be staying in until she finishes it. But I'll send over the schedule and…"

David trailed off as they entered the reception area. Daisy was sitting next to Anna and the two of them were bent over her binder. Anna wrote something on the paper and Daisy's face broke out into a grin.

"Perfect! That's the answer."

"You're kidding." Anna stared at her in disbelief.

"I'm not. You did it," Daisy said.

"Holy shit!" Anna said before dropping her pencil and binder in the empty chair beside her and hugging Daisy. "I did it! You're a friggin miracle worker, Daisy."

Daisy laughed. "You solved the equation, not me."

"Yeah, but you explained it in a way that I, like, actually understood," Anna said.

She glanced up, a grin crossing her face when she saw her father. "Dad, I actually understood math for a change."

"That's great, honey," David said.

"It's because of Daisy," Anna said. "She, like, explains math so much better than you."

Daisy flushed and stood up, clearing her throat awkwardly as David walked toward her. He held his hand out and Cooper's lion growled angrily when Daisy shook it. His lion didn't like the way David was looking at Daisy and, to be honest, Cooper didn't like it either.

His lion surged forward, taking control just enough to

make Cooper stride jerkily across the reception area. She had already dropped David's hand, but Cooper took Daisy's arm, tugging her up against him before putting his arm around her waist in a clear 'the woman belongs to me' gesture.

Daisy tried to step discreetly away, and Cooper held her closer before holding his hand out to David. "Good to meet you, Mr. Landon. Remember to email the information to the office this afternoon."

"I will." David shook his hand. With a look of amusement on his face, he nodded to Daisy before turning and ushering Anna toward the door.

"It was nice to meet you, Daisy," Anna said. "Thank you for your help."

"You're welcome, Anna," Daisy replied.

When the door closed behind them and the rival for his mate was gone, his lion relinquished control. Cooper stared blankly at the way his hand gripped Daisy's hip. Daisy tugged at his hand and he released her and stepped back.

"Sorry," he said. "I shouldn't have done that. My lion, uh… sorry."

She rubbed at the scar on her forearm. "That's okay. But I think we need to talk about -"

"Hey, Coop?" Lusa walked into reception. "Do you have a few minutes to talk?"

"Can you give me five minutes?" Cooper said.

"I'm leaving in seven," Lusa said with a glance at her watch.

"It's fine," Daisy said. "We can talk later."

Cooper frowned. "I'm out of the office all afternoon and -"

"We can talk on Monday." Daisy walked back to her desk and cursing inwardly at his stupidity, Cooper followed Lusa to his office.

CHAPTER 9

"**D**aisy! Over here!"

Daisy turned and smiled at Ryan before threading her way through the busy coffee shop, holding her hot coffee carefully. A few people, their noses wrinkling, immediately stepped out of her way or made a wide berth around her, and a tiny thrill went through her.

She thought she'd gotten pretty good at figuring out who was a shifter but being marked by Cooper made it incredibly easy to know for certain. Last night while grocery shopping, the number of shifters who actively avoided her had both surprised her and made her jittery with excitement. For the first time in years, she hadn't been afraid while out in public.

She'd felt strong and a little invincible, and definitely awed by the power that Cooper's scent seemed to have. A couple of the shifters had even looked distinctly nervous when she walked by them.

Worried that Cooper's scent might have worn off by now, her nervousness reappeared when she walked into the coffee shop. But it was quickly apparent that Cooper's scent still covered her, and her newfound confidence returned.

She sat down in the chair across from Ryan. "Hi, Ryan."

She was feeling nervous for an entirely different reason now. Not only was Ryan drop dead gorgeous, but she was a celebrity. The sci-fi show she'd starred in as a teenager was a cult classic, and Daisy had no doubt that Ryan was still asked for autographs on a daily basis.

"Hi." Ryan smiled at her. "You look… different."

"Do I?" Daisy said. Ryan may have only seen her a couple of times before at the office, but Daisy had no trouble believing that she looked different to her. She felt different. All because of Cooper marking her.

"Yeah." Ryan sipped at her drink. "Thank you for meeting me for coffee."

"Thanks for inviting me." Daisy took a sip of her own drink. It was Saturday afternoon and the coffee shop was jam packed with people. Now that she didn't have to worry about a shifter potentially approaching her, Daisy didn't mind how busy it was. It would help conceal the conversation she was about to have with Ryan.

She hadn't been at all surprised when Ryan called her this morning and invited her for coffee. After overhearing Grayson and the other guys' conversation, she'd expected it. What she hadn't expected was that it would be only Ryan and not Grayson as well.

"So, how's your weekend going?" Ryan said.

"Fine," Daisy said. "I went grocery shopping last night and, um, just relaxing today."

She really needed to make more friends, but it was hard to make friends without revealing her fear of shifters. Not only was it embarrassing to admit, but it was hard to do normal things with other people when you were constantly worried that a shifter might be close by. Going for coffee or a movie, hell, even a round of mini golf was an exercise in torture for her. It was almost impossible for her to act natural and normal when out in public. Megan had understood and very sweetly worked around Daisy's fear, but her best friend was one of a kind.

That's not a problem anymore. You can be normal in public now, thanks to Cooper.

That feeling of giddiness washed over her along with a healthy dose of surrealness. The idea that she could walk around in public without being afraid was intoxicating.

If Cooper agrees to keep marking you.

She wanted to drown out sensible inner Daisy, but it kept right on talking.

He probably won't. Not after you practically throw yourself at him every time he does and then freak out and run away. It's like you want to be fired. Then you'll be homeless. How would that feel? To be living on the street, not knowing who's a shifter and who isn't?

"Daisy?" Ryan touched her hand. "You okay?"

"Yes, sorry." God, she'd been sitting there for over a minute, lost in her thoughts. Ryan must think she was a complete moron. "Um, how is your weekend?"

"Good. Grayson and I had dinner last night with my friend Shay, and we're having games night with my sister and her boyfriend tonight."

"Sounds like fun," Daisy said.

There was uncomfortable silence and then Ryan said, "So, I wanted to chat with you about something that's a little awkward, but I hope you'll hear me out. You know that Grayson and Cooper are best friends, right? Grayson loves Cooper a lot and he asked me to -"

"Talk to me about spending time with Cooper because his lion thinks I'm his mate. His lion is going mad because I was spending time with Cooper when he was injured and now I'm not."

Ryan's mouth dropped open, but she recovered quick. "Yes, that sums it up. How did you know?"

Daisy traced the top of her coffee lid with her finger. "I overheard Grayson and the others talking in the office. Grayson said that the two of you would talk to me about spending time with Cooper outside of work. Why isn't Grayson here?"

"I thought it would go better with just me," Ryan said. "Grayson is trying to hide it, but he's really worried about Cooper and that makes him and his tiger a little tense. And I know that you can be a bit nervous around shifters, so I thought just you and me would be easier on you."

Daisy couldn't help her small laugh. "A bit nervous? Is that what Grayson told you? Because he's being kind if that's what he said. I'm terrified of them."

Ryan sipped at her coffee. "Can I ask you something personal?"

At Daisy's nod, she said, "Why did you take a reception job in an office full of shifters when you're so scared of them?"

Daisy took a deep breath. "I'm trying to get over my fear. I've gone most of my life being afraid and I thought maybe if I worked with them, if I was around them every day, it would help me manage the fear. It was my therapist's idea."

Ryan mulled that over. "I can see the logic behind that. It must be very difficult on you though."

"At first, it was," Daisy admitted. "Honestly, I almost vomited during the job interview. How I even got the nerve to join Cooper and Wes and Grayson in the boardroom… I don't know. I remember answering their questions but don't remember what my replies were. I could hardly talk I was so afraid."

She traced the scar on her forearm. "I knew I wouldn't be hired, you know? I could see it on Grayson and Wes's faces. They could smell my fear. When Cooper offered me the job right there in the boardroom, I – I almost fell out of the chair. I croaked out a yes and two days later I was working in an office of shifters."

"That's pretty brave of you," Ryan said.

"Not really. The first month was horrible. I vomited every morning before going into the office. I wouldn't have lasted that first week if the person I was replacing hadn't been human. Having Amanda there training me, seeing how well she got along with the shifters and how unafraid she was, helped me a lot."

She smiled a little at Ryan. "Of course, it also helped that every shifter in the office actively avoided me the first few weeks. They could smell how scared I was of them and they deliberately emailed me rather than talking to me in person and kept their distance from reception."

"That was Cooper's idea," Ryan said. "Grayson told me last night that Cooper talked to everyone in the office after that first week about giving you your space until you were more comfortable."

"He's a really good boss," Daisy said, and then shook her head at how stupid she sounded. "I mean, he's … well, he's a good guy."

"He is," Ryan said. "I don't know him super well, Grayson and I haven't been dating for that long, but Cooper risked his life to save Gray's, and I will never forget that."

"The last couple of months, I've been doing a lot better," Daisy said. "I know Grayson probably doesn't think that because I still get kind of anxious and sweaty around him and the other guys, but I can eat lunch with Lusa now and have normal conversations with her."

"That's great," Ryan said. "Grayson said that Cooper was marking you?"

Daisy nodded, feeling weirdly embarrassed. "Yes. I had an... incident with a shifter in a coffee shop and when I talked to Cooper about it, he suggested marking me to keep other shifters away from me. It's very effective."

"Don't I know it," Ryan said with a laugh. "Grayson marks me all the time now and I swear, any shifter who gets within two feet of me acts like I have the plague."

As she spoke, a man was heading for the empty table beside their table. He was on the smaller side and Daisy would never have guessed he was a shifter, until he paused in pulling out his chair, and inhaled deeply in their direction. An uneasy look crossed his face and he studied first Ryan and then Daisy before pushing the chair in and walking away.

Ryan gestured in his direction. "See what I mean?"

"I like it," Daisy said abruptly. "I'm always so afraid and now I don't have to be afraid. Shifters avoid me. It's … it's like being released from prison."

She sounded like a drama queen and she grimaced. "Sorry, I don't mean to sound so melodramatic."

"You're allowed to feel how you feel," Ryan said. "And honestly, I can only imagine what a relief it must be to know that shifters won't go near you after spending a lifetime being afraid of them. It's a sweet thing that Cooper has done for you."

"It is," Daisy said.

Now Ryan would ask her why she was so afraid of shifters, and Daisy would have to be rude. She liked Ryan but she didn't know her very well. She wasn't about to share her life story with someone who was practically a stranger.

Instead of asking why she was afraid, Ryan said, "So, would you be open to helping Cooper?"

"Yes," Daisy said. "Whatever he needs."

Oh yeah? So, you're gonna fuck the madness right out of him?

Her cheeks grew hot again and she took a big gulp of coffee, hoping Ryan would think her red face was from the hot coffee.

Ryan visibly relaxed. "That's great. Thank you, Daisy. I know this will be hard for you, but I promise you that Cooper won't hurt you. It doesn't have to be every night. If you could spend even two or three evenings with him a week, I think that will make a huge difference. And if you'd like, Grayson and I can be there too. We can have dinner at our place or at Cooper's. Or yours, if that's where you're most comfortable."

It would be a cold day in hell before she let any of them see the shitty building she lived in. It was two crumbling walls away from being condemned, as far as she was concerned. She kept her apartment clean, but it was a tiny studio apartment with cracked ceilings, leaking faucets, and mold growing in her bathroom no matter how much she cleaned. The furniture was... well, her furniture consisted of a lumpy loveseat, a gouged and stained coffee table, a bookshelf with a missing shelf, and an air mattress as her bed.

Jeff had drained her bank account and maxed out her credit card, and she'd spent the last of her cash moving here to California. Most of her paycheque went to paying her credit card debt, leaving the bare minimum to cover living expenses, but really, she had no one to blame but herself. At the end of the day, she'd believed Jeff's lies about the inheritance, believed him when he said the money she was spending on him would be paid back in full.

"Daisy?"

Jesus, she'd zoned out again. Ryan was going to think she was a real idiot.

"Sorry. I'm happy to help Cooper and I think I'll be okay spending time alone with him, but if not, I'll definitely call you."

"Okay," Ryan said. "Thank you, Daisy."

"What if it isn't enough?" Daisy said.

"What do you mean?" Ryan said, but her look suggested she knew exactly what Daisy was talking about.

"What if he goes mad anyway because I won't, uh, have sex with him. I heard what Grayson said about a friendship not being enough. If Cooper's lion thinks I'm his mate, he'll push Cooper to ask me for more. To… to sleep with him. Right?"

She held her breath, a weird part of her hoping that Ryan would tell her that yes, she was right and if Daisy was a real team player, she'd climb into Cooper's bed, spread her legs, and let Cooper have his deliciously dirty way with her.

For the greater good, of course.

Instead of trying to convince Daisy to fuck Cooper, Ryan said, "That's true, but we have a plan for that as well, so don't worry. We're not going to ask you to be anything more than friends with Cooper so don't stress about having to do anything else. Cooper won't pressure you for sex, I promise."

"You have a plan for that too?" Daisy echoed. She waited, jealousy gnawing at her insides, for Ryan to elaborate. Grayson had said something about finding another woman to sleep with Cooper. Had they already found someone?

"Yes," Ryan said. Instead of sharing the plan, she said, "So, are you originally from California?"

Knowing a subject change when she heard one, Daisy swallowed down her disappointment and said, "No. I grew up in Connecticut."

"WHAT? HOLY SHIT. ARE YOU ALL RIGHT?"

Cooper paused outside of Lusa's office. It was Monday morning and although Daisy wasn't in the office yet – slightly unusual as she normally was the first one at the office – his lion was in a fantastic mood. Ryan's conversation with Daisy on the weekend was a success. Daisy had agreed to spend time with him outside of the office. While his human side was struggling with some shame about looking so weak, his lion side was practically euphoric over the news and had been purring like a kitten for hours.

The first thing we'll do is mark her again, his lion rumbled. *You should let me do it this time. You don't do it right.*

He ignored his lion and stuck his head into Lusa's office as she said, "All right. No, I'll let Coop know. Are you sure you don't want me to pick you up once you're done with the police? I'll be at the Landon's place this morning for an hour or so and can swing by when I'm done. You sure? Okay. See you later."

"Everything okay?" Cooper said when she ended the call.

"Hey, that was Daisy," Lusa said. "She's going to be late to work."

"What's wrong?" His stomach clenched and his lion stopped purring.

"Her car was broken into last night. She said she didn't have anything worth stealing in the car, but they broke all the windows and slashed her tires. She's waiting for the police to arrive to take her statement and then she has to arrange for her car to be towed. I told her I'd pick her up, but she said she'd take the – Coop? Where are you going?"

She followed him to his office and watched as he

103

unlocked the drawer that held the employee's personnel files and yanked it open. He grabbed Daisy's and flipped it open, rifling through the documents until he found the paper with her address on it.

His eyes widened. Holy fuck... Daisy lived in the goddamn Bartwell neighbourhood.

"She lives in Bartwell," he said.

Lusa made a face. "Half of those apartment buildings are run by slumlords. It's a terrible neighbourhood. I'm not surprised her car was broken into."

He stuffed her file back into the drawer and locked the drawer before heading toward the cubicles in the middle of the office. "Chase! Hey, Chase, you here yet?"

Chase's head popped up above his cubicle wall. "Yeah, boss. What's up?"

"Can you listen for phones? Daisy won't be in until later."

"Sure." Chase followed him toward reception. "You going out?"

He nodded as Lusa said, "Coop, you're supposed to be going with me to the Landon client at nine."

"You can handle it on your own," he said. "I trust you."

His lion growling and pacing restlessly within him, Cooper left the office.

CHAPTER 10

Daisy didn't know if the police officer was a shifter or not and she was kind of freaking out about it. He was tall and broad shouldered like a shifter but that didn't mean he was one. He wasn't sniffing her and backing away, but that didn't mean he wasn't a shifter. She hadn't been marked by Cooper since Friday. It was highly probable that his scent had faded on her.

The police officer walked around her car and she backed up a few steps when he drew closer, trying not to flinch. The officer being a shifter or not was the least of her damn worries. Not when she had a destroyed car and a letter shoved under her door early this morning with a written notice of immediate termination of lease.

She clapped her hand over her mouth to block the hysterical laughter that wanted to escape. Jesus, what did she do now? She had twenty-four hours to find a new place to live, and maybe enough money in the bank for a week at a motel if she ate nothing but crackers and peanut butter.

She'd have to quit her job. She'd have to quit her job and ask Megan for a loan for a plane ticket back to Connecticut.

She could crash on Megan's couch for a month or so while she looked for another job.

You'll never see Cooper again.

"Ma'am?" The police officer had stopped circling the car and was standing next to her. She backed up a step and tried to smile at him. God, she hoped he wasn't a shifter.

"My car is pretty much toast, right?" she said.

He nodded. "I'm not a mechanic but it's not looking great. It looks like in addition to slashing your tires and breaking your windows, they put sugar in your fuel tank. It's gonna cost more to fix than your car is worth, I think."

She blinked back the tears and stared at her ruined car as the officer said, "Is there anyone angry with you?"

"What?" she said.

"An ex-boyfriend, maybe? A co-worker that you got into a fight with," the officer said. "You'd be surprised at what people will do when they're pissed off."

"No, I... no, there isn't anyone," she said in a low voice.

He took a step closer. Although her rational mind said he was only doing it because he couldn't hear her, her fear was clawing at her insides now and she knew she was about to lose it. She couldn't stand here a moment longer, not knowing if the officer was a shifter or not, not knowing if he might hurt her or –

"Daisy?"

She whirled around, staring wide-eyed at Cooper before crowding up against him and wrapping her arms around his waist. He hugged her tight and kissed the top of her head before rubbing her back. "It's all right, baby. You're okay."

"What are you doing here?" she said.

"Lusa told me what happened."

"How do you know where I live?"

"I looked it up in your personnel file." Keeping his arm

around her waist, he studied her car before glancing at the police officer. "Do you think this was deliberate?"

"And you are?" the police officer said.

"My boss," Daisy said.

"Her mate," Cooper said.

Her face flushed as the officer raised an eyebrow before saying, "It could be deliberate if Ms. Martin thinks there may be someone who's upset with her. That being said, we've had a rash of these types of car break-ins in the last month, so it fits the pattern."

"There isn't anyone," Daisy said.

"Then probably just bad luck," the officer said. "I have a few more boxes to fill in on the report and then we'll be finished. Give me a minute." He walked back to his car and glanced over his clipboard, filling in some information as Daisy stared up at Cooper.

"Is he a shifter?" she said.

"No, baby, he isn't," Cooper said.

She relaxed a tiny bit. "I didn't know if he was a shifter or not because I think your scent has probably worn off and I... will you mark me again when I get to the office, Cooper? Please?"

She hated the pleading sound of her voice but God, it had been so nice not to have to be afraid.

"I will," Cooper said. "I promise."

"Okay." She took a deep breath and made herself step away from his comforting solidness. "Thank you for checking on me, I appreciate it. I'll be in as soon as I'm finished here. It'll take me a little longer to get there on the bus, but I'll work through my lunch and I can make up the rest of the time on the weekend or -"

"Daisy, stop," Cooper said. "You're not taking the bus. I'll give you a ride to the office."

She swallowed hard, her throat burning with unshed tears. "Thank you, Cooper."

"You're welcome."

She wanted to hug him again, but she wrapped her arms around her own torso instead as the officer returned. He handed over her licence and the clipboard. "Sign and date at the bottom please."

She signed the report, and he took the clipboard back. "I'll get this filed and we'll contact you if we catch the person who did this."

Cooper snorted and the police officer shrugged. "Yeah, I know, but we do what we can."

He climbed into his car and drove out of the parking lot. Daisy rubbed at her forehead as Cooper studied her car.

"It's wrecked," she said. "They put sugar in the gas tank. Even if I could afford to get it fixed, it would cost more to fix it than it's worth."

She studied the rows of cars in the parking lot. Most of them were as old and crappy as hers and she shook her head. "All these cars and they pick mine to break into."

"It's shitty luck," Cooper said.

"Yeah. I need to run to my apartment and grab my purse and my lunch. I'll call a tow truck from the office. I'll be right back."

She stopped when Cooper followed her across the parking lot, staring up at him. "What are you doing?"

"Going with you," he said.

"Oh, um, that's okay. I'll only be a minute."

He studied her apartment building and the man sitting on the front step who was swaying back and forth. "If you think I'm letting you go near that drunk and coked out guy on the front steps, you're wrong."

"That's just Robert. He's harmless," Daisy said. "He lives here."

"I don't care. He could hurt you."

"He won't," she said. "He doesn't do drugs. He just drinks too much."

"Either you let me go with you or you don't go in at all," Cooper said.

"I need my purse," she said.

He didn't reply and she glared at him. "You're not the boss of me, Cooper Brooks."

"I kind of am," he said with a small grin.

"Only during working hours."

"It's twenty after eight," he said. "You start work at eight. Haven't we had this conversation before?"

"You're kind of being a jerk," she said.

"I know."

She rolled her eyes and contemplated whether she could sprint to her building before he could catch her. Probably not in this skirt and heels.

As if he could read her thoughts, he leaned down and said, "I'm faster than you, little Daisy, but you're welcome to try and outrun me."

She scowled at him and he laughed before purring and cupping the back of her neck so he could rub his face against her throat. It sent an immediate tingle of need through her belly. She bit back her moan as he purred again and said, "The sooner we get back to the office, the sooner I can mark you."

"You could mark me now," she said.

"I could." He straightened and dropped his hand from her neck, smiling at her as she scowled again.

"You're not playing fair."

"Maybe not. C'mon let's get your stuff."

She sighed and let him follow her to the building.

"Daisy? Is that you?" Robert squinted at her when she stopped at the bottom of the steps.

"Hi, Robert. How are you?" she said.

He shrugged before drinking from the bottle he held in his left hand. "Shitty. Bad news about the building, huh? I don't know what I'm gonna do… I ain't got nowhere else to go."

She glanced nervously at Cooper before hurrying up the stairs past Robert. "I'm sorry, Robert, I'm late for work. I'll chat with you tonight."

"Sure, yeah, okay," Robert mumbled. He paid no attention to Cooper as he stepped past him.

Embarrassment brewing in her belly, she opened the door to her lobby and stepped inside.

"Jesus," Cooper said before covering his nose. "Are you fucking kidding me? Daisy, this place needs to be condemned."

She pressed her lips together and headed for the stairs. There was an elevator, but it'd been broken the entire three months she lived here. As they climbed the stairs, she said, "It's not that bad."

She almost sounded like she believed it.

"You can't stay here anymore," Cooper said.

She coughed to hide her bitter laughter. He had no idea how right he was.

"I'm on the second floor," she said as she pulled open the door and stepped into the hallway.

Cooper covered his nose again and muttered a curse. She supposed the smell of urine and weed and mold was much stronger to him. She breathed through her mouth and walked briskly toward her apartment.

Before she could get to her door, the door to the apartment beside hers swung open. An old woman with a scarf covering the curlers in her silver hair and a moth eaten velvet robe tied around her thin frame, stepped into the hallway.

"Daisy! Daisy, have you heard? Did you get the notice?"

"I did, Mrs. Treaton," Daisy said. "Listen, I can't stay and talk right now but I'll talk to you after work, okay?"

Mrs. Treaton clutched at Daisy's arm. "What are you going to do? I already talked to my daughter and she said I can live with her – although I don't relish the idea of listening to her and that useless man of hers having sex night and day – but what will you do? Where will you go?"

"Can we talk after work?" Daisy patted the old woman's hand. "I'm running really late."

"But did you get the notice?" Mrs. Treaton said. "Did you, Daisy?"

"I did," she repeated.

"What notice?" Cooper said.

"Nothing," Daisy said quickly. "Mrs. Treaton, go back inside and -"

"The building's been condemned!" Mrs. Treaton released Daisy and clamped her bony fingers around Cooper's arm instead. "We got a notice this morning that we gotta be out by tomorrow at noon. They aren't giving us a choice. They said the whole building failed code and it's a health hazard to live here. I ain't surprised to tell you the truth. I got enough mold growing in my bathroom to perform multiple science experiments. Black mold too... it ain't good for you, you know."

"I know," Cooper said.

"Where is Daisy gonna go?" Mrs. Treaton said. "She ain't got no family here and she obviously don't have money if she lives in this dump."

"Mrs. Treaton," Daisy said loudly. "Go back inside please."

"She's a sweet girl," Mrs. Treaton said to Cooper. "She

shouldn't be living out on the street. Why, she'll be raped and murdered!"

"She won't be living on the street." Cooper patted the old woman's hand. "I'll take care of her."

"You promise?" Mrs. Treaton said. "She's been real good to me since she moved in. She brings me my mail and cooks my dinner some nights. And she helps me shower when my arthritis acts up. I'd hate to see her out on the street."

"She won't be," Cooper said. "I promise. She's moving out of her apartment today. I have a place for her to stay."

"That's real good. My daughter is flying in this afternoon to help me pack my shit and then she's renting a car and we're driving back to Oregon. I ain't got much, but I ain't leaving it behind." Mrs. Treaton reached up and patted Cooper's cheek. "You're a good boy then, aren't you? You one of them shifters? You're big like a shifter."

"I am," Cooper said. "I'm a lion shifter."

"Whoo-ee, I thought so," Mrs. Treaton said. "My daughter is married to a jaguar shifter. All they do is have sex night and day. It's like listening to two cats in heat, I swear to God. I tell you what, I ain't looking forward to having to listen to that in my twilight years, but an old woman like me don't got much choice. Colleen's been begging me for years to move in with her, but I liked my independence you know?"

"Yes, ma'am," Cooper said.

"Anyway, you take good care of my sweet flower, all right?" Mrs. Treaton said.

"I will," Cooper replied.

Mrs. Treaton shuffled past him to hug Daisy. "Be a good girl, Daisy. You got my email, make sure you check in with me every once in a while."

"I will," Daisy said. "Plus, we're Facebook friends, remember?"

"Ayuh, I remember," Mrs. Treaton said. "I ain't been on there much since I accidentally posted that nude selfie on my main page instead of sending it in private message like I meant to."

Behind her, Daisy could hear Cooper choking back laughter and she pressed her lips together to stop her own laughter. "Okay, well, take care, Mrs. Treaton. I'll email you."

"All right then. Be a good girl." Mrs. Treaton kissed Daisy's cheek before returning to her apartment and slamming the door shut.

Cooper stared at Daisy and, flushing, she unlocked her apartment and stepped inside. Cooper followed her in and made another grunt of disapproval. "You don't have a bed."

"I have a bed."

"An air mattress on the floor is not a bed."

"Yes, it is." She grabbed her purse from the counter in the kitchenette and grabbed her lunch from the fridge. "Okay, I'm ready to go. Let's – Cooper, what are you doing?"

He'd taken off his suit jacket and opened the tiny closet next to her air mattress. He pulled out her suitcase and dropped it on the air mattress. "You start packing your clothes. I'll call Boone and get him to pick up some boxes and bring them by so we can pack your other stuff."

He studied the loveseat and the broken bookshelf. "How attached are you to your furniture?"

"I'm not," she said. "But you're not helping me pack."

"Yes, I am," he said. "We'll load it into my truck. If you don't want your furniture, then," he glanced around her small apartment, "everything will fit in one load."

She sighed, hating what she had to say next, and a big part of her worried about what would happen to Cooper when she left. But what choice did she have? She couldn't live on the street just so she could stick around and stop Cooper from going mad.

"Cooper, you're my boss. I'm already embarrassed enough that you know my building has been condemned. I'm not getting you to pack my stuff and move it to the motel. Also, I, um, I know this is terrible timing, but I need to give you my notice of resignation."

"No," Cooper said.

She blinked at him. "What?"

"I'm not accepting your resignation."

"You have to," she said.

"No, I don't."

"Look, I don't want to quit, I really don't. But…" God, she really hated having to admit this to him, "I don't have enough money to live in a motel until I find another place to live. Which means my only option is to go back to Connecticut. So, I'm quitting. I know it's shitty of me. I wish I could give you two weeks notice but maybe we could Facetime every night to help you with your um… problem."

"You don't have to live in a motel," Cooper said. He opened the cupboards in the kitchen and pulled out some of her glassware. "You can stay with me."

She gaped at him. "I – what?"

"I have an extra bedroom. You can stay with me," he said.

"I can't stay with you."

"Why not?"

"You're my boss."

"I am," he said. "Think of it as a temporary thing until you find something else. You've already agreed to spend time with me outside of work, right? Living with me will make that easier."

She stared silently at him as he crossed his arms over his

chest and leaned against the counter. "I promise to give you space, Daisy. You know I won't hurt you, right?"

"I know," she said.

"Look, Grayson mentioned yesterday that you told Ryan you were trying to get over your fear of shifters. Being room-mates, even temporarily, will help both of us with our... problems."

She rubbed at the scar on her forearm. "What if I – what if I'm too afraid? I don't want to be scared but..."

"If you are, we'll come up with another solution that doesn't involve you quitting and moving back to Connecticut. Okay?"

She didn't reply and Cooper said in a low and cajoling voice, "You don't have much of a choice, baby. Even if this place wasn't condemned, I wouldn't let you stay here. It isn't safe."

She didn't object when he stepped closer and took her hand, rubbing his thumb over the pulse point in her wrist. "It's only until you find a new apartment, Daisy. A month at most, right?"

"What will everyone else at work say?" she said.

"I don't care, and you shouldn't either," he said. "If they ask, I'll tell them you're doing it to help me. They all think I'm on the verge of going insane anyway, remember?"

He smiled at her, but she scowled and squeezed his hand. "Don't joke about that, Cooper. It isn't funny."

He sobered and rubbed her wrist again. "Will you try, Daisy?"

She stared into his gorgeous blue eyes and nodded. "Yes, I'll try."

CHAPTER 11

"God, that is some craptastic luck." Lusa grabbed her sandwich from the fridge and plopped into the chair next to Daisy. "Car broken into and your building condemned. Although, honestly, not surprised about the condemned building thing. Your neighbourhood is terrible. Why did you rent there, Daisy?"

Daisy poked at her sandwich. "It was the only thing I could afford. I have some, uh… debt."

Her face heated with embarrassment but Lusa nodded. "Tell me about it. Between rent, car payment, and my student loan debt, some months I barely have enough money for food. It's frustrating as hell. What are you going to do for a place to stay? I only have a one bedroom, but you're welcome to crash on my couch if you need it."

"Oh, that's, um, okay. I have a place to stay for now," Daisy said.

"With Cooper?" Lusa bit into her sandwich.

Daisy poked a hole right through the bread of her sandwich. "How did you know?"

"Girl, please, you are covered in his scent. Figured Coop

would have you stay with him. It's easier for you to bang him when you're at his place, right?"

Daisy's mouth dropped open. "I'm not... I ...what?"

Lusa sipped some water before pulling out a piece of lunch meat from her sandwich and popping it into her mouth. "It's really nice of you to sleep with Cooper so he doesn't go mad, Daisy, especially considering how terrified you are of shifters. Talk about taking one for the team."

She laughed. "Although, my friend Kara told me that just because I don't find Cooper attractive, doesn't mean that other women don't. Apparently, according to her, he's fine as hell. Me, I like brunettes. You're into blonds though, huh?"

Daisy gulped down some water before clearing her throat. "I'm not having sex with Cooper."

Lusa paused with her sandwich to her mouth. "Oh. Shit. Sorry. I thought you were because you're covered in Coop's scent and because Boone..."

Her face went red and she set her sandwich down. "Oh fuck. I'm gonna kill Boone. I'm sorry, Daisy."

"It's okay," Daisy said. "I, uh, I smell like him because I asked him to mark me."

She touched her throat a bit self-consciously. Thanks to how few personal possessions she'd brought with her from Connecticut, after Boone dropped off some boxes, it had taken her and Cooper less than an hour to pack up her stuff. They'd gone to his place, put her stuff in his spare bedroom, and then Cooper drove her back to the office. He was late for a client meeting, but he'd still taken the time to mark her like he'd promised before leaving with Gray and Wes for the meeting.

"Earth to Daisy," Lusa said.

"Sorry, what did you say?" Daisy said.

"Why are you asking him to mark you?" Lusa said.

"Because I'm afraid," Daisy said. "I'm afraid of shifters I don't know and even most of the ones I do know, but when Cooper marks me with his scent, it keeps other shifters away from me. I go to the grocery store and they avoid me. I have no problem telling who's a shifter and who isn't because the shifters so obviously avoid me. It's like… magic."

Lusa nodded. "Coop's a pretty powerful lion shifter and you stink like him. I'm not surprised other shifters are staying the hell out of your way."

"So, they really can tell just by his scent that he's, um, strong and stuff?" Daisy said.

Lusa nodded. "Oh, for sure. Are female shifters giving you," she grinned, "excuse the expression… catty looks?"

"I don't think so?" Daisy said. "But he hasn't been marking me for very long."

"You'll start getting the looks from them," Lusa said. "We female shifters like the big powerful males, and Coop's scent will be a damn aphrodisiac to some females. They're gonna be pissed that he has a mate. Or they think he does."

Daisy's throat closed up to a pinhole and she stared down at the sandwich she could no longer eat. "Will they go after me?"

She could hear the fear in her voice. Lusa made a soothing motion with her hand. "No, no. That isn't what I meant. I mean, yeah, they'll be annoyed that a powerful lion shifter is taken by a human, but they're not going to go after you. No one wants a pissed off lion shifter on the hunt for them. Especially one like Coop."

"What do you mean – one like Coop?" Daisy said.

"He's over the top possessive and can be jealous," Lusa said. "You can smell it in his scent. It's another reason his marking is so effective on you. Other males can smell that he's the possessive and jealous type."

Daisy stared at her and Lusa ate another bite of her sandwich before saying, "You okay?"

"This is… I mean, it's fascinating."

"It isn't anything you can't find out by Googling," Lusa said. "Although with your fear of us, you probably avoid anything to do with us at all. Except for working with us… which, hey, I've wanted to ask this forever but why are you working with an office full of shifters when you're so terrified of us?"

"An immersion thing," Daisy said. "My therapist suggested it."

"Makes sense. Although, a few of us had a bet going in the office the first month you worked here about when you would have a panic attack and sprint out of the office and never return," Lusa said.

Daisy laughed because really, it was funny when you thought about it. She sipped some water and took a small bite of her sandwich. "It's helped a certain amount, and I think spending time with Cooper will help too. But I can't… I mean, having sex with him is too much immersion. Forgetting that he's my boss and it's inappropriate, I don't think I'll ever be over my fear enough to be, um, intimate with a shifter."

"That's fair." Lusa smiled at her. "But you have come a long way in only three months. Hell, you never smell afraid when we have lunch together now, and only smell slightly terrified when Boone and the others come near you."

Daisy made a face and Lusa's smile widened. "That was meant to be encouraging. You really are doing better and I'm proud of you, girl."

"Thanks, Lusa. I'm glad we're friends."

"Me too."

There was some awkward silence before Lusa said, "I'm

really sorry about what I said about fucking Cooper. That was totally over the line."

"No, it's fine," Daisy said. "I'm not sleeping with him, but, like I said, I am spending more time with him to try and, uh, help him."

"Well, it's working," Lusa said. "Honestly, I was super worried about him last week, all of us were. He was," she paused, "not good. The change in him has been so dramatic that it's why I thought you were sleeping with him, even though I know how terrified you are of shifters. I figured you had to be giving it to him on the regular for his lion to calm down so quickly."

She winced and tossed the crusts of her sandwich into the garbage. "Christ, I am batting a thousand today. Sorry to be so crude."

"It's okay," Daisy said. "I think letting him mark me helps his lion too so maybe that's why he's better?"

"Oh, for sure, it does. Our cats fucking live to mark our mates. It's ridiculous. Honestly, this whole mate thing is kind of ridiculous, but what are you going to do, you know? Our cat falls for someone and that's it... we're gonzo for them."

"So, do you mate for life then?" Daisy said.

"Some do," Lusa said. "But our cats can fall out of love with their mates, just like humans do. Shifters can and do get divorces."

"Oh," Daisy said. "What happens if you're, um, cat falls for someone but you don't?"

"Doesn't happen," Lusa said. "Our human side is always, at the very least, attracted to the human or shifter our cat is hot for. It doesn't take long before we fall as hard for the person as our cat has. And it works the opposite way too. I can be super attracted to someone that my cat only finds a little attractive, but her feelings can intensify to match mine as she gets to know the guy better."

"Holy crap," Daisy said. "It's like you have a whole second personality."

Lusa laughed. "Not quite, and the relationship between our human side and our cat side is hard to explain to humans but trust me… most of the time we are in complete harmony."

"But if you're not…"

"It's bad if we're not. Go insane bad if we're not," Lusa said. "Coop's lion is super powerful which is why the madness was happening so quickly."

Her expression turned serious. "I know I'm making light of it, but what you're doing for Cooper is incredibly kind and generous. Coop is a great boss and an amazing person. Watching him descend into madness was terrifying for all of us. Thank you for working through your fear to help him. Even spending extra time will help him until he can find another woman that he and his cat find attractive. With any luck, he'll convince his cat that she's mate material and you'll be off the hook."

"Right," Daisy said. Her stomach was churning, and she reminded herself it was completely ridiculous to be jealous of some unknown woman who may or may not become Cooper's mate. It shouldn't and didn't bother her to think about Cooper calling someone else his 'little mate' in that deep sexy voice of his, or of him marking another woman instead of her. That was the end goal, right? For him to find his actual mate.

"You okay?" Lusa said. "You look kind of pissed."

"Yeah. I," she took a deep breath and decided to say it, "I'm worried that me spending more time with Cooper will actually do more harm than good. Assuming we get along okay, won't it just make his cat more, uh, attracted to me?

Make him think I'm his mate even more than he already does?"

Lusa shrugged. "Maybe, maybe not. You won't be sleeping with Cooper so if he can find another woman to sleep with, that might transfer his cat's, uh, affections, over to her. I know it sounds fucked up, but our cat sides are controlled by base urges. Eating, fucking, procreating, and protecting their mate and cubs are really all they think about it. So, if Cooper finds another woman to have sex with and it's good between them, then the chances of his cat seeing that woman as his mate are really high."

"Oh," Daisy said. "Well, that's, uh, good. I think the other guys have a plan to help Cooper meet someone else."

"Yeah, they do," Lusa said. "Boone told me that if you didn't sleep with Cooper, they had a potential woman lined up who knew the score and was happy to try and help."

"Do you know -"

Chase stuck his head into the lunchroom. "Hey, sorry to interrupt, but David Landon is on the line and -"

Lusa sighed. "God help me. He's a nice guy but the questions… we're installing the system tomorrow morning and I hope like hell he's not there. It'll take twice as long."

She tossed her lunch trash in the can and smiled at Chase. "Give me two minutes to get back to my desk and then transfer the call, would you, Chase?"

"He's not asking for you," Chase said. "He's asking for Daisy."

"YOU SERIOUSLY CONVINCED HER TO LIVE WITH YOU?" Grayson twisted in the passenger seat of the SUV and stared at Cooper like he was some sort of dark wizard. "How the fuck did you do that?"

"I told you, her building is condemned and she's short on cash." Cooper pulled out of the parking lot and headed for the freeway.

"Yeah, but she doesn't have any friends she can stay with?" Grayson said.

Cooper shrugged, his face flushing when Wes spoke from the back seat. "Did you give her a choice?"

"Yes... mostly."

"What does that mean?" Grayson said.

"It means I told her she was staying with me but if it was too much for her, we'd find somewhere else. I had to do something. She was gonna quit and move back to Connecticut. I can't live in fucking Connecticut, Gray. Do you know how goddamn cold it gets there?"

Coop didn't miss the alarmed look that Gray gave Wes in the back seat. He merged onto the freeway. "I'm not trying to freak you out."

"Well, you are," Gray said. "I know we said it would be good to have Daisy spend more time with you but this... this isn't good, buddy. If she's living with you, sleeping down the damn hall from you, it's only going to make things worse when she won't sleep with you. Tell him, Wes."

"Gray's right, Cooper," Wes said. "Think about how pissed your lion will be when Daisy is sleeping in your house and you won't mate with her."

"Look, it probably won't work anyway, and I'll have to rent her an apartment or something.

Gray's eyebrows almost disappeared into his hairline. "Now you're going to rent her an apartment? You suddenly win the lottery or get an inheritance you didn't mention?"

Cooper just snorted before flicking on the turn signal to merge off the freeway.

"Where are you doing?" Grayson said.

"Back to the office," Cooper said.

"Not so fast. We have a dinner meeting with Roger Standen about security for his work trip. Did you forget?"

"Shit," Cooper said. "I did." He flicked off his turn signal. "I'll drop you guys off at the restaurant and then come back after I drive Daisy home from the office."

"It's a forty minute drive to the office from the restaurant and with rush hour traffic, it'll take you closer to an hour and a half," Grayson said. "The meeting will be over by the time you get back."

"Daisy doesn't have a car, and I'm not letting her take public transportation," Cooper said. "She's little and any asshole could hurt her."

"No shifter will go near her," Grayson said. "Not with the way she smells like you."

"Humans can't smell it," Cooper said.

"Cooper, you can't keep blowing off meetings to -"

"The safety of my mate is more important than a fucking meeting," Cooper growled. His hands clenched around the steering wheel and he gave his best friend a quick, but he hoped effective, glare. "Don't you dare try and tell me it isn't."

Wes leaned forward, his phone in his hand. "I asked Eleanor to pick her up."

"Your driver?" Gray said.

"She's not *my* driver," Wes said. "She's *a* driver. But she's used to picking me up at the office around this time, so she might have an open spot."

His phone dinged and he nodded. "She does. Problem

solved, Cooper. Eleanor will give Daisy a ride to your place from the office."

"Is she a safe driver?" Cooper said.

"Oh my God, Coop," Grayson said.

Cooper handed him his cell phone. "Text Daisy and let her know that Eleanor will be picking her up after work and driving her home. Tell her Eleanor is a human," he glanced at Wes who nodded in confirmation, "and not to worry about the cost, I'm paying for it."

"HEY, YOU'RE DAISY?" THE YOUNG AND PERKY BRUNETTE sitting behind the wheel of the black Camry was not at all what Daisy expected.

"Yes, um, you're Eleanor?"

The woman laughed. "Sure am. Let me guess – you were expecting a little old lady driver, right?"

Daisy grinned as she clicked her seatbelt in place. "Maybe."

Eleanor twisted in the seat to look at Daisy, hooking one slender arm over the head rest. "My mom named me after her favourite aunt. Her favourite *dead* aunt."

She rolled her pretty brown eyes before smiling at Daisy. "Honestly, most of my friends call me El. Unless my mom is around. She gives them shit if they shorten it."

"Well, it's very nice to meet you, Eleanor. Thank you for the ride home." Daisy flushed. She was acting like Eleanor was doing her a favour instead of doing her job.

"Don't mention it. I'm normally here every day picking up Wes anyway, so it was no problem."

"You drive Wes home?" Daisy said.

"Yeah, he doesn't drive. You didn't know that?" Eleanor checked her mirrors before pulling out into the traffic. With rush hour, it was slow going, and she glanced at Daisy in the rear-view mirror as they inched along. "You work with him, right?"

"I do, but Wes doesn't really…"

"Talk?" Eleanor said.

"Exactly."

"Well, at least it's not only me. I've been driving him to and from work for over a year and swear to God, he's said less than five sentences to me. The most I've heard him talk was when he got a phone call on the way to work one day."

Daisy laughed. "That sounds like Wes."

Eleanor glanced at her in the rear-view mirror again, her cheeks a little too red, her eyes a little too bright. "He seems like a good guy though."

"He is," Daisy agreed. "He, uh, he cares a lot about his friends."

"Yeah, I'm not surprised. He's a tiger shifter, is that right?"

"Lion," Daisy said.

"Oh. I figured it had to be one or the other. He's so big. Anyway, I'm glad to hear that he is a good guy. I mean, I figured he was… he's a fantastic tipper."

"You really drive him to work and home every day?" Daisy said.

"I really do." Eleanor turned left and then slammed her hand down on her horn when a woman in a red Mercedes cut her off. "C'mon, lady! I'm driving here!"

She smiled at Daisy. "Sorry."

"No problem. Do you know why Wes doesn't drive?"

Eleanor shook her head. "Not a clue. He doesn't do small talk, remember? I was hoping you might know."

"I wonder what he does when he has to go to client meetings on his own," Daisy said.

Eleanor stepped on the gas and zoomed through a yellow light. "Oh, I drive him to those too. Some days he books me for the entire day and I drive him to different meetings and stuff. He's definitely my best customer."

"Sounds like it," Daisy said with a small grin.

There was silence for a few minutes before Eleanor said, "I've even driven him to some personal stuff as well. Like bars and shit. Kind of weird that he doesn't get his girlfriend to drive him."

Eleanor was trying to sound casual and doing a really terrible job of it, Daisy decided. Hiding her smile, she said, "Wes doesn't have a girlfriend."

"Oh yeah? Boyfriend then?"

"Nope, he's straight."

"Cool, cool, cool," Eleanor said and then cleared her throat. "So, you know he doesn't have a girlfriend and that's he's straight, but not that he doesn't drive. That's sort of strange."

"One of our coworkers, Lusa, was trying to set him up with a friend of hers last month. She talked to me about it. She wouldn't have set him up if he had a girlfriend."

"Oh. Did he, uh, like Lusa's friend?"

"He didn't go out with her. Wes said thanks but no thanks."

Eleanor didn't say anything, but Daisy could almost see the tension ease from her shoulders. Adopting her own casual tone, Daisy said, "Wes is good looking, huh?"

Wes *was* good looking. Just because his dark eyes and dark hair with the threads of silver at the temples didn't do anything for Daisy, didn't make him unattractive. He had a fantastic body, tall and lean with broad shoulders and a narrow waist, and he always had the perfect amount of stubble on his strong jaw. Daisy might be more obsessed with the blond clean-shaven type, but she could see how other women would find Wes attractive.

Eleanor shrugged. "Not bad for an old man."

Daisy laughed. "He's not that old. He's only forty-something. How old are you?"

"Twenty-seven," Eleanor said. "You?"

"Twenty-six," Daisy said.

"You ever seen Wes go out with someone our age?" Eleanor said. That false casualness was back in her voice.

"Honestly, I've never seen Wes go out with anyone," Daisy said. "I think Wes is a bit of a loner."

"Yeah, sounds like it." Eleanor shrugged but she wasn't very good at hiding her emotions on her face. Daisy could see the disappointment even in the narrow rear-view mirror.

As if Eleanor suddenly realized what was written across her face, she forced a bright and cheerful smile at Daisy. "So, you originally from California?"

CHAPTER 12

"This is delicious." Cooper dipped the biscuit into the steaming bowl of chicken stew sitting in front of him. "I didn't expect you to make dinner but holy shit, I'm fucking glad you did."

Daisy laughed and he said, "Sorry about the cursing. I swear a lot and it's a nasty habit, I know."

"I don't care," Daisy said. "People who swear a lot are more intelligent."

"So, what you're saying is I'm a fucking genius?" Cooper said.

Daisy laughed again and his lion purred happily at the sound. Hell, it hadn't stopped purring since he got home to find Daisy in the kitchen wearing a loose t-shirt and shorts that showed off her pretty pale legs, standing by the stove and stirring a delicious smelling stew.

You should put our cub in her belly, his lion said.

Knock it off, Cooper snapped at him.

His lion retreated with a growl, and Cooper ate a few more bites of stew. If his lion knew that Cooper also wanted Daisy pregnant and barefoot in his kitchen like it was the goddamn 1950s, he'd never stop hounding Cooper to make it happen.

Cooper smiled again at Daisy. "Thank you for making dinner."

"It wasn't a problem. But, um, wasn't your meeting tonight a dinner meeting?" Daisy spooned some stew into her mouth.

"Yeah, I didn't eat much," he said. Not exactly the truth, but he had a big appetite and a fast metabolism, always had. But the last couple of weeks he'd been so focused on trying to keep his lion from going insane, that he hadn't been eating the amount he normally did.

"Okay, well I made enough for lunch leftovers too," Daisy said. "Are you sure you don't mind that I used your groceries? The potatoes and turnips and carrots were left over from when I bought you groceries and they were going to go bad soon so -"

"My food is your food," he said. "Eat whatever you want, whenever you want."

She scraped the last of the stew out of her bowl and swallowed the final spoonful. God, he loved having Daisy in his house. He selfishly hoped it took her months to find a place to live. Of course, if her new place was as big of a shithole as her last one, he wouldn't let her leave anyway.

Cool it, big guy. Daisy doesn't belong to you.

His inner voice was right, but it wouldn't stop him from refusing to let Daisy live in an unsafe neighbourhood or building. He'd move out of his own fucking house and let Daisy live here if he had to. He'd do whatever it took to keep her safe.

"So, I know I won't be here that long," Daisy said, "but we should talk about the cost of renting a room from you. I looked at some local ads and most rooms cost -"

"No," he said.

She wiped her mouth with her napkin. He could smell her annoyance with him, but it actually made him happy. Better annoyance than fear, right?

"Cooper, let me finish, please."

"I'm not charging you rent to live here, Daisy. You're doing me a favour by staying with me, remember?"

She fiddled with the corner of her napkin. "No, I'm staying here because my crappy apartment was condemned, and you felt sorry for me because I was about to be homeless."

"One hundred percent wrong," he said.

She shook her head, a small smile playing on her lips. "You're so stubborn."

"One hundred percent right," Cooper said with a grin.

"At least let me pay for my share of food," Daisy said.

"Are you planning on cooking dinner every night?"

"Probably. If you don't mind that I do. I like to cook and it's nice to have someone else to cook for," Daisy said.

"Then consider it even. I buy the food, you cook it."

"Cooper." Her annoyance and exasperation deepened.

"I love to eat and hate to cook," he said. "I know it's cliché that a single guy can't cook, but it's true. You can call my mom and ask. She tried to get me to be self-sufficient by teaching me to cook as a teenager, but it didn't stick. You cooking will save me a ton of money on food. I normally order takeout five nights a week."

"That's so bad for you," she said. "There's so much sodium in the food."

He grinned at her. "So, you living here will be good for my wallet and my health – physical and mental."

She picked at her napkin again. "Is it helping, Cooper? Be honest with me. Do you, um, feel better when I'm around?"

"Yes," he said. "I do. It's made a huge difference, Daisy."

"Even if we're never more than… friends?" She accented the word 'friends' lightly and Cooper kept the smile pasted on his face with nothing but pure willpower.

"Yes," he said. "Just friends is fine."

It wasn't fine, but he couldn't say that to her. It was nice of her to help him out by spending time with him, but at the end of the day, it wasn't her problem that his lion thought she was his mate. Or that Cooper would go mad without her.

"Are you sure?" She was giving him a look he couldn't quite read. If he hadn't known better, he would have thought she was fishing for him to say no. Maybe waiting for him to say something along the lines of, "Actually, Daisy, you're also required to spread those pretty pale thighs of yours and let me bury my face in what I'm sure is the sweetest fucking pussy I'll ever taste."

He immediately sported a hard on and he shifted in his chair, the pressure at his groin taunting him. After what happened in his office on Friday, even thinking about being with Daisy was a mistake. The fear in her eyes had killed his desire immediately. She might have wanted him for a few brief glorious minutes, but the second she was reminded of what he really was, her fear had driven out her lust for him just like that.

He hadn't been close to shifting but his eyes changing colour and his fangs descending were something that was always going to happen when he was with a woman unless he really concentrated on controlling it. And he didn't have a chance in hell of controlling it around Daisy. His need for her was too strong, too overwhelming. None of that was her fault, of course, but it was a real kick in the ass that he couldn't be with her *because* he wanted her so much.

"Cooper?" Daisy said. "Are you sure?"

"Yes," he said, forcing his smile wider until his cheeks hurt. "And I have some other, uh, ideas I'm working on so that hopefully you won't have to disrupt your life much longer."

"Right." Daisy stood up abruptly, grabbing her soup bowl and her water glass and putting them both in the dishwasher. "It's getting late and I'm pretty tired. I think I'll go to bed."

"Sure, okay. Good night, Daisy."

"Night, Cooper."

She left the kitchen, and he sniffed the air delicately, a frown crossing his face before he stood up and put his own bowl in the dishwasher and the leftover stew in the fridge. It had almost smelled like jealousy radiating from Daisy before she left the kitchen. He snorted and flicked off the lights before heading toward his own bedroom. He was an idiot.

He paused outside of Daisy's bedroom door, tempted to knock and ask her if she needed anything. His lion pushed forward, urging him on, and he raised his hand to knock before thinking better of it.

Staying overnight with him was bound to be stressful and overwhelming and scary for her. He wouldn't make it worse by invading her personal space after she'd made it clear she wanted to be left alone.

Ignoring his lion's whining to go to his mate, he walked into his bedroom and shut the door. He brushed his teeth and stripped off his clothes before climbing into bed. He stared at the wall separating him from his mate before staring up at the ceiling. Daisy in the room right next to his was both heaven and hell.

"DAISY? WHY ARE YOU UP SO EARLY?"

Cooper stumbled into the kitchen in, God help her, nothing but a pair of shorts and the most adorable case of bedhead she'd ever seen. She looked away from his magnificent chest and concentrated on pouring her coffee into a travel mug without spilling it.

"I didn't mean to wake you," she said. "Go back to bed, it's early."

"I just said that." He squinted at her before dropping into a chair and yawning hugely. "Please don't tell me you're a morning person."

He rubbed at his chest and heat flared in her belly. Jesus, she needed to get control of herself. But it would be really great if the man would put a damn shirt on. She considered saying something to him before dropping the idea. This was Cooper's house. If he wanted to walk around in nothing but a pair of shorts, it was his right. It wasn't his fault that she was suddenly acting like a horny housewife.

"I'm not," she said. "I'm definitely not. But I have to take three buses to get to the office in time for eight so -"

"You're not taking the bus." He yawned again. "Is there any coffee left?"

"Yes." She poured him a cup and handed it to him, barely registering that she didn't flinch or jerk away when their fingers touched.

He took a sip of it and she pulled some milk from the fridge and set it on the table in front of him.

"Thanks, Daisy." He poured some milk in and sipped at the coffee again. "Jesus, even your coffee tastes better than mine."

She glanced at her watch before grabbing a container of stew from the fridge. "I put some stew and a couple of biscuits into a container for you for lunch. I'll see you at the office."

His long fingers wrapped around her wrist, pulling her gently to a stop. Instead of fear, an almost overwhelming amount of lust went through her. Cooper's nostrils flared and she flushed dully. He could smell her lust, she knew he could, but it wasn't like she could control it.

Sure you could. You could think about how Cooper looked with glowing eyes and fangs, and how it would feel when he used his sharp claws to shred through your chest cavity.

Normally those types of thoughts sent adrenaline rushing to her body and brought on her fight or flight instinct. But today… nothing. Cooper wouldn't hurt her. He just wouldn't. And honestly, she could kick herself for her reaction when he kissed her on Friday. So, his eyes had changed colour and he showed a little fang. He was a lion shifter…it was bound to happen, right?

Who are you and what have you done with the real Daisy?

He dropped her wrist. "You're not taking the bus. You can drive in with me."

"I don't want to be a bother or -"

"You're not," he said. "There's no need for you to take the bus to and from work when you can hitch a ride with me. And you can borrow my truck anytime you want for personal errands or whatever until you find a new car."

"Well, thank you, that's very nice of you. I appreciate the rides to work and the offer to borrow your truck but I'm not getting another car. I don't want a car loan and I don't have enough cash to buy one so, I'm investing in a bus pass and a good pair of shoes." She forced a smile at him and tried to pretend that she wasn't almost crushed with shame at the poor state of her finances.

"No," he said and then took another sip of coffee.

"What do you mean no?"

"You're not taking public transportation. I'll help you find a decent car and loan you the cash to buy it."

"Um, like hell you are," she said.

He shrugged. "You're not taking public transportation, baby. It isn't safe."

"It's perfectly safe," she said. "Thousands of people take the bus, Cooper. And now that shifters avoid me, I don't -"

"Humans can't smell my scent," he said.

"I'm not afraid of humans."

That stubborn look crossed his face and he shook his head with a finality that was kind of cute. "My mate is not taking the bus. End of story."

She popped her fists on her hips and glared at him. "Your mate will take the bus if she wants to, Cooper Brooks."

He studied her and when he began to purr, she shook her head. "Don't you dare try and... and sweet-purr me into getting what you want."

His purr turned into a laugh. "Sweet-purr?"

"You know what I mean," she said. "I appreciate you wanting to keep me safe but taking the bus is not some precarious mission that puts me in mortal danger."

He leaned back in his chair and shrugged lazily. "Fine. If you want to take the bus, you can take the bus."

She wrinkled her nose at him. "Gee, thanks for your permission."

He laughed. "You're welcome. When you buy your bus pass, grab me one too, would you? I'll stop at the ATM and get some cash for it on the way to work."

"What? Why do you need a bus pass?"

He gave her an adorably innocent look. "Because I'll be on the bus with you."

"Cooper, you... are you being serious right now?"

"Yep."

"You're going to get on the bus every time I get on the bus?"

"Yep."

"Oh my God. You realize you're being a total ass, right?"

"Yep."

She covered her mouth with her hand and manufactured a small coughing fit to hide her stupid grin. She wanted to be annoyed with him. Wanted to act like she was pissed off that he was going all macho lion shifter on her, but the truth was... she liked it. When was the last time someone had looked after her? Growing up in foster care, she'd been treated more like a cheque than a child. More often than not, she couldn't count on any of her foster parents to take care of her beyond her basic needs of being fed and clothed.

She had Megan, of course, but it wasn't the same as having parents or a partner who loved her. Her loneliness, her need to have someone who loved her and cared for her, had blinded her to Jeff's true nature. And even though she'd been the one who looked after him in the relationship, she'd told herself that when push came to shove, Jeff would be there for her.

Only, he hadn't been there for her. He hadn't loved her or cared for her the way he was supposed to. The only thing he'd cared about was her good credit and trusting nature.

She realized that while she'd been thinking, Cooper had stood and poured her a glass of water. He handed it to her, and she took a small sip. "Thank you."

"You're welcome."

She studied his bare chest, beyond tempted to trail her fingers through that light layer of golden coloured hair. Jeff was the first and only man she'd slept with and he'd waxed his chest on the regular. She'd asked him once to let his chest hair grow in and he'd given her a look like she'd asked him to put a hive of bees on his head.

"So, we stopping at the ATM for cash for a bus pass or not?" Cooper said with a small grin.

"No," she said, "but you're not buying me a stupid car."

"That's fine, I can compromise," he said. "If I can't give you a ride somewhere or my truck isn't available for you to use, I'll pay for a rideshare."

"That's not a compromise," she said.

"Sure, it is."

She huffed out an angry snort and he grinned and purred to her. She watched in fascination when his blue eyes turned a dark yellow and his voice deepened and thickened into a rasp. "Our mate is adorable when she's annoyed with us."

It was his lion speaking. She knew that instinctively and while it made her a little nervous, she was more captivated by the little flecks of blue she could see in the dark yellow of his iris. Were those flecks of blue always there or –

"I'm sorry, baby." There was remorse in Cooper's voice, and she blinked in confusion when he backed away, the dark yellow turning back to blue. "I didn't mean to scare you."

"You didn't," she said. "That, um, that was your lion, wasn't it?"

He hesitated and then nodded. "Yes."

"I didn't know your cat side could talk."

"It's more like they talk through us, it's kind of hard to explain. It doesn't happen very often, to be honest."

His pupils turned to slits and she waited patiently until he returned to her. "Sorry."

"It's fine. I don't mind if you talk to your lion around me. You know that, right?"

He didn't reply and she flushed. "Okay, I used to mind

because it made me nervous. But it doesn't anymore, I promise. What did your lion say to you?"

He looked a little embarrassed. "Nothing important."

"Does he talk a lot to you?" Daisy said.

"Depends on his mood. In general, no. But if he wants something, he never shuts up about it."

She smiled. "Lusa told me that if a shifter talks a lot, then normally their cat is talkative too. She said Boone's cat probably talks all the time to him and Wes's cat probably barely says two words in a day."

"That sounds about right." He glanced at the clock on the wall. "I'm gonna have a shower and get dressed."

"Do you eat breakfast?" she said. "I could make some pancakes."

His stomach growled and he grinned at her. "I love pancakes."

"All right. Um, before you go to shower, should you, uh, mark me again?"

When he didn't say anything, she cleared her throat. "I figured it would be better to do it here than at the office."

Red was creeping up his neck and she could feel her own flush of embarrassment when he said, "I don't need to mark you today. You're still covered pretty heavily in my scent."

"Oh, okay. Right. Well, uh, I'll start making pancakes then."

"Thanks, Daisy."

She made herself smile at him. "You're welcome, Cooper."

CHAPTER 13

"I seriously can't believe you're living with a shifter. And not just a shifter but your boss." Megan's voice was too loud, and Daisy glanced at the wall that separated her bedroom from Cooper's before making a shushing motion.

"What? I thought you said he went to bed." Megan lowered her voice.

"He did," Daisy said. "But our rooms are right next to each other."

Megan cocked her head. "Is there a lock on your door?"

"Yeah," Daisy said.

"Are you using it?"

She blinked at her. "No, of course not. Why would I?"

Megan's face broke out into a broad smile and Daisy could see her clapping her hands even through the small screen of her phone. "Daze, babe, I'm so proud of you!"

"For what?"

Megan leaned forward until her lips were all that were in view. "You are sleeping in a room right next to a shifter and you're not locking the door, you're not afraid, you're acting like it's no big thing, girl. Why the fuck do you think I'm proud of you?"

Daisy laughed quietly. "Well, thank you. I'm not trying to burst your bubble here, but I think it's more to do with who the shifter is. I'm still afraid of shifters."

She stretched out on the bed, propping the pillows behind her back, happy all over again to have a bed to sleep in instead of a stupid air mattress on the floor. "Today at work, Chase came into the supply room when I was in there and I didn't realize it. When I turned around and saw him blocking the door, I almost had a damn panic attack. I was definitely shaking, and I know he could smell my fear because he started apologizing and practically ran out of the room."

She sighed. "I felt so stupid. Chase is a really nice guy. Cooper makes him cover reception during my lunch hour and he never complains even though it isn't really his job. I think I hurt his feelings when I got so scared."

"Small steps, babe. Small steps. Three months ago, you would have started screaming if he was in the room with you, right?"

"Yeah, I guess so."

Megan smiled at her. "I'm really sorry that your shithole apartment got condemned and your shithole car broken into, but I'm also really happy that you're living somewhere safe."

"It is nice to have a bed again," Daisy admitted.

"You gonna invite your boss into that bed?"

"Megan!" Daisy glanced at the wall again. "You know I'm not."

Megan shrugged. "No, actually I don't. You're living with him, cooking him pancakes for breakfast, and driving to and from work with him. Hell, you're practically fucking engaged at this point."

Daisy rolled her eyes. "I told you – we're only doing all

of these things because it's beneficial for both of us. I have a place to stay while I look for a new apartment and Cooper's lion is happy."

"What will you say when he asks for sex?" Megan said.

"He won't." Daisy folded her legs under her and hiked the quilt a little higher. "He told me himself that he's looking for another woman to have sex with."

"Seriously? He said that to you?"

"Well, not in those words but the message was clear," Daisy said.

"You sound jealous," Megan said.

"I'm not."

"Aren't you?"

"Shut up, Meg-head."

She expected that would make Megan laugh, it normally did, but her best friend just stared solemnly at her through the phone. "You should try sleeping with him, Daze."

"What? You know I can't."

Megan shrugged. "I'm starting to think you could. It's obvious you're attracted to him. Hell, you made out with him in his office, remember? Maybe sleeping with him would help you get over your fear of him."

"I'm not afraid of him," Daisy said. "I used to be but now I'm... well, I'm not. I don't think. Jesus... this is confusing."

"I know I told you it wasn't a good idea before, but I've changed my mind. I think you should try sleeping with him. You'll know then for certain if you're still afraid of him and if you're not, maybe banging him will help you get over your fear of other shifters."

Daisy laughed. "How exactly would that help me?"

Megan grinned at her. "For God's sake, girl, I'm trying to get you laid. Work with me here. You need to find out how amazing sex can be, and you know that lion shifter will be game."

"You don't know he'll be good at sex," Daisy said.

"He will be," Megan said. "Trust me on this."

"How many lion shifters have you slept with?" Daisy asked.

"Enough. Look, obviously you shouldn't do anything you don't want to, but I do think you should at least consider the idea. Honestly, I haven't seen you looking this happy and relaxed since... well, ever, to be blunt. You don't have that pinched look on your face anymore, you don't jump at every little sound... Cooper is good for you, babe."

"I had a pinched look on my face?" Daisy said.

Megan waved her statement off. "Just consider it, okay? You could get some good sex for once in your life, and from the sounds of it, maybe an awesome boyfriend too."

"I can't date my boss. That's weird."

"No, what's weird is letting him mark you until you're so horny that you're making out with him in his office," Megan said.

Daisy cocked her head, listening intently as Megan peered at her through the screen. "What? What's going on?"

"I thought I heard the stairs creak," Daisy said in a low voice. "I don't want Cooper hearing us discuss my sex life."

"More like lack of sex life," Megan said.

"Ha, ha," Daisy said. She listened for a few seconds more but when it was completely silent, decided the noise she heard was her imagination. "What if I try and I can't actually go through with it? I would feel like a horrible tease. Or what if the sex isn't good and I don't want to keep sleeping with him? That wouldn't be fair to Cooper. It would be basically leading him on. His lion already thinks I'm his mate. If I slept with Cooper and I didn't like it and never did it again, it would be even harder to convince his lion that I'm not his mate. I don't want Cooper going crazy just because I don't like the way he, uh, bangs me."

Megan tugged absently at her hair. "Well, you make a good point. But, Jesus, girl, don't you want to experience good sex at least once in your life? Maybe have a man actually make you come?"

"Jeff made me come," Daisy said.

"Once," Megan said. "He made you come once in how many years of sleeping with him? Face it, babe, you have no idea what good sex is."

"Maybe not," Daisy said. "But, again, you don't know that Cooper is good at it."

"I stand by my statement that he will be awesome at sex. I've only slept with one shifter who wasn't great at it."

"Seriously, how many shifters have you slept with?"

"Wouldn't you like to know, you perv," Megan said. "I gotta go, I have an early day tomorrow and I want to relax in the tub for a bit. Love you, babe. Call me if you need anything."

"Love you too." Daisy ended the call and tossed her phone on the bed before lying back and staring at the ceiling.

Tonight had been very… pleasant. After work, she and Cooper had stopped at the grocery store and picked up groceries for the week. She grinned up at the ceiling. If she thought Cooper's scent had kept shifters away, it was nothing compared to having the actual Cooper with her. It had been crystal clear which shoppers were shifters and which were humans just by their reaction to Cooper. For the first time in her life she'd felt strong and almost powerful, which was stupid because she was small and weak.

Cooper makes you feel strong.

She rolled onto her side and stared at their shared wall.

Yes, she supposed that was true. She did feel strong when she was around him. Maybe it had something to do with him being literally the only shifter she didn't feel nervous around. Even her anxiety over certain actions – like when he talked to his lion and his pupils changed, or when he growled, or his eyes changed colour – had faded and been replaced with a weird kind of fascination.

And the purring. Don't forget how awesome his purring is.

She sat up in bed and pushed the covers back before swinging her feet over the side. Even though it was after ten, she wasn't tired. After dinner, she and Cooper had watched TV for a couple of hours and kept any conversation related to the shows they watched. She'd sat on the couch, a small part of her hoping that Cooper would sit beside her, but he'd sat in the armchair across the room.

She ran her hands through her hair before standing. She'd make herself a cup of tea, maybe that would help relax her enough to sleep. She walked toward the door, pausing when she caught a glimpse of herself in the mirror on the wall. She was wearing just a pair of sleep shorts and tank top, but she didn't bother grabbing her robe. Cooper had gone to bed over an hour ago and it would only take her a few minutes to make her tea.

She walked down the staircase in the dark, keeping her steps light, and walked to the kitchen. She stepped inside, her breath catching in her throat when she saw Cooper standing next to the sink. Shit. He had been walking down the stairs earlier.

He was wearing just a pair of shorts again and the moon-light shining through the window over the sink highlighted the utter perfection that was his chest.

"Can't sleep?' Cooper's deep voice washed over her, and

a shiver went down her back. He sounded like he did when he told her he could smell how wet she was for him. Heat flashed in her pelvis and zipped down her legs.

Jesus, she was losing it.

"Uh, thirsty." She hovered in the doorway, acutely aware of the way her nipples had hardened and pressed against the thin cotton of her tank top. She wanted to put her arms over her chest but that would draw attention to them. Maybe Cooper wouldn't notice.

His face hidden in the shadows, he stepped back from the sink. She took a deep breath and walked to the sink, grabbing a glass from the cupboard and filling it with water then taking a sip.

She made herself turn to face him, leaning one hip against the counter. Her face flushed red. Her eyes had adjusted to the dim light and she could see Cooper staring at her tits. She cleared her throat. "You couldn't sleep either, huh?"

He cocked his head and sniffed the air before rasping out a purr that sent another wave of shivers up and down her spine. "Your friend was right, my little mate."

"I…what?"

He took a step closer. The moonlight filtered across his face and although his eyes were still blue, she could see the desire and the lust stamped across his features.

"I can make you come," he said. "I can make you come until you're crying my name and begging me to fuck you."

The muscles in her belly cramped in a spasm of pleasure and her pussy was immediately wet. He sniffed the air again as she said, "You… you heard us on the phone?"

He nodded. He hadn't touched her at all, but the heat in his gaze made her feel like she was on fire with need. "The wall between our rooms is thin and I have excellent hearing, sweet Daisy."

She turned to face the window and gripped the edge of the sink, staring blankly out the window. "I'm so embarrassed."

He moved closer. She felt the heat of his body when he stepped behind her and rested his hands on the sink beside hers, caging her in. Instead of feeling fear, another rush of desire rocketed through her.

He bent his head and nuzzled the side of her throat. "Don't be."

He marked her neck, and the roughness of his stubble made her moan and arch. Something hard brushed against her ass and she pressed against it instinctively, gasping when Cooper immediately cupped one breast in his big hand.

He rubbed his erection against her ass and pulled at her nipple through the thin cotton. "Would you like me to show you how easily I can make you come, little mate?"

"I… yeah, sure, okay."

He laughed and then purred to her, plucking gently at her nipple before sliding both hands under her tank top and cupping her tits. She cried out when he rubbed his thumbs across her aching nipples, and he purred and kissed her throat.

"I've wanted to touch your perfect breasts since the day you walked into the office." He kissed her throat again. "Lift your shirt, baby, and show me how gorgeous your breasts are."

Blushing, feeling a little self-conscious, she grabbed the hem of her tank top and lifted it to her collarbone. Cooper made a growl of approval and she stared at the contrast of his tanned hands and her pale breasts, another slow spasm of desire rolling across her lower body.

"So beautiful," Cooper said. "My mate has such pretty pink nipples."

He pinched her nipples lightly before rubbing them again

with his thumbs. She arched her back as pleasure radiated down to her pelvis. She knew her nipples were sensitive, but the rough feel of Cooper's fingers was raising her desire to a level she'd never experienced before.

"Cooper," she moaned, "please."

"Tell me what you want." Cooper marked the top of her shoulder before kissing along the curve of it. His hot wet mouth against her skin made her cry out and rub her ass against his cock again.

"Kiss me, please," she said and turned her face toward his.

"Yes, my mate."

He captured her mouth in a hard kiss, one that stole both her breath and any lingering trepidation. She kissed him back frantically, thrusting her tongue into his mouth with a shameful lack of finesse. She didn't care. She needed him, needed his kisses and his touch.

He sucked on her tongue, his hands kneading her small breasts, his cock rubbing against her ass. He purred to her before teasing her bottom lip with the tip of his tongue.

"Does my mate want me to make her come?" Cooper said teasingly.

"Yes, yes she really does," Daisy said.

His low chuckle made her flush. Or maybe it was the feel of his fingers circling around her belly button. He traced the waistband of her shorts. She was getting ready to beg in a decidedly undignified manner when he slipped his hand inside her shorts.

To her relief, he didn't tease. He cupped her pussy, his warm fingers pressing against her folds, his thumb stroking the small patch of hair at the top of her mound.

"Your pussy is so wet for me," he breathed into her ear. "Good mate."

She moaned and spread her thighs wide, hoping he'd get the message. She clutched at his forearm when he immediately rubbed her clit with his fingertips. Her head fell back with a heavy clunk against his chest, and she bit at her bottom lip as she rocked her hips back and forth, working herself against his hard, rough fingers.

"Oh God," she moaned. "You're so good at this."

"I am." His smug tone brought a smile to her lips. "Your clit is very swollen and wet, sweet Daisy."

His touch on her clit turned light, and she dug her nails into his forearm. "Cooper, no. Harder."

He purred and marked her neck repeatedly as his left hand kneaded her breasts and his right hand rubbed her clit. He slid one thick finger into her, and she clenched hard around him, the sound of his low groan making her feel powerful in an entirely different way.

He rubbed hard at her clit and she was shocked to realize how close she was to coming. It never happened this way. She never felt this needy, this desperate for an orgasm. She dug her nails into his arm again and made a pleading, mewling sound that sounded nothing like her.

Cooper purred to her. She could feel the vibration from his chest against her back and she moaned his name as she pumped her hips faster against his fingers.

"Come for me, my mate," Cooper breathed into her ear.

She cried his name, her orgasm bursting through her in a rush of heat and light and pleasure. She shook wildly, sagging against his broad chest as her legs trembled and her breath heaved in and out of her chest.

Cooper purred again, his big hand squeezing her breast before he slid his hand out of her shorts. With a low growl, he pulled her to the table and boosted her up onto it before placing his hand against her sternum and pushing her onto her back.

He crowded between her thighs. The front of his shorts was tented, and when he made another low growl, she glanced at his face. His eyes were dark yellow and glowing brightly in the darkness and she could see the tips of his fangs gleaming in the soft moonlight.

A flash of fear went through her. It was brief but it was enough to make Cooper stiffen and push away from her. She sat up, shoving her tank top down as he clenched his big hands into fists and backed toward the doorway of the kitchen.

"Cooper, wait."

He shook his head. "You're afraid. You're afraid because of me and I can't -"

"I'm not," she said. "I'm not afraid of you."

He slammed his fist against his thigh. "You are. I can smell it, Daisy. I'm sorry… this was a mistake."

She slid off the table and he backed out into the hallway. She felt like she was the big cat stalking her prey as she went after him. "Cooper, no, let me explain. I was afraid but only -"

He muttered a curse and shook his head. "I shouldn't have done that. I shouldn't have – look, just go to bed, okay?"

"We need to talk," she said. "You need to listen to me."

"In the morning. I can't… I can't talk tonight. My lion is too riled up and I – please, Daisy." He gave her a pleading look that hurt her heart. "Go to your room. Please, baby."

"Okay," she whispered.

He took the stairs two at a time. She heard his bedroom door slam shut and she leaned against the wall, covering her face with her shaking hands. She'd just had the best orgasm of her life and then managed to ruin everything.

CHAPTER 14

"This isn't any of my business, but are you okay?" Eleanor glanced at Daisy in the rear-view mirror.

Daisy managed a wan smile. "Fine."

She wasn't fine. Not by a long shot. She'd woken this morning to an empty house and a note from Cooper saying he had to go in early and Eleanor would pick her up and drive her to work.

"You sure?"

"How come you didn't pick up Wes this morning?" Daisy said.

"Oh, he texted me and said his boss was picking him up, but could I pick you up instead," Eleanor said.

Daisy rubbed at her aching forehead. Cooper was avoiding her and dragging poor Wes into their stupid drama as well.

"I'm sorry," she said to Eleanor.

"For what?" Eleanor said.

"You normally drive Wes to work and now you're stuck with me."

"I get paid either way, right?" Eleanor grimaced. "Sorry,

that came out wrong. What I meant is, I know I don't know you very well, but I'm kind of worried about you this morning. Are you sure you don't want to talk about what's upsetting you?"

Feeling miserable and lonelier than she'd ever felt since moving to California, Daisy said, "I don't have very many friends here, and the one friend I do have, I messed up with him and now he's avoiding me."

She could feel the sting of tears and she wiped at her eyes as Eleanor stopped at a light and twisted in her seat to face her. "I'm sorry, Daisy. He probably needs time. I know I tend to need space when I'm upset with someone."

"Maybe," Daisy said. "But it sucks because it was so nice to have a friend and now…"

The light turned green and Eleanor stepped on the gas. They sat in silence for a few minutes before Eleanor said, "What are you doing Friday night? You wanna have drinks or something? I know a hole in the wall pub not too far from your office. It's got a great vibe to it."

Daisy grimaced. "Thank you, but I don't want a pity friendship, Eleanor."

"It isn't," Eleanor said. "Look, honestly, I don't have that many friends either. I'm kind of a lot to take and you either end up loving me or hating me, you know? I talk too much and I'm awkward in social situations and my dad always said that my filter is broken. So, like, I always say the wrong thing at the wrong time."

She turned left on the street that their office building was on. "If you don't want to hang out with me, that's cool. But my invitation for drinks on Friday had nothing to do with pity, and everything to do with me being a little lonely myself."

She parked in front of their office building and turned to

smile at Daisy. "So, what do you say? Drinks on Friday? I promise to try and rein in the weird."

Daisy smiled at her, the depression lifting a little for the first time since she woke up to Cooper's empty house. "Yes to the drinks and you can be as weird as you want."

A smile lit up Eleanor's pretty face. "Awesome, give me your number."

DAISY GLANCED UP FROM HER COMPUTER WHEN THE OFFICE door opened. Mr. Landon stepped into reception and she smiled at him. "Hello, Mr. Landon."

"Good afternoon, Daisy. How are you?"

"Good, thank you. Do you have a meeting with Cooper?"

Normally, when Cooper booked a meeting, he asked Daisy to add it to the calendar for him because he had a history of accidentally deleting the calendar program. But he'd done a stellar job of avoiding her all day, so it wasn't surprising to her that he'd booked a meeting without letting her know.

"No, I was in the area and thought I would drop in and see if you'd come to a decision regarding our phone call about tutoring Anna. I know three nights a week is a lot, but Anna is really struggling, and you were so great with her that day here in the office."

Daisy smiled at him. "I'm so sorry, Mr. Landon. I meant to call you this morning, but it's been a little busy in the office."

"That's all right. If you still haven't made your decision, I can -"

"No, I have," she said quickly. "I'm happy to tutor Anna, as long as you understand that I have no formal training in

157

teaching or tutoring or anything like that. I've just always loved math and been good at it."

"That's fine," he said. "You made that clear on the phone on Monday. What's important is that Anna is comfortable with you and she can learn from you. Do you think you could start tonight?"

"Start what tonight?"

Cooper's deep voice filled the reception. He stopped at Daisy's desk, reached to cup the back of her neck before seeming to think better of it and holding his hand out to Mr. Landon instead. "David, it's good to see you again. Is there a problem with the security system?"

"No, no," David said as he shook Cooper's hand. "It was installed yesterday and Lusa was very thorough in explaining how to operate it. I'm here to talk to Daisy."

"About what?" Cooper said.

She frowned up at him and he had the good grace to look a bit sheepish.

Before she could ask David if she could call him later to continue the conversation, David said, "Daisy has agreed to tutor my Anna in math. She'll start tonight if that's agreeable to her."

"No," Cooper said.

David blinked at him. "I'm sorry?"

"She's not tutoring Anna."

Daisy stood and put a hand on Cooper's arm before smiling at David. "I can start tonight. What time would you like me there?"

Cooper's low growl died out when Daisy squeezed his arm and gave him a look that would wither plant life.

David studied them before saying, "Around seven? I can text you my address."

"Perfect. Tell Anna I'll see her then."

158

She squeezed Cooper's arm again when it looked like he was about to say something else. David gave Cooper an amused look and headed toward the door. "Thank you, Daisy. See you tonight."

"Bye, David."

When the door closed behind him, she dropped Cooper's arm and glared at him. "Don't you dare say it, Cooper."

"Daisy," Cooper's look suggested he thought she'd gone completely mad, "what are you doing? You can't tutor Anna. She is being stalked by a shifter. If you're at her house, you're in danger. Do you get that?"

"There's a state of the art security system just installed by your company," she said. "No one can get into that house without David and Anna's knowledge. Isn't that right? That's what you told David, wasn't it?"

He growled, his face turning red, and she tapped him on the chest. "Don't you growl at me. Was that not what you said?"

"Yes," he snapped.

"Then I'll be perfectly safe," she said.

"I don't want you doing this," he said. "You can't expect me to be okay with my mate putting herself in danger like this."

A little thrill went through her but she quickly stomped it out. Just because Cooper called her his mate didn't mean that their problems were solved. They needed to talk about what happened last night. Still, it didn't stop her from referring to herself as his mate as well. "I expect you to trust that your mate will be smart and not put herself in dangerous situations."

"*This* is a dangerous situation." He wasn't yelling but he was clearly agitated, and his eyes were starting to transition from blue to yellow. His pupils turned to slits and she waited as he spoke with his lion for nearly thirty seconds before returning to her.

"No." He crossed his arms over his chest. "No, it isn't safe, and we won't let you do this. No arguing, my mate. It's for your own protection."

She laughed in disbelief. "Cooper, are you freaking serious right now? I'm doing this and you can't stop me."

"Do you like him? Do you want him as your mate instead of me? I am your mate, little human. Not him. Me." His voice had deepened and thickened into the rasp of his lion, his eyes had completely changed to dark yellow, and his pupils were slits.

She stroked his chest and his thick arms, petting and soothing him like he was, well... a cat. "I know."

"Say it," he demanded, his voice growing thicker and harder to understand. "Say that I am your mate."

"You're my mate," she said, rubbing his chest again. "I'm not interested in David and he isn't interested in me. You know that. You would smell if we were into each other, right?"

"Maybe." Cooper looked away and when he returned his gaze to her, it was human Cooper fully in charge again. A very pissed off human Cooper. "Why the hell do you want to tutor some teenage brat anyway?"

"Not that it's any of your business, but I need the money." She dropped her hands from his chest. "Is spending my free time tutoring something I *want* to do? Maybe not, but I don't have much of a choice, okay? I have some consumer debt that -"

He snorted angrily. "Maybe if you were better with your money, you wouldn't need a second job. You didn't seem to own anything worth shit at your apartment, how the hell did you get consumer debt?"

Hurt washed over like her a tidal wave. She took a step back from Cooper as Grayson's voice said, "Cooper, enough."

Cooper was still glaring at her and she turned away, sitting down in her chair and staring at her computer. Grayson stepped up to the reception desk and took Cooper's arm. "Let's go, Coop."

"I'm having a discussion with Daisy," Cooper said.

"I'm done talking to you," Daisy said without looking away from her screen.

"Coop, time to leave," Grayson said.

With another loud growl, Cooper turned and stomped away. She glanced up to see Grayson standing there. "What can I do for you, Grayson?"

"You okay?"

"I'm fine."

"Cooper didn't mean what he said. Sometimes -"

"I have a lot of work to do," she said.

Grayson looked like he was going to say something else before nodding and leaving reception. Her stomach in knots, her hands shaking, Daisy slumped in her chair and tried to stem the hot tears that wanted free.

"BUDDY, YOU FUCKED UP."

"Boone," Grayson said.

"What? He did. No point in sugar coating it." Boone took a drink of beer.

"Keep being an asshole, and you won't be invited to the Wednesday beer nights anymore," Grayson said.

"One of us needs to be the voice of reason," Boone said.

"He's a big boy, he can handle the truth that he acted like an idiot with Daisy today."

"I know. I fucking know, all right?" Cooper crossed the living room, handing a fresh beer to Grayson before he collapsed on the couch and stared moodily at the beer in his hand. "It's my fucking lion's fault. He lost his shit when he saw Landon talking to Daisy."

"You gotta rein in that possessive jealousy shit," Boone said. "The ladies hate it."

"You think I like being this way?" Cooper growled at him. "You think I like being driven crazy by the idea that my mate is in danger or is spending time with another male? Because I fucking don't. It's fucking hell and it is taking everything in me not to drive to Landon's house and carry Daisy the fuck out of there."

Boone laughed. "Oh my God, if you actually do that, call me. I wanna be there to watch when Daisy kicks you so hard in the nuts, I gotta fish 'em out of your throat for you."

"Daisy's too afraid to do something like that," Wes said. He stretched his long legs out in front of him and sipped at his whiskey.

"Good point." Boone tipped his beer to him.

"She's not afraid anymore," Grayson said.

"Bullshit," Boone replied. "Just this afternoon, I could smell her fear when I walked into the kitchen while she was getting a coffee."

"Correction, she's not afraid of Cooper anymore," Gray said.

When Boone and Wes gave him skeptical looks, he shrugged. "It's true. When I came into reception this afternoon, I heard Cooper's lion talking to Daisy. He wasn't exactly being sweet, but there wasn't a hint of fear coming from her. She was weirdly calm about it."

Boone sat up straight on the couch and stared at Cooper. "Your lion fucking talked to her?"

"He's done it twice now," Coop said.

"Holy shit." Boone stared at Grayson. "Your cat ever talk to a human before?"

Grayson shook his head and Boone turned to Wes. "You?" He paused. "Shit, what am I saying... your cat probably barely talks to you."

Wes didn't reply and Boone sat back, staring again at Cooper. "My tiger never shuts the fuck up and he's never had the urge to talk to a human."

"What do you want me to say?" Cooper said. "I don't know why the fuck he's doing it, other than he thinks I keep screwing shit up."

"You kind of are," Boone said.

"Yeah, thanks," Coop said.

Boone clinked his bottle against Cooper's. "Cheer up, buddy. Daisy's a sweet girl. Say you're sorry for trying to control her and she'll forgive you. Then don't ever fucking do it again."

"At this point, I don't even know if she's coming back home," Cooper said.

"Eleanor is bringing her back here after she's finished her tutoring," Wes said.

"Daisy could ask her to take her to a hotel," Cooper said.

"True," Wes acknowledged.

Cooper's lion whined in misery. He tried to soothe it as Gray leaned forward from his spot in the armchair. "Coop, she'll come back here. Her stuff is here, and one fight doesn't mean she's not going to help you anymore. She doesn't want you going mad anymore than we do. Forgetting that she needs her job, she likes you. She wants to help you."

"She did," Cooper said. "But maybe not now and honestly, I can't fucking blame her for it."

"When she comes back, say you're sorry like Boone suggested, and promise Daisy you won't interfere in her life again," Gray said. "It's the only thing you can do."

"I'm not sure I can stop my lion – myself – from trying to keep her safe. I don't want to control her, Gray, I really don't, but I want to keep her safe," Coop said.

"She still smells like you, buddy. That'll keep her safe," Grayson said.

"It won't last forever. What if she won't let me mark her again?" Cooper said.

Grayson took another drink of his beer. "She will, Coop."

His stomach churning, the hops bitter on his tongue, Cooper stared at the beer bottle. He wished he had the same kind of faith that Gray did, but he was certain he'd lost Daisy forever. Maybe she hadn't been afraid of him this afternoon, but anytime they were intimate, she certainly was. He wanted to believe that he could just be friends with Daisy and that would be enough, but the part of him that refused to lie, knew better. If he couldn't touch her, couldn't have her in his bed, he would go mad.

CHAPTER 15

"Thanks for helping me, Daisy. I'm sorry I'm so stupid."

Daisy stopped on the staircase and turned to stare up at Anna. "Stop that. You're not stupid. Math is a difficult subject for a lot of people. Besides, you're much better at it than you give yourself credit."

Anna shrugged and they finished walking down the staircase into the foyer. Daisy had never been in such a large house before. It was a beautiful home with art on the walls that probably cost more than her yearly salary, a tasteful and classic decorating style, and a seemingly endless number of rooms. She'd been sorely tempted to ask Anna just how rich her father was, even knowing how tacky that was.

He had to be a millionaire though, right? No one with a house this size could be anything less than a millionaire. Plus, he had a gardener, a personal chef, and a live-in housekeeper. Neither the gardener nor the personal chef were at the house when Daisy arrived for tutoring, but Anna had introduced her to the housekeeper, Tabitha, before they'd gone to Anna's room to study.

"Holy crap, how many rooms does this place have anyway?"

The familiar voice had Daisy spinning around to see Eleanor coming from the direction of the kitchen with Tabitha beside her.

Tabitha laughed. "Twenty-seven. Why do you think he hired me to clean?"

"Hey, Daisy!" Eleanor grinned at her as they joined her and Anna in the foyer. "You must be Anna. I'm Eleanor, Daisy's friend. It's nice to meet you."

"Nice to meet you too," Anna said. Her cell phone buzzed, and she pulled it out of her pocket, a smile crossing her face as she texted, her thumbs flying across the tiny keyboard.

"Um, what are you doing in here?" Daisy said.

Eleanor laughed. "I got here a little early and Tabitha saw me waiting in the driveway and invited me in."

"I saw her drop you off, so I knew she was safe and not, like, connected to that crazy shifter stalking Anna," Tabitha said. The housekeeper was pretty with long blonde hair and light blue eyes, and she looked to be about Daisy's age.

"Tabitha gave me a tour of the place while we waited and she told me all about her boyfriend," Eleanor said.

Tabitha laughed. "I'm sorry. It's a new relationship so I'm totally in that stage where everything he does is magical. Plus, I've never dated a shifter before so it's kind of exciting to me."

"What kind of shifter is he?" Daisy glanced at Anna.

The young girl was still staring at her phone screen, but her body had gone stiff and her thumbs had stopped moving. She relaxed, her thumbs tapping away again when Tabitha said, "A lynx shifter. He's so handsome and funny. I can't believe how lucky I am that I met someone like him."

"Good for you," Eleanor said. "We should probably get going, right, Daisy?"

"Yes," Daisy said. "Anna, I'll see you tomorrow night, okay?"

"Yup. Thanks again, Daisy."

"You're welcome."

HE WAS IN THE SHOWER WHEN SHE GOT HOME. HE COULD hear her in the kitchen even over the sound of the running water. The tension in his shoulders eased but was immediately replaced by nausea in his stomach. What if she was only here to pick up her stuff and leave?

He hurriedly rinsed and turned off the shower, toweling dry in record time and throwing on a pair of shorts and a t-shirt. He took the stairs two at a time and hurried into the kitchen. The nausea settled a touch when he saw Daisy reheating some leftovers.

"Hi," he said.

"Hello." She opened the microwave and pulled out the plate, stirring the potatoes and poking at the roast beef before setting the plate on the table and sitting down. "You didn't eat dinner."

"I wasn't that hungry," he said.

She glanced at the six empty beer bottles sitting on the counter and he said, "I didn't drink all of those. The guys and me, uh, have a beer together every Wednesday after work. We call it Wednesday beer night. Because we drink beers."

His lion growled at how stupid he was acting.

I know, I know.

"I wasn't judging." She took a bite of potatoes. "Drink as

many beers as you want, I don't have the right to tell you what to do."

He winced. Fuck, she was still pissed with him which he totally deserved.

"I'm sorry, Daisy," he said. "I shouldn't have said what I did about the money thing. That was awful and I am truly sorry."

She set her fork down and took a sip of water. "What about when you tried to tell me what to do with my life?"

He ran a hand through his wet hair. "I apologize for trying to put my foot down on something that was none of my business, but I won't apologize for trying to keep you safe. In the future, I will be better at asking you not to do something that puts you in danger, rather than telling you not to do it."

It was a lame ass apology, but the best he could do. Keeping his mate safe was both his and his lion's number one priority, and as far as his lion was concerned, Daisy should never leave Cooper's side.

"In the future," Daisy said.

Jesus, this was not going well. He decided to skip over the future comment. "Anyway, I'm sorry and I hope you won't move out."

"I can't." She stared down at her food. "I'm too broke, remember? Poor money management skills."

He winced. "Daisy, I -"

She pushed her plate away and rubbed at the scar on her arm. "Fuck. I'm sorry. That was a bitchy thing to say."

"I deserved it," he said.

"You didn't," she sighed. "I don't have poor money management skills, okay? I have poor judgement when it comes to men."

"You don't have to explain," he said. "It isn't any of my business."

"No, it isn't," she said. "But I also hate that you think I'm dumb with money, so you're getting the explanation whether you want it or not."

He could smell her anger and her frustration with him. Hating that he was upsetting her, he kept his mouth shut as she took another drink of water before staring at the scar on her arm.

"I used to date this guy named Jeff and he, well, he wasn't a good guy."

Anger turned his vision red. Was this Jeff guy the reason she was so afraid of shifters?

We find him, his lion growled. *We find him and show him what happens to men who hurt our mate.*

"Was he a shifter?" Cooper's voice was thick and on the verge of a growl. "Did he give you that scar on your arm? Is he why you're afraid of us?"

She stared blankly at him before shaking her head. "No. Jeff was human, not a shifter. Calm down, Cooper."

"I'm calm," he said.

"Your fangs are out and you're growing a beard," she said.

He retracted his fangs and scrubbed at his face as if he could simply rub the hair off. She waited a beat and then said, "He was human, but he was a real... jerk. We were together for a few years though. He was my first real boyfriend, and he was understanding about my fear of going out in public. I was tired of being alone and I... well, I was weak."

"You're not weak, baby," he said.

She shrugged. "I am. Anyway, Jeff's grandmother had died about two months before we started dating. He was getting a massive inheritance from her, over two million, but it was tied up in some legal disputes with a cousin. But Jeff knew he was getting the money, his grandmother's will was very clear that he was to get the money. His cousin was being greedy, Jeff said."

She stared out the window at the darkness before rubbing at the scar again. "Jeff had expensive taste and I had a good credit rating. We ate through my savings with vacations and I helped Jeff buy a new car. He would pay me back, of course, when the inheritance came through, so I didn't worry too much about it. Jeff was very charming and persuasive, you know? My friend Megan said Jeff could sell water to a drowning man."

Coop nodded. "Yeah, I know people like him."

"Anyway, we burned through my savings within the first two years we dated and then we racked up my credit card. My limit was modest, and Jeff tried to get me to up it, but I didn't. I mean, I was still believing that he would pay me back but there was apparently a tiny part of me that wasn't completely stupid."

"You're not stupid," he said. "Guys like Jeff are very good at what they do."

"Yeah," she said. "It didn't matter anyway. I didn't know this, but he opened up three credit cards in my name and maxed them out. When I found out, I freaked out and demanded that Jeff pay me back immediately. Demanded that he go to the lawyers and finally get the inheritance thing sorted out. After hours of arguing, Jeff finally admitted the truth to me."

"His cousin got the inheritance," Cooper said.

She laughed bitterly. "There was no inheritance at all."

"Holy fuck," Cooper said.

"Yeah. It was all a lie. I kicked him out and I reported him to the police for fraud and identity theft. He was furious with me, sent me a few texts that were... unpleasant. I blocked his number and got a restraining order, but he had already disappeared anyway. The police said he had a history of doing this to women. He had a few different names. I knew him as Jeff Colberg, but his real name was Anthony Biswell. He has, I don't know how many, warrants out for his arrest. Once the woman wises up to what he's doing, he disappears and assumes another identity."

Cooper's lion was growling and the hair on the back of his neck was standing up. "How angry was he with you?"

"Why?"

"Your car was broken into," he said.

"It wasn't him."

"You can't know that for sure."

"I know it wasn't him," she said. "A few of the women he's scammed have been trying to find him and I'm in the email group. The night my car was broken into, we got an email from the private investigator the women hired to find him. They had pictures of him in Mexico taken that day. He's living with a woman there and, no doubt, running his scam on her."

"You're sure it was him?" Cooper said.

"Yes," she said. "It's not how he works, Cooper. He doesn't harass his victims. He just moves on to the next one."

"Just to be safe, I'll assign Chase to keep an eye on you when you're -"

"No," she said. "That's not necessary."

"Daisy -"

"I said no," she snapped and then rubbed at her forehead. "Thank you, but it isn't necessary." She stood and put plastic wrap over her plate of food and shoved it back in the fridge. "It's late and I'm tired. I'm going to bed. I just wanted you to know that I'm not broke because I'm bad with money. I'm broke because I was stupid and naïve and… and lonely."

She looked upset and close to tears and he wanted to pull

her into his arms and hold her until the weariness and defeat he could smell on her were gone. But under the defeat, he could catch a hint of her frustration with him and he knew instinctively that trying to soothe her now would be a mistake.

"I'm sorry," he said again.

"Thank you. I accept your apology," she said. "Good night, Cooper. I'll see you in the morning."

She left the kitchen and he rubbed at the back of his neck. Well, that was it. Daisy might have forgiven him for what he'd said, but he was a fool if he thought she might consider him to be her mate now. Hell, if she could, she'd move out of his house and not have to deal with his sorry ass at all except for at work.

His lion made a mournful whine that Cooper tuned out. Enough was enough. He had to stop thinking of Daisy as his mate and move on. Even if she could look past his jealous and possessive nature, history had proven that she couldn't sleep with him. Whatever had happened in her past couldn't be fixed by him and he had to stop thinking that it could. And no matter what he tried to tell himself, he couldn't be with a mate who he couldn't sleep with. His lion needed a woman who was his mate in every sense of the word to be happy. And, if he was being honest, so did Cooper.

Maybe if you asked her what happened, we could help her get over her fear.

She wouldn't tell him. He knew that as well as he knew his own name. No, the best thing to do was move on and try and convince his lion to find another mate. He pulled his cell phone from his pocket and thumbed through the texts until he found the one from Ryan's friend Shay. She had texted him a few days ago. He hadn't replied yet, not sure what to say, and too wrapped up in Daisy.

He listened to the faint sounds of Daisy walking across her bedroom and the telltale creak of the mattress when she climbed into bed, before texting Shay.

YOU'RE EAVESDROPPING AGAIN, DAISY.

She ignored her inner voice as she hovered outside of Cooper's office. She wasn't eavesdropping, she was simply waiting for him to finish his conversation with Grayson before she dropped off the document she had for him.

Besides, if a person didn't want a conversation overheard, a person should close their damn door.

She rubbed at the scar on her arm and leaned against the wall outside Cooper's door. It was only midafternoon Thursday, but she was worried about Cooper. He'd driven her to work this morning but barely said a word and didn't look at her once. Her annoyance with his behaviour yesterday had faded but now he was the one who seemed upset with her.

"Okay, so I'll talk to Chase about the Dalton file and let you know if we have any questions." Gray's voice drifted out of the open door.

"Sounds good," Cooper said.

She leaned a little closer to the doorway when Grayson lowered his voice and said, "So, Ryan said you texted Shay?"

"Yeah," Cooper said.

"You're having dinner with her tomorrow night?"

Jealousy pierced through her stomach like a hot needle. She gripped the document hard and held her breath, straining to hear the two shifters' low voices.

"Yeah."

There was a beat of silence and then Gray said, "You

don't think it'll work with Daisy? Even though she's not afraid of you now?"

"She's afraid of me still," Cooper said.

"Doesn't smell like she is."

She heard the creak of Cooper's leather chair as he leaned back. "When we're, uh, intimate, she's afraid."

"Shit," Grayson said.

She wanted to burst into his office and deny it, but what good would that do? She did sometimes get afraid. If Cooper wasn't even willing to try and help her work through it, she couldn't force him to sit there and wait while she deep breathed her way through the fear. She didn't even know for certain that she wouldn't become more afraid the closer she got to being naked with him. What if she had to stop? It wouldn't be fair to Cooper.

Yeah, yeah, we know, her inner voice said. *But you won't know what will happen until you try and maybe if you actually talked to Cooper about it, told him what you're worried about, he'd be more understanding than you think. It's called a conversation, moron.*

"It kills me to smell her fear," Cooper said. "Do you have any idea what it's like to have your mate be afraid of you?"

"No," Grayson said.

Cooper sighed loudly. "Anyway, I texted Shay because I've finally realized that Daisy and I will never be mates. At best, we can be friends. But just being friends with her is a bit tricky until I can convince my lion that we can find someone else to be our mate."

"You know that Shay isn't looking for a relationship, right?" Grayson said. "She agreed to meet with you *because* you only want no commitment sex."

"I know," Cooper said. "But maybe sleeping with Shay

will help keep my lion from losing his fucking shit while I look for someone else. I signed up for that dating site for shifters this morning."

"Seriously?" Grayson said.

"Yeah. And I paid extra to get access to the females specifically looking for mates. There has to be someone there who will catch my lion's eye, right?"

A dating site for shifters? Daisy wanted to throw up. Had she ever felt such stabbing, blinding jealousy before? It was bad enough thinking about Cooper having meaningless sex with a woman, but for him to find someone he loved and wanted to spend the rest of his life with? The reality that she was on the verge of losing Cooper landed on her like a meteorite and she could barely stand under it's weight.

She leaned against the wall, her throat tight and her stomach churning. A vision of Cooper touching some other woman, calling her his little mate, being his stubborn, possessive, jealous self over her instead of Daisy, ran through her head.

She clenched the paper in a tighter fist, her hatred for the fear that had ruled her life since she was nine years old a burning coal in the pit of her stomach. The fear had cost her jobs and friends, and now she was going to lose the man she loved.

She wanted to scream but she concentrated on her breathing, pulling in the good air and shoving out the bad, until her anger and sadness were somewhat under control. She wouldn't cry at the office, and she wouldn't beg Cooper to try and work with her fear in order to sleep with him. It wasn't his problem. It was hers and always would be.

She straightened, pasting a smile on her face when she heard Grayson approach the open door. She skittered back a few steps and then walked toward Cooper's door, trying to look natural as Grayson stepped into the hallway.

"Hi, Daisy."

"Hey, Grayson." She ducked past him and knocked briskly on Cooper's door. "Cooper, I have the letter you asked me to type."

He was sitting at his desk and his smile looked false and out of place. "Thank you."

She set it on his desk and smoothed out the wrinkles from where she'd gripped it. Telling herself to get the fuck out already, said, "So, I'm doing the tutoring thing tonight at six but there are still leftovers in the fridge for dinner."

"Sure, okay. Thank you."

She paused. "Do you like ham? I was thinking I might make a ham tomorrow night for dinner."

"Oh, uh," he suddenly became very interested in a chip on his desk, "actually, I have plans for dinner tomorrow night."

"Oh," she said. "Going out with Grayson and the guys?"

Daisy, stop it!

"No," Cooper cleared his throat, "a different friend."

"That sounds nice," she said.

"Yes." When she didn't move, he glanced at her. "I'm pretty busy this afternoon. Was there something else?"

Her throat got tight again, and she blinked rapidly. "Nope, I'll head back to my desk now."

She was halfway to the door when Cooper said, "Daisy, wait."

She stopped, her hands clenched into a tight fist at her abdomen. "Yes?"

"My scent has faded. I should – that is, would you like me to mark you again?"

"Yes," she said, a little ashamed by the eagerness in her voice.

She reached to close the door, disappointment flooding through her when Cooper said, "Leave it open. It'll only take a couple minutes."

She turned, making herself smile at him as he approached her like she might be the one who was a dangerous big cat.

"You ready?" he said.

"Yes." Something that was part relief and part smugness flooded through her. Once he touched her, he wouldn't be able to resist her. He never could. Maybe, once he was marking her, she would tell him to lock his office door. Maybe she'd take him back to his desk, sit him down in his chair and unzip his pants. Maybe once she was on her knees in front of him, once she was sucking his cock, he'd forget all about his plan to have sex with Shay. Maybe he'd –

"Daisy." Cooper's voice was tight, and his nostrils were flaring. She knew he could smell her sudden lust for him.

Good, she wanted him to smell it. Wanted him to know how much it turned her on to think about sucking his dick.

"Yes?" Her voice was low and thick with need.

"Tilt your head back," he rasped.

She tilted her head back and closed her eyes, already anticipating the firm grip of his hand on the back of her neck, the brush of his body against hers, the strength of his arm around her waist as he drew her in close.

Her eyes popped open when he brushed his face against her throat. He wasn't touching her at all except with his face. Too shocked to process what exactly was happening, she stood there numbly as he rubbed his face against both sides of her throat in a decidedly brisk and unsexy way before straightening.

She stared blankly at him as he returned to his desk and sat down, pulling the chair in tight until his flat abdomen brushed against the edge of the desk. When she didn't move, he said, "What's wrong?"

"Nothing," she said. "Thank you for marking me."

"You're welcome." He stared at his computer screen, clearly dismissing her. Feeling horny and stupid and embarrassed, she turned and nearly ran out of his office.

CHAPTER 16

"Expecting me to concentrate on fractions is impossible when I'm this hungry." Anna flopped down face first on her bed.

Daisy smiled at her. "We can take a quick break so you can grab a snack."

"A snack isn't gonna cut it," Anna said. "I didn't eat dinner."

Daisy hadn't eaten dinner either, too upset by Cooper's obvious rejection to have much of an appetite.

"Why didn't you eat?" Daisy said.

Anna's voice was muffled by the quilt. "Dad's at some charity thing tonight and Patricia made one of my least favourite meals."

She turned her head enough to give Daisy a one-eyed stare. "That makes me sound like a spoiled brat, right? Complaining about what our personal chef made for dinner."

Daisy laughed. "Maybe a little."

Anna flopped onto her back, staring at the ceiling as she tapped her pencil against her forehead. "I could go for a burger. There's an amazing burger joint not too far from here."

"I don't have a car," Daisy said.

"It's literally like three blocks away. We can walk," Anna said. "My dad and I go there a lot. We should go. I'm starving."

"Nope," Daisy said. "It's too dangerous."

"It's a super popular place," Anna said. "Even if Xander showed up, there's always a ton of people around. He wouldn't try and do anything with that many witnesses."

"Still not a good idea," Daisy said. "Why don't we grab a snack from the kitchen and -"

Her stomach growled so loudly that Anna heard it from across the room. She laughed and sat up on the bed. "A snack isn't gonna cut it for you either. I won't be able to concentrate on fractions without a burger and fries in me, Daisy. It's not possible. Please? I'm feeling a little stir-crazy tonight."

Daisy rubbed at the scar on her arm before fishing her cell phone out of her purse. She called a number as Anna said, "If you're calling to ask my dad, he's not going to answer. He keeps his phone on silent when he's at the charity stuff."

"It's not your dad I'm calling," Daisy said. When Wes answered the phone, she said "Hey, it's Daisy. How exactly does this personal security thing work for Anna?"

"IS THIS THE BEST BURGER YOU'VE EVER TASTED OR IS THIS the best burger you've ever tasted?" Anna said.

Daisy grinned and stuffed some more fries into her mouth, chewing and swallowing before saying, "Fine, you were right. The burger and the fries are amazing."

"My dad and I come here, like, twice a week." Anna's

phone buzzed and she glanced at the screen. A smile broke out across her face.

"Do you need to answer the text?" Daisy said. "I don't mind."

"Nah, it's okay." Anna pushed her phone to the side. "It's just my friend Scott."

She looked around the busy restaurant, her gaze landing on Wes who was sitting at a table about twenty-five feet away. Anna lowered her voice, even though Daisy was pretty certain Wes couldn't hear them, not with the din of the other patrons, the two flat TVs blaring sports, and the chatter of the servers. "Scott wants to be more than friends."

"Do you want to be more than friends?" Daisy dipped a fry into the pool of ketchup on her plate.

"I think so. I mean, he's my age which will make Dad and Mom happy and he's really smart and funny. He's not, like, the best looking guy around, but Xander was super hot and look how that turned out."

"Is Scott a human or shifter?"

"Human," Anna said. "I don't think I'll ever date a shifter again."

"I'm sorry you're going through this," Daisy said.

"It does suck." Anna picked at the sesame seeds on her bun. "Xander seemed like a good guy at first, you know? He was so nice to me and he told me how mature I was for my age and stuff. But, like, only a few months after we started dating, he was talking about wanting me to be his mate, and what kind of wedding we would have, and how many kids did I want, and it got weird. I broke up with him and then the shit really hit the fan."

She took a sip of her soda before glancing at Daisy. "I had to leave my mom and all my friends because of him, and,

181

like, he still won't leave me alone. I don't get it. I'm not that special or pretty… why won't he leave me alone?"

Daisy reached across and took her hand. "You're smart and gorgeous and any guy would be lucky to have you. But it sounds like Xander has some mental health issues. And I'm not trying to suggest you're immature, but you are too young for him. Xander is an adult and he took advantage of you, honey."

"Yeah, that's what my parents say too. I'm not a child though, Daisy."

"But you're not an adult yet either," Daisy said gently.

Anna shrugged. "I guess. But I thought I loved him and that he loved me. But now…"

"What?" Daisy said, squeezing her hand gently.

"I'm afraid of him."

"It'll be okay, honey. Your dad won't let anything happen to you, and Xander won't be able to hide forever. Sooner or later, he'll mess up and the police will find him."

"Maybe," Anna said. "He's pretty smart though."

"Even smart people make mistakes," Daisy said.

She released Anna's hand and took a drink of her own soda. Anna pushed back her chair. "I'm gonna use the washroom. Be right back."

Daisy watched her weave her way around the tables, smiling when Anna studiously avoided looking at Wes as she passed by his table. She'd have to tell Anna that she didn't have to pretend Wes wasn't watching her, and that in fact, it might be better if she didn't.

She took out her cell phone and studied her text messages. Cooper hadn't texted her, but it wasn't like she expected him to, right? After his reaction to her this afternoon, after his *non-reaction* to marking her, she'd be a fool to think he would. He was looking for a new mate and when he found her, Daisy would become nothing more than a –

"I need you to give her a message for me."

She glanced up, staring curiously at the good looking guy standing next to Anna's empty seat. He was wearing jeans and a t-shirt with a blue hoodie layered over it. He had black hair and a dark brown beard and gorgeous green eyes.

"I'm sorry?" she said.

"You need to give her a message," he said.

He cracked his knuckles nervously as Daisy stared at him in confusion. "Who?"

"Jesus, are you fucking stupid?" The man stepped closer. "Tell her that I love her and -"

He stopped and sniffed at Daisy, anxiety flashing across his face. "Fuck, you're a lion's mate."

She swallowed hard. The man was a shifter. She pushed her chair back as he took a step back. "Just tell Anna that -"

"Oh my God…"

Anna's voice was faint and barely legible above the noise in the restaurant. The man spun around. Adrenaline rushed through Daisy, making her feel lightheaded and her legs shake as she shoved her way to her feet.

Anna was staring up at the shifter with terror in her eyes. She cringed when the shifter cupped her face. "Xander, don't."

"Wes!" Daisy screamed. "Wes, it's him!"

She strained to see around Xander's broad body, relief rushing through her. Wes must have sensed something was wrong when Xander approached the table. He was already halfway to them, shoving his way through the large group of people blocking his route.

"I miss you," the man whispered.

Anna pulled away from his touch, stumbling back as Wes cleared the group of people.

"Fuck," Xander growled, glancing at Wes before spinning back to face Daisy. He pushed past her, knocking her flat on her ass as, moving fast, he ran toward the back of the restaurant. Wes ran by Daisy without a word and Anna helped her to her feet.

"Daisy! Are you okay?"

Daisy rubbed her elbow before putting her arm around Anna's waist. They'd already lost sight of Xander and Wes in the restaurant and Anna gave Daisy a frightened look. "What do we do?"

"Stay right here where there are plenty of people," Daisy said. "If Wes isn't back in five minutes, I'll call Cooper."

She put her arm around the frightened teenager, ignoring the looks from the people at the table next to theirs. "You okay, honey?"

"Yeah, I think so," Anna said before hugging Daisy hard and burying her face in Daisy's shoulder.

IF ANYTHING COULD CONVINCE DAISY THAT COOPER WAS already halfway to believing she wasn't his mate anymore, it was his reaction when he walked into the Landon mansion. Or rather... his lack of reaction.

Her expectation that he would either be completely freaking out and worried about her or be cranky and spilling out *I told you so's* left and right, was completely mistaken.

Looking calm and completely in control, he said, "Are you hurt?"

"No," she said.

"He pushed her down," Anna said. "Hard."

"Do you need to go to the hospital?" Cooper asked in that calm tone of voice that, honestly, was starting to freak *her* out a little.

"No," she said. "I'll have a bruised elbow, nothing more."

"All right." He turned to Anna and smiled at her. "How are you doing, kid? Okay?"

"Yeah," Anna said. "He's changed. He dyed his hair and he grew a beard and he's thinner now. It's why I didn't recognize him when I was walking back from the bathroom. It wasn't until I heard his voice that I..." she took a deep breath, leaning against her father, "I'm really sorry, Daisy. This is all my fault."

"It isn't," Cooper said. "You're allowed to go out, and you and Daisy did the right thing by calling Wes to go with you."

He turned to Wes. "Did you get a good look at his new appearance?"

Wes nodded. "Good enough."

"Why didn't you catch him?" David said to Wes. "He was right there in the restaurant. If you had caught him, all this would be over."

"Dad," Anna said, "be cool."

"Xander is a cheetah shifter," Cooper said.

"And he's a lion shifter." David pointed at Wes.

"Yes," Cooper said, "he is. But cheetah shifters are incredibly fast. As soon as he was out of the restaurant, he shifted to his cheetah. Once that happened, once Xander had a clear and open path, there was no way Wes, or anyone who isn't a cheetah, would have caught him."

David scrubbed his hand over his face. "Fuck, sorry." He looked down at Anna before kissing her forehead. "She's our world and if something happened to her..."

"Oh my God, Dad," Anna said with an embarrassed grimace, "you and Mom gotta get hobbies."

Daisy laughed, and even Wes and Cooper cracked smiles as David kissed Anna's forehead again. "I love you, kid."

"I love you too," Anna said.

The doorbell rang and David said, "That'll be the police."

As David opened the door, Cooper glanced down at Daisy. She smiled tentatively at him, the smile dying when he nodded briskly before turning away. She was aching to hug him, wanted the comfort that only he could give her. Instead she crossed her arms over her torso and stared at his broad back.

COOPER KEPT IT TOGETHER AT THE CLIENT'S. HE EVEN KEPT it together on the drive home with Daisy, despite the way his lion was growling and whining and demanding.

But his control wavered in the house, wavered and then disappeared under the overwhelming desire of both his and his lion's need to touch his mate. To assure himself that she really was okay.

His entire body shaking, he followed Daisy into the kitchen. She set her purse on the table before opening the cupboard for a glass. His legs weirdly weak, he walked toward her as she said, "Do you want a glass of water?"

She gasped when he turned her around and boosted her onto the counter so they were face to face. Without speaking, he hugged her hard, wrapping his arms around her slender body and burying his face in her neck. He was probably crushing her, probably making it impossible for her to breathe. But the panic that settled over him like a slab of cement the second he got Wes' phone call finally broke when he had his mate in his arms.

He purred to her, stroking her back and reminding himself that he couldn't kiss her.

His lion purred louder when Daisy returned his hug. She hooked her legs around his hips and pulled him in even closer, her small hands smoothing up and down his back. His body was still shaking, and she pressed a kiss against his shoulder through his t-shirt. "I'm all right, Cooper. I'm okay, honey."

"Are you sure?" he rasped against her throat.

"Yes. Your scent scared him. He knew I was your mate and it kept him away," she said.

She wasn't his mate, couldn't be his mate, but hearing her say it soothed his lion in a way that Cooper could never replicate. He marked her throat again, cupping the back of her neck and tilting her head back so he could mark every inch of her pale skin.

She didn't protest, not even when her throat was bright red, not even when he could see faint scratches from his stubble rising on her skin. She let him mark her until he was satisfied, until his scent on her was so overpowering, that every shifter within twenty feet of her would smell Cooper.

His lion growled its approval as Cooper marked her a final time before cupping her face and staring into her eyes. He could get lost in their gorgeous green depths, *wanted* to get lost. She made a soft sound of encouragement, her lips parting as her gaze dropped to his mouth.

His cock hardened as the scent of her need infused the air between them.

He wanted to kiss her. He wanted to touch her. He wanted to take her upstairs, undress her, and make her come repeatedly until she was warm and sated and utterly satisfied. He wanted to bury himself deep in her warmth and forget all the reasons why she couldn't be his mate.

Instead, knowing it would crush him when her desire turned to fear, he made himself pull away from the warmth of her body, tugging free of her limbs as she stared at him with hurt and disappointment.

"Cooper -"

"I'm glad you're okay," he said. "It's late and I have a busy day tomorrow. Good night, Daisy."

His lion roared angrily and tried to surge forward. He held it back grimly, digging deep for control, as Daisy swallowed hard and looked away.

If she asked him to stay, he would. He could deny his mate nothing. His lion growling furiously, Coop clenched his hands into tight fists behind his back.

Instead of asking him to stay with her, Daisy said, "Good night, Cooper."

He walked out of the kitchen with stiff and jerky strides. By the time he reached his bedroom, his lion was growling so loudly, he could hear nothing else. He dropped onto his bed and ignored his lion's pleading to go to their mate.

CHAPTER 17

"You okay, boss?" The worried look Boone gave him, indicated just how fucking terrible Cooper looked. It wasn't that Boone didn't care about Coop or the others, he just often masked his worry or concern under humour or sarcasm. If he was concerned enough to drop the humour, he obviously thought Cooper was about to lose it.

"Fine," he said. "Didn't sleep well."

That was the fucking understatement of the year. He hadn't slept a goddamn wink all night. He'd laid in bed, staring at the ceiling, straining to hear the soft sound of Daisy's breathing through the wall, until the sun rose.

"Maybe you should take the day off," Grayson said. "The office won't fall apart if you take a day off, Coop."

"I'm fine, I said." Cooper stared at Wes sitting next to Grayson. "Tell me what you found out from your friend in the police department."

Wes took a sip of coffee. "I talked to Roberto this morning. He said there were four separate calls last night about a streaking complaint in the Rose Valley neighbourhood, near the cross streets of Moncton and Torrance."

"Bing-fucking-o," Boone said. "It has to be Xander."

"Not necessarily," Grayson said. "But it's probably the best lead we've got right now." He glanced at Cooper. "You sure you want to use resources to find this guy? Landon asked us for security, not to hunt the guy down."

Coop wanted to bare his teeth at his best friend. Wanted to snarl at him that he didn't give a fuck what Landon had hired them for. What mattered was finding the man who had dared to go near his mate.

Instead, he took a deep breath and made his voice calm. "I'm sure. Boone and Wes, you're on stakeout duty. Chase will replace Wes in watching Anna when she leaves the house. Unless Daisy is with her and then I'm on watch."

He waited for the others to protest. To tell him that his ability to keep them safe would be compromised by his feelings for Daisy. Wisely, everyone kept their mouth shut.

"You want us to head over to Rose Valley today?" Boone asked.

"Yes. Start at Moncton and Torrance."

"There are a lot of apartment buildings in Rose Valley," Boone said. "This could take a while."

"I don't care how fucking long it takes or if you have to sit outside every goddamn apartment building in the neighbourhood. You find this asshole and then call me."

"No, call the police," Grayson said.

Cooper glared at him and Gray shook his head. "If you think I'm going to let you go to prison for life just because your lion is pissed that Daisy was shoved by this guy, you really are going mad."

"I just want to talk to him before I call the cops," Cooper said.

Boone burst into laughter. "Bullshit, Coop. Gray is right,

you're not getting anywhere near Xander. It's for your own good, big guy."

Coop growled at him, but Boone only laughed again before standing and clapping Wes on the back. "C'mon, buddy, we'll hit the grocery store and stock up on some munchies before we head over to Rose Valley."

The two shifters left Cooper's office. Coop frowned at Grayson when he didn't move. "Is there something else? I have a lot of work to do today."

"Are you still planning on going out with Shay tonight?" Grayson said.

Cooper glanced at the open door. "Yes, why?"

"Because Daisy smells so strongly like you that there's no way you didn't have sex with her last night."

"We didn't," Cooper said shortly. "I marked her again to be on the safe side."

"Coop -"

"She can't be my mate," he snarled at Grayson. "Jesus Christ, we've talked about this how many fucking times? Give it a rest, will you?"

"Yeah, okay." Grayson stood and guilt rolled through Cooper like dark clouds before a storm.

"Gray, I'm sorry. I didn't sleep last night and I'm exhausted. I have a lot of shit on my plate right now."

"I know." Grayson leaned across the desk and squeezed his shoulder. "Text me tomorrow and let me know how it goes with Shay, all right?"

"I will." Cooper sat back in his chair, rubbing at his eyes before tilting his head back and staring at the ceiling. He was doing the right thing, he told himself, as his lion growled a constant litany of demands to go to Daisy.

"Okay, I know what you're thinking," Eleanor said, "but give it a chance. The food here is amazing and they have, like, forty-two different craft beers. Do you drink?"

Daisy slid into the booth, setting her purse down beside her and studying the large and, frankly, dingy looking pub that Eleanor had driven them too. Despite the grungy look of the place, it was packed full of people and she had to raise her voice to be heard over the noise. "I drink a little."

"Cool." Eleanor leaned back against her seat and smiled at her. "So, how come Wes texted me and said I didn't have to pick you up after you were finished tutoring? Did the two of you hook up last night or something?"

She was trying to sound casual, but even though she didn't know Eleanor very well, Daisy could see the falseness of her smile. She quickly shook her head. "No. Wes and I are coworkers, nothing more. There was an incident with Anna."

"Shit, she okay? Was it the stalker guy?"

Before Daisy could answer, their server arrived. They each ordered a beer and when he'd left, Daisy said, "She's fine. But Xander showed up at a burger place we were at."

"Oh my God. You're kidding?" Eleanor said.

"No. Wes was with us and he almost caught him, but the guy is a cheetah shifter and I guess they're incredibly fast. He shifted and took off and Wes didn't have a chance of catching him."

The server brought back their beers and set them on the table. Eleanor glanced at the menu in front of her. "We'll need a couple more minutes, please."

She waited until he left again before saying, "So, that must have been terrifying for both you and Anna."

"It was scary, but he didn't get too close to me because I smell like Cooper, and Anna was in the bathroom when he first came up to the table so -"

"Wait, go back to the smell like Cooper thing," Eleanor said. "Cooper as in, yours and Wes's boss, Cooper?"

"Yeah."

"Why do you smell like him?" Eleanor said. She leaned forward and sniffed at her. "Like, you mean his cologne or something? Because if so, his cologne smells like vanilla."

"No, not his cologne. His scent. It's kind of a long story," Daisy said.

"Now I'm even more intrigued," Eleanor said before flipping open her menu. "C'mon, let's figure out what we're going to eat first and then you can tell me exactly why you smell like your boss."

"CAN I ASK WHY YOU'RE SO AFRAID OF SHIFTERS?" ELEANOR said as she ate the last forkful of pasta on her plate.

Daisy stared at her barely touched meal. "I don't... I can't talk about it. I'm sorry."

"Don't be. I'm sorry for being nosy," Eleanor said. She took a swallow of beer. "So, you said that Cooper is the one shifter you're not afraid of anymore and you're kind of horny for him, so I'm not getting the problem. Are you afraid you'll lose your job if you guys break up?"

"No, not at all. Cooper isn't like that," Daisy said. "I'm not afraid of Cooper, I'm really not. I am worried that I'll try to sleep with him and maybe have to stop and take a break because I'm starting to get nervous. Or that with more intimacy, it'll bring outright fear back and I won't be able to go through with it. If that happens, at best, I'll look like an idiot and at worst, a tease."

"Maybe if you talked to Cooper about your concerns -"

"I tried but he's basically avoiding me now. If I even have

a whiff of anxiety when we're making out, it freaks him out and he stops everything."

"Well, it's sweet that he's so worried about scaring you, but also, if he thinks you're his mate, not having sex with you is gonna make him go mad, like you said, right?"

"Maybe." Daisy poked at her salad. "He's actively looking for another mate though. He's on a date with another woman as we speak."

"Shit," Eleanor said.

"Yeah. It's not, like, a real date. This woman – Shay – doesn't want anything but sex. But Cooper hopes that if his lion is having sex even with another woman, that it will help convince his lion that I'm not his mate."

"Jesus, shifters are fucking weird," Eleanor said.

"He signed up on a shifter's dating site," Daisy said. "He's hoping to find another woman to be his mate."

"Which upsets you," Eleanor said.

"Yes, because he's my friend and if it doesn't work, he'll go crazy and maybe kill himself," Daisy said.

"He's your friend and that's why you're upset about him dating other women," Eleanor repeated.

Daisy threw her napkin over her food. "Yes, that's what I said."

"You sure that's the reason. Or are you upset because you're in love with him and want to be his mate?" Eleanor said.

"No, I… why would you think that?" Daisy said. "I barely know him."

"Don't take this the wrong way, but you can't lie worth shit," Eleanor said, "and you have a very expressive face. You can practically see your love for him on your face when you say his name. It's gross and also kind of adorable."

"It doesn't matter. It's too late now. He's on a date with

Shay and she's probably gorgeous. They'll probably have sex a billion times tonight, and she'll probably have, like, a magical vagina or something and he'll forget all about me."

"Magical vaginas are hard to compete with," Eleanor said solemnly.

Daisy smiled a little. "God, I'm an idiot."

"No," Eleanor reached across and patted her hand, "you're in love."

———

"How's your steak?"

"Really good," Cooper said. "Yours?"

Shay ate another large bite of her rare steak before smiling at him. "Delicious. Thanks for meeting me here. I know it doesn't look like much, but the food is amazing."

Cooper smiled at her before sipping at his beer. Shay was right. The pub was a definite hole in the wall type of place, but the steak on his plate was probably one of the best steaks he'd ever eaten. Too bad he could barely taste it. Of course, if his goddamn lion would shut the fuck up for one goddamn second, maybe he could actually enjoy his meal.

I hate her, his lion growled grumpily. *She smells funny and she talks too much.*

Stop it, Cooper snapped. *You're being ridiculous. Shay smells normal and she absolutely does not talk too much. You're just being a dick.*

I want to go home to my mate, his lion said.

He tuned his lion out, smiling apologetically at Shay. "Sorry."

"That's all right," Shay said. "Honestly, I get a little fasci-nated by the whole pupils turning to slits thing. So, I should probably apologize for staring at you while it happens."

He forced himself to eat another bite of steak. Shay was a beautiful woman, gorgeous in fact, and contrary to what his lion said, she smelled amazing and her body was perfect, and he really, really should be attracted to her.

He wasn't.

Give it time, he told himself. *Once you're in her bed, you'll feel something.*

"So," he cleared his throat, "Gray said that you used to do some acting and that's how you and Ryan became friends. Were you in any shows I would know?"

She smiled. "I did a few commercials and had a couple of cameos on Ryan's TV show, *Alien Hunter*. Honestly, I wasn't that great of an actor."

"I'm sure you were amazing," he said. "What commercials?"

Jesus, could he sound less interested if he tried?

Apparently not, because Shay finished the last bite of her steak before wiping her mouth with her napkin. "So, not to make this awkward, because if you want to do small talk and get to know each other a little better, I'm fine with that. But, if you want to skip the small talk and go back to my house and into my bed, I'm also perfectly fine with *that*."

He could feel the heat rising in his cheeks. "Are you always this blunt?"

She shrugged. "Depends on the situation, I suppose. We're both adults and we both know why we went out tonight. I'm not interested in a relationship and you're looking for a distraction. I'm sure you can smell my attraction to you but in the interest of saving time, let me be clear that I am absolutely interested in seeing you naked and in my bed."

He tried to formulate a response as Shay sipped some wine.

"That is, assuming you're attracted to me as well," she said.

"You're a beautiful woman," he said.

"But?"

"But I'd be thinking about someone else while we're having sex."

She smiled at him, the sadness in it making him wonder if her seemingly happy nature wasn't a sham. "It wouldn't be you I'm thinking of either."

"What's his name?" Cooper said.

"It doesn't matter. He's moved on and I'm trying to," Shay said. "You're one of the few men I've been attracted to since the relationship ended, so I'm willing to try this, if you are. Cooper?"

He knew Shay was talking, but her voice was distant and unimportant. What was important was the fact that he could smell Daisy's scent, smell it even over his own. It was coming closer and holy shit…

He stared in shock at Daisy, his hand shooting out to catch her wrist when she would have walked by him. She jumped and jerked to a stop, her mouth dropping open when she saw him. "Cooper? What – what are you doing here?"

"What are you doing here?" he said.

Was she on a date? If she was on a date, he'd rip the asshole into fucking shreds before he let him touch his mate.

"I'm – I'm here with a friend."

"What's his name?" Cooper knew he was starting to growl, knew that his eyes were turning yellow and a beard was growing on his face, but he couldn't control it. Daisy was his mate. She belonged to him and it would be a cold fucking day in hell before another man took what was his.

"It's Eleanor," Daisy said. "Wes's driver."

He relaxed, his lion settling down and purring to Daisy, as

she pointed to a booth across the pub. He'd never met the woman who drove Wes to work practically every day, and he was a little shocked to see how young she was. He'd expected a woman in her fifties.

"That's Eleanor?" he said.

"Yes." Daisy tugged at his hand and he realized he was still holding her wrist, his thumb brushing over the pulse point.

He released her and cleared his throat. "Daisy, this is Shay. Shay, this is Daisy. She's our receptionist at work."

Daisy's face was pale, but she smiled at Shay. "Nice to meet you."

"You as well," Shay said.

There was a moment of awkward silence and then Daisy said, "I should go. Cooper, will you be home late tonight?"

He glanced at Shay as Daisy's weird smile grew larger. "I'm staying with Cooper while I look for an apartment."

"That's nice," Shay said.

"It is," Daisy said. "Separate bedrooms, of course. I'm in the guest room... not his room. I mean, I've been in his room, but not for..."

Her face turned bright red and Cooper inhaled deeply as Daisy rubbed hard at the scar on her arm. "Anyway, nice to meet you, Shay."

"Nice to meet you too, Daisy," Shay said.

With one last look at Cooper, Daisy walked back to her booth. Pride and a certain sense of possessiveness washed over Cooper as the shifters she walked past noticeably avoided her.

"So, that's Daisy, huh?" Shay said.

"Yes." He watched as she slid into the booth across from Eleanor. She said something to Eleanor and the pretty dark-haired woman looked his way before turning back to Daisy.

"Cooper?" Shay said.

"Sorry. Um… what were we talking about?"

She smiled at him. "Why are you doing this, Cooper? Daisy's into you."

"She isn't," he said.

"Please. She's been giving me the death stare since she sat down in her booth," Shay said.

He looked over at Daisy, he couldn't help it. She was staring at Shay. Although she looked like her normal sweet self to him, she turned away when she realized he was watching her.

"See what I mean," Shay said. "That girl's so jealous, she's practically glowing green."

"She's not jealous," Cooper said.

Shay laughed so hard, the couple at the table next to them stopped talking and looked over. "I know you could smell her jealousy, Cooper."

He flushed. He *had* smelled her jealousy. It made his lion go nearly crazy with excitement, but he was currently trying to convince himself and his lion that he was wrong.

"You could, couldn't you?" Shay said.

"Yes, but I'm trying to convince myself I was mistaken. You're not helping," he said.

She laughed again, her blue eyes dancing with mischief. She really was a gorgeous woman. Too bad he felt absolutely no attraction to her.

"The two of you are adorable, and you need to go and talk to her instead of sitting here with me," she said.

"I can't," he said.

"You can. Being too chicken to do it is not the same as not being able to do it," Shay said.

"She's afraid of me."

"Is she?" Shay said. "Because, again, that look she's

aiming my way screams 'get away from my man' more than 'you're in terrible danger, lady'."

He glanced over again. Daisy was staring at them and even though she looked away immediately, this time he couldn't miss the way she was glaring at Shay.

"There's no way you're just friends," Shay said. "Am I wrong?"

"We've been," he could feel his cheeks burning, "partially intimate."

"Partially intimate," Shay said with a small smile. "You're so cute. Okay, you've made out with her, so you know she wants you. So, why are you trying to work up the interest to have sex with me when it's clear the two of you want to bang like bunnies?"

"She's scared of me when we're…"

Shit. What was he doing? He couldn't tell Shay this kind of information. He didn't even know her.

"When you're about to…" Shay made a circle with her left thumb and forefinger and poked her right forefinger in and out of it.

Cooper couldn't help but laugh and Shay grinned up at him. "Look, if she's as afraid of shifters as Ryan said she is, then yeah, she's probably gonna be a little nervous about being naked with one. Have you tried talking to her about her fear? Maybe asking her if there's something you could do that would help when she starts to be afraid?"

"No," Cooper admitted. "I leave when she's afraid so that she isn't afraid anymore."

"That's sweet but I suggest you try talking to her instead," Shay said.

"If she's afraid, she's afraid," he said. "Me telling her I'm not going to hurt her won't make her believe it."

"Maybe not but showing her you're willing to do whatever she wants or needs, might."

When he just stared at her blankly, she said teasingly, "Lord, it's a good job you're so pretty. Look, you could tell her that if she starts to be afraid, you guys can slow down or stop completely and take a break. You can let her set the pace, tell her she's in charge and you won't do anything without her express permission first. Maybe your first time won't be as sexy as you both want it to be, but maybe what your first time needs to be is just – for her – getting through it without freaking the fuck out. You know?"

"I want it to be good for her," he said.

"Which is awesome, and you should tell her that. But also make it clear that it's her decision how it happens. Hell, tell her she can handcuff you to the damn bed if that makes her less nervous."

He laughed and she winked at him. "Don't knock it, until you try it, handsome. Anyway, my point is, have a conversation with her about her fear instead of trying to pretend it doesn't exist. Because, buddy, that woman might be anxious around you, but she also has it bad for you."

She stood and when she pulled her wallet out of her purse, Cooper said, "I'm buying dinner."

"Thank you," she said.

"Thank you for the advice. I'm sorry I wasted your time tonight."

"A handsome man and a delicious steak are never a waste of time," she said. "Good luck. I hope your get the girl, Cooper Brooks."

She leaned down and brushed her lips across his cheek before making her way toward the exit. Cooper flagged their server down and paid for the meal then glanced toward Daisy.

She was still sitting in the booth with Eleanor and he crossed the pub to them.

Feeling awkward as shit, he said, "Hi, ladies."

Daisy's look was decidedly frosty. "Hello."

When she didn't introduce him to Eleanor, Cooper turned to the dark-haired human and said, "Hello, I'm Cooper."

"Eleanor. Nice to meet you, Cooper. I've heard good things about you."

"Uh, thanks. Wes says you're a very competent driver."

She laughed, her dark eyes sparkling with amusement. "Thanks."

"Daisy, could I speak to you for a few minutes?" Cooper said.

"I'm visiting with Eleanor." Daisy crossed her arms over her chest and smiled thinly at him.

Well shit, this wasn't going well.

His lion whined in misery. The smell of Daisy's irritation was upsetting him. His headache was returning, a heavy pulse of pain in his temples that would turn agonizing over the next few hours.

"Actually," Eleanor said, "I have to get going. I just remembered I have a... thing."

"What thing?" Daisy said.

"A secret thing," Eleanor said with a devilish grin. "Cooper, would you mind giving Daisy a ride home?"

"Not at all." Holy fuck, he could goddamn kiss Eleanor right now.

Daisy stared pointedly at Eleanor who smiled at her and plucked her wallet from her purse. "Sorry, beautiful, I completely forgot about the thing."

"Sure, you did," Daisy said, but Cooper could smell amusement rather than irritation drifting from her soft skin.

Before Eleanor could signal their server, Cooper said, "I'd like to pay for yours and Daisy's dinner."

"No," Daisy said.

"Sweet," Eleanor said at the same time. She grinned at Daisy. "Girl, never turn down a free meal."

She stood and held out her hand to Cooper. He shook it and she said, "Nice to meet you, Cooper. Thanks for the dinner."

"Thank *you*," he said, hoping she understood how grateful he was to her.

"Bye, Daisy. Text me tomorrow." Eleanor walked away and Cooper slid into her spot in the booth.

Daisy was shredding her napkin and refusing to look at him. Cooper studied her half-eaten plate of food. "You didn't eat very much."

She glared at him. "I lost my appetite."

"Shay is only a friend," he said.

"Don't do that," she said. "Don't lie to me. I know exactly why you're having dinner with her. What I don't understand is why you're sitting here instead of going home with her so she can bang your brains out and help you forget about me."

"I don't want to forget about you," he said.

"Oh yeah? So, you had dinner with her because you thought it would be fun to make me jealous?"

"No, that isn't it. But I will admit that I like that you're jealous. I know how it makes me sound, but..." he shrugged.

She tossed her shredded napkin on her plate. "Of course I'm jealous, Cooper. Why wouldn't I be? You call me your mate all the damn time, you take care of me, you gave me the best orgasm of my life. Of course I'm going to be freaking jealous!"

Her voice was rising, and she looked around to see if

anyone was watching them. "I hate that you're going to sleep with her."

"I'm not, baby. I only want to sleep with you," he said.

"Yeah, well, we tried that, and it didn't work."

"It's my fault," he said. "I left the other night because you were afraid, but -"

"You didn't even give me a chance to explain," she said, her beautiful face red with frustration. "I was afraid for, like, two seconds, but you wouldn't even give me the chance to work through it. You just walked away."

"I know," he said. "I won't do that again."

"Do you think I like having those moments of fear with you? I don't." She was working herself up, her tiny hands clenched into fists, and the flush in her face flowing down her neck and across her chest. "I hate it! But I can't guarantee it won't happen again, and maybe I won't be able to go through with sex, I don't know. The only way to find out is if we try, but I don't want to act like a tease. It isn't fair to you, but I don't know what else to do. If we don't try, it'll never happen. But if we try and I'm afraid and have to stop, you're going to be disappointed and maybe even upset and -"

"Baby, stop." He reached out and took her hands, massaging them open from their tight fists before purring to her. She closed her eyes and took some deep breaths. He continued to purr until the tension eased from her body and the flush in her face faded.

When she opened her eyes, he squeezed her hands. "I want to be with you, Daisy. If that means we take things really slow, I am one hundred percent on board. Whatever you need from me, I'll give you. If that means nothing more than kissing and touching, I can do that."

"What if we have to stop?" she said. "What if we're about to… and I'm afraid and want to stop."

"Then we'll stop," he said.

"It's not that simple," she said.

"It is."

"It isn't. I'll be a… a tease and it isn't fair to you if I keep having orgasms and you don't."

He grinned at her. "Baby, my new favourite thing is giving you orgasms so if that's all we do for the next six months, I'm perfectly fine with that."

"You're crazy, Cooper. You can't go that long without…" She flushed and lowered her gaze to the table.

"Look at me, my mate," Cooper said.

She stared up at him and he rubbed his thumbs over the inner skin of her wrists. "Not to brag, but I'm pretty good at masturbating. If I need to take care of myself until you're comfortable in lending me a hand, I can do that."

Her mouth dropped open and he purred to her when she started to giggle. "Oh my God, I can't believe we're sitting in a pub talking about sex and masturbation."

"I've had weirder conversations in a pub," he said.

"You have not," she said.

"I'm friends with Boone, remember?"

She giggled again, and the tension in his chest eased when she turned her hands in his and linked their fingers together. "Are you sure you want to try this, Cooper? I really don't know if I'll be able to go through with it. At least not at first."

"I'm positive," Cooper said. "You are my mate, and I'll do whatever it takes to make you happy."

She stared at their linked hands before smiling at him. "Let's go home."

CHAPTER 18

Daisy didn't need a shifter's sense of smell to know that Cooper was nervous. His big body was stiff, his face was pinched, and she wondered if he would call the whole thing off. He might, she decided, despite what he'd said to her in the pub. When he led her into the living room, instead of his bedroom, her stomach sank.

He sat down on the couch and tugged on her hand. "Sit with me, Daisy."

"Why don't we go to the bedroom instead?" she said.

"In a bit. Do you want to watch a movie?"

She sat down next to him, shoving away her disappointment. "One of your romantic comedies?"

He flushed bright red – God, he was adorable when he blushed – and said, "Fucking Boone. I'm gonna kill him. He told you, didn't he?"

She grinned at him, settling back into the couch beside him, liking the heat of his big body next to hers. "He did."

"I suppose he also told you I crochet."

"Nope." She folded her legs under her and leaned against Cooper. Maybe if he could see and not just smell that she was relaxed, he'd be more open to trying to have sex. "You told me that yourself."

He stared at her before understanding dawned. "That night you drugged me."

She burst into laughter. "I did not *drug* you, Cooper. But yes, that's when you told me. You're making a granny square blanket for Wes, you said."

He nodded and she took his hand. "I like that you crochet. I've always wanted to learn. Maybe you could teach me."

He raised her hand to his lips and kissed the back of it. The firm warmth of his mouth sent shivers down her spine. "I'm too new at it to teach anyone. But we can watch the YouTube tutorials I watched, and I can give you some tips."

"I'd like that," she said. "Will you ever give me my scarf?"

He blushed again. "I told you about the scarf?"

"It matches the colour of my hair," she said.

"Jesus," he groaned, "did I say that?"

"Yes. I thought it was sweet."

He studied her and then reached out with his free hand and smoothed a lock of her hair between his fingers. "I love your hair. It's so soft and the colour is beautiful."

"Thank you." She reached up and slid her hand around the back of his thick neck, tugging until he bent his head toward her. She pressed her lips against his, smiling at the way he immediately purred.

She rested her hand on his chest, that deep vibration making her fingertips tingle as she licked his bottom lip. When he parted his lips, she slipped her tongue into his mouth, feeling bold and horny. She touched his tongue delicately with hers. His low groan and the way his purring increased in sound sent warmth from her belly to her pelvis.

He took the kiss deeper, angling his mouth over hers and

cupping her face with one warm hand. She crowded in close, resting her hand on his thick thigh and rubbing gently. When he cupped her breast, she arched into him and moaned when he rubbed his thumb over her nipple.

He pulled back. "Is this okay?"

"Yes," she said before tugging on the hem of his shirt. "Take this off."

He yanked his t-shirt over his head and dropped it on the floor. She stared in awe at his amazing chest, her fingers itching to thread through the light layer of hair.

Do it. He's your mate, remember?

She shuddered with pleasure when he kissed her neck before sucking on her earlobe. Her heart thumping, she rested one hand on his chest, smiling delightedly at the feel of the coarse hair. His hand had slid under her shirt and he cupped her breast through her bra. His fingers traced the edge of her bra before he leaned back.

"This okay, baby?"

Irritation threaded past the desire. If he was going to check in with her every thirty seconds, it would take forever to get her damn orgasm.

"You don't have to ask every time you touch me," she said. "My God, you've seen me half naked and touched my…"

A deliciously dirty grin crossed his face, and he slid his fingers under her bra to caress her throbbing nipple. "Your pussy?"

She blushed, her fingers curling into the hair on his chest. "Yes."

He nipped her neck. "I loved the way you moaned when my finger was in your pussy, baby. You're so tight and wet. I can't wait to feel you tighten around my dick."

She gasped, fresh hot desire slamming into her. When

Cooper pulled on her shirt, she raised her arms so he could strip it off. Before he could ask, she took off her bra, tossing it aside as he stared greedily at her naked breasts.

"So pretty," he growled before purring to her. His big hands cupped both her breasts and he pulled lightly on her nipples.

"Oh God," she moaned. "Cooper, take me to your bed."

"Not yet, little mate."

"But I want to go," she said with an embarrassing pout.

He smiled at her but shook his head. "We're taking things slow, remember?"

"We can be slow in the bedroom," she said.

He ignored her and she clutched at his thick blond hair when he dipped his head and pressed a kiss between her breasts. He licked and nipped at the underside of each breast until she couldn't stand the teasing.

"Cooper, please!" She pushed his head in the direction of her nipple, not even ashamed when he made a low laugh.

His hot wet mouth closed around her nipple and sucked. Pleasure speared straight to her pussy and her hips arched. Her pussy was aching and throbbing and she wanted, no *needed*, him to touch her.

His lips were still teasing her nipples, moving from one to the other, sucking and licking and driving her mad with desire. She grabbed his hand and tried to shove it between her legs. He resisted and she moaned in frustration.

"Patience, my mate," he said against her breast.

She pushed her own hand between her legs, scowling when he immediately pulled her hand away. He held her wrist and she could hear the smile in his voice when he said, "You can wait a little longer to come."

She uttered a curse before squirming over until she was straddling him. She needed friction against her clit and... she moaned, rubbing her pussy against that perfect hard length of him behind the denim.

It wasn't completely ideal... ideal would be both of them naked so she could drag his length directly against her clit, but it was better than nothing. She was so turned on, if she rubbed hard enough, she could come this way, and she was definitely motivated enough to do just that. She finally understood the appeal of dry humping.

Cooper hissed out a breath that turned into a purr as his big hands clamped down on her hips. She squirmed again, trying to find the right position and Cooper said, "Baby, wait."

"I don't want to wait. I want to..."

Her breath caught in her throat when she glanced up. Cooper's eyes were dark yellow and while she couldn't see them with his mouth closed, she had no doubt that his fangs were out. She stared at the pretty blue flecks in the yellow of his iris as his pupils narrowed.

"My mate," Cooper's voice had lowered. "Don't be afraid."

"I'm not afraid," she said. "I'm annoyed because I want to come, and you won't let me."

The tension she could feel developing between them disappeared with his laughter. He pressed a kiss against her collarbone before squeezing her denim-clad ass. "I'll let you, I just think we should take it slow."

"Well, I think we should both be naked," she said.

His nostrils flared and his hands tightened on her ass again. "Are you certain that's what you want? We don't have to -"

"I'm positive," she said.

She hopped off his lap, pulling off her socks and then

reaching for the button on her jeans. Cooper leaned forward and pushed her hands away. "Let me."

He unbuttoned and unzipped her jeans before tugging them down her legs. She stepped out of them and kicked them inside, gasping when Cooper brushed his mouth just below her belly button. His hands gripped her ass and squeezed before he ran his fingers up and down the backs of her thighs. He stared up at her. She brushed his hair back from his face and smiled at him.

"Are you sure, my mate?" His fingers curled around the waistband of her panties. She stared at his beautiful golden eyes and nodded.

He pulled her panties down her thighs, helping her to step out of them before he tossed them on top of her discarded jeans. Nerves and shyness were starting to creep in, and she tensed when he leaned forward again and kissed the small patch of auburn curls at the top of her mound.

He pulled back immediately, staring up at her before leaning back against the couch. "We can stop, baby."

"I don't want to," she said.

"All right," he said. "Straddle me."

"Aren't you going to, um…" She couldn't bring herself to say the words 'eat my pussy'. That was for women who were brave and confident in their sexuality.

Apparently, he knew what she meant. "Not right now."

"But I want you to, um, do that. I don't have a lot of experience in bed so that's why I'm nervous. I'm not afraid of you."

He smiled at her and tugged on her wrists until she straddled him again. "I still think it's better if we wait."

"You're not even naked," she complained. "Didn't we agree to both be naked… oh! Oh my God!"

Cooper had slipped his hand between her thighs, and she

immediately forgot about her annoyance when his rough fingers rubbed across her clit. She rubbed herself shamelessly against his hand, grabbing onto his shoulders for support.

He splayed his other hand across her lower back and bent his head to capture one nipple in his mouth. He worried it with his tongue and his teeth and when she felt his fangs scrape lightly against her nipple, pleasure exploded inside of her.

"Holy fuck," she said.

He laughed against her breast before licking the hollow between them while his thumb brushed repeatedly against her clit. "I love my mate's reaction to my touch."

"Touch harder," she demanded.

She hardly recognized herself. It wasn't like her to be so bossy or needy, but she was finally starting to understand why people acted so crazy about sex. She was feeling halfway to crazy herself and they hadn't even had sex yet.

Speaking of which...

"I want you naked," she said. "Right now."

"Soon," he said before nuzzling her nipple.

"No, now," she said. "Right... oh... oh fuck!"

He laughed and slid a second finger inside of her while his thumb continued to rub her clit. "Feel good, baby?"

She ground herself against his hand, her nails digging into his shoulders and her breath coming in harsh, hot pants. She rocked back and forth, the pleasure steadily building, reaching for that peak.

She was riding a man's hand. She, the girl who thought sex was barely worth the effort, was riding Cooper's hand like a woman possessed and not the least bit ashamed by it. She wanted her orgasm, needed it, and –

"Cooper, no!" she wailed in frustration and need when he moved his hand away.

He kissed the tip of one nipple. "Shh, baby, I'll give you want you want. Stand up for a second."

He helped her stand. Her legs felt weirdly shaky and her lower body was throbbing with need to the point where it was almost painful.

"Can we please go to the bedroom," she said.

He'd taken his wallet out of his back pocket and she watched as he pulled out a condom. "I think we should stay here."

"Why?" She should have felt self-conscious standing completely naked in front of Cooper. Instead she felt impatient and needy.

"I think it's best. You can be on top, all right? You're in charge, my mate," he said as he unbuckled his belt.

She nodded. A little of her common sense was returning and while she wasn't afraid now, it didn't mean she wouldn't be when she saw his dick, or they started to have sex. Cooper was bigger and stronger than her but being on top would give her a sense of control, even if it wasn't really true.

He paused in unbuttoning his jeans. "Are you certain this is what you want, Daisy?"

"Yes," she said.

He didn't wait for her to say anything else. He unzipped his jeans and lifted his hips, shoving both his jeans and his briefs down past his knees. He bent and removed them and his socks with a fluid grace she envied before straightening and sitting back.

Her gaze dropped to his dick. He was big and thick which wasn't surprising. What surprised her was her lack of fear. Hell, she didn't even feel a lick of trepidation. She bit her bottom lip when Cooper fisted his shaft slowly, making a bead of precum appear at the tip.

"We can stop, my mate." His voice was low and reassuring.

She believed him, despite the look of need on his face and the hardness of his cock. If she said she wanted to stop, he would stop, and he wouldn't make her feel guilty or like a tease.

"You really are the best. You know that, right?" she said.

He smiled at her. "I want to make you happy."

"I want you to put on that condom," she said.

He laughed and tore open the condom, rolling it onto his dick. He held his hand out to her and she took it, linking their fingers together as she straddled him again.

"You're in control," he repeated. "Go as slow as you want or need."

She appreciated what he was doing but going slow was the last thing she wanted. She was aching and empty, and she needed his cock. She grasped the base of his dick, barely hearing his low groan as she tried to straighten to her knees. She kept sinking into the couch and she muttered a frustrated curse.

"Cooper, help me."

His big hands cupped her hips and lifted her up, easing her forward until his dick pressed against her pussy. She knew he was strong, knew that he was powerful, but his ability to lift her so easily made her pause. She studied his face, one hand still wrapped around his dick, the other gripping his shoulder for balance.

He inhaled deeply and said, "We can stop, my mate."

His voice was hoarse, and the need on his face matched the intensity on her own. She guided his cock to her entrance. "No, I don't want to stop."

The relief that crossed his face sent a giggle bubbling up her throat. It disappeared when the head of Cooper's cock slid into her. She clutched at his shoulders, staring at his gorgeous face as he carefully eased her down onto his cock until she was sitting in his lap and stuffed full of his glorious dick.

"Still good?" he said before purring to her.

"So good," she breathed and tried an experimental squeeze.

He groaned, his hands tightening on her hips. "Fuck! Be a good girl, my mate."

She leaned forward and pressed a kiss against his mouth. "You feel so good, Cooper."

"So do you. So tight and wet." He purred again before resting his hands on the couch on either side of him. "You're in control, baby."

She braced her hands on his shoulders before riding him with slow and languid thrusts. He purred loudly, his hands digging into the couch cushions as she traced one flat nipple with the ball of her thumb. She leaned forward and kissed his thick neck before licking her way to his ear.

"Does this feel okay?" she whispered into his ear.

"Yes," he groaned. "Can you go a little faster?"

"Not yet," she said.

He groaned again, and she was a little surprised at how much she was enjoying taking the lead. That foreign feeling of power rippled through her and she gripped the back of Cooper's neck, staring into his golden eyes as she thrust a little harder.

"Good mate." He purred to her, and she moaned when his hands cupped her ass and squeezed. "This okay?"

"Yes," she panted as he kneaded and squeezed. "Will you rub my clit?"

"Whatever you want, my mate." He traced a path across her ribs and down her hip with his rough fingers before slipping them between her legs.

The slow and lazy circles he made on her clit sent flames licking along her nerve endings. She thrust harder and faster. She was suddenly on the edge of her climax and she wanted him there with her, wanted to watch Cooper fall over that cliff with her.

His hips were thrusting now, rising up to meet each of her strokes, and his purring had taken on an erratic breathless quality that was somehow even sexier. He groaned her name and rubbed harder at her clit. "Baby, you're so tight. You have to come for me. I'm not gonna last."

She clutched at his shoulders, crying his name when his free hand cupped one breast and he teased her nipple with his thumb. She ground herself against his hand and his cock, throwing her head back and digging her nails into his warm skin when her climax washed over her. His purrs turned deafening, and the pace of his thrusts turned hard and fast. She clung to him as his purr became a roar. He clamped his hands around her hips and held her tight as he pumped in and out.

Her body shaking with pleasure, she collapsed against him, listening to the purrs vibrating out of his chest as he relaxed against the couch. He stroked her back and kissed her shoulder. "That was incredible, Daisy."

"Hmm," she said sleepily. "I need a nap."

He laughed and kissed her shoulder again before easing her off of him and onto the couch. "Be right back."

He disappeared out of the living room and she heard the tell-tale squeak of the guest bathroom door. She relaxed on the couch, wondering if she should throw on Cooper's t-shirt to hide her nakedness before deciding she didn't care. She'd just be taking it off again once she was in Cooper's bed.

He returned to the living room and without speaking, scooped her up off the couch. She giggled and put her arms around his shoulders. "I feel very princess-ish."

He purred to her and she rubbed her nose against his as he climbed the stairs. When he went left toward her bedroom, she shook her head. "No, your bed."

"Are you sure?" he said.

"Yes. Unless you don't want me in your bed for anything other than sex?" Doubt was pushing past the contentment and the sleepiness. Shit, she was being awfully presumptuous.

"You're always welcome in my bed for whatever you want," he said as he walked to his bedroom instead. "Sleeping, sex, watching movies. You name it."

"Eating cookies?"

He laughed. "You like eating cookies in bed?"

"Sometimes." She rested her head on his chest. There was so much they didn't know about each other. She hoped he wanted to learn about her as much as she wanted to learn about him.

"Cookie eating is fine." He laid her down on the right side of the bed. "As long as you eat them on your side of the bed only."

"My side of the bed," she said as he pulled the sheet and quilt over her and then slid into bed beside her. "I like the sound of that."

"I do too." Cooper pulled her into his arms. She rested her head on his chest again, listening to the low sound of his purrs as she slung one leg over his.

"Cooper?"

"Yeah?"

"I wasn't afraid. Not once."

"I'm glad, baby."

"Me too. You were right." She lifted her head to smile at him. The gold in his eyes had faded to blue and she stroked her fingers across his strong jaw.

"About what?" he said.

"You're really good at sex."

He laughed and kissed her. "Baby, I haven't even shown you half of what I can do."

She wiggled her eyebrows at him. "I'm ready for round two if you are."

"I am. But I think," he grinned at her when she tried to stifle her yawn, "you really do need a nap before we start round two."

She snuggled into him. "Just a little cat nap. Wake me in twenty minutes. Okay?"

"Yes. Sleep, my mate."

CHAPTER 19

Cooper woke up to the early morning sun sending rays of light across his bedroom and an empty bed. He ignored his feeling of unease and headed to the bathroom.

He hadn't woken Daisy like she'd asked. Despite what she said, she looked tired and worn out, and she'd been sleeping deeply within five minutes. He'd been tired too and having his mate in his arms had given his lion its first restful sleep in months.

He was regretting it now though. He finished using the bathroom and washed his hands before grabbing his toothbrush. He hadn't expected to wake up to an empty bed. How the hell had Daisy even snuck out of his bed without him hearing her?

Maybe because it wasn't only your lion who hadn't slept well for months?

He brushed his teeth and spit toothpaste into the sink, then rinsed his mouth. Maybe. But what if Daisy left his bed because she regretted what happened? What if she didn't want to sleep with him again? What if last night was a one-time thing?

His lion roared angrily at the thought. Cooper had to control his very childish urge to punch the wall. If Daisy was finished with him, she was finished with him, and there wasn't anything he could do about it.

She is our mate! His lion was pouting worse than a three-year-old who was denied candy.

He wiped his mouth and opened the bathroom door. He needed to find Daisy.

"Oh shoot. You're awake."

His lion purred happily, the sound rumbling out of his chest and throat. Wearing his t-shirt, Daisy stepped into the bedroom. He stared at the tray in her hands. It held two cups of coffee, two plates of pancakes dripping with syrup and butter, and - his stomach growled - a pile of delicious fragrant bacon.

"I wanted to surprise you with breakfast in bed," Daisy said as she shamelessly eyed his dick. "But you're not in bed anymore."

He grinned at her and sat on the bed, leaning back against the headboard. "Problem solved."

She laughed and carried the tray over, setting it on the bed next to him. He held the tray steady as she sat on the bed beside him and propped some pillows behind her back. "I hope you're hungry. I got carried away with making pancakes."

"Famished."

She piled some bacon onto the plate closest to him before handing it to him. "Eat up while it's still hot."

They ate in comfortable silence. The bacon was perfectly crisp, the pancakes perfectly fluffy, the coffee perfectly brewed. There was a probability that he was seeing every-thing Daisy did through rose-coloured glasses, but he didn't care. He was happy and content and so was his lion, and it was because of Daisy.

Daisy set her plate down on the tray and sipped at her coffee. "You didn't wake me up."

"You were tired," he said.

She gave him a mock scowl and he leaned over to press a kiss against her lips. She tasted like sweet syrup and bitter coffee, and he found the combination weirdly intoxicating. He nuzzled her damp hair. "I was tired too."

"You must have been," she said. "I got up and had a shower and made breakfast all without you waking up. Don't cat shifters normally have, like, super sonic hearing?"

"Yes," he said. "I'm not sure what happened."

He finished his breakfast and when Daisy went to grab the tray, he lifted it. "I'll take it to the kitchen. You stay here."

"You got it, boss."

He laughed and cringed at the same time. "God, please don't do a Boone imitation while you're in my bed."

He left her giggling in his bed and carried the tray to the kitchen. He grabbed a couple of bottles of water and returned to the bedroom. Daisy was lying on the bed, scrolling through her phone. He stared at her pale legs stretched out on the bed. Was she naked under his shirt?

It was about time he found out.

His cock already starting to harden, he set the water on the nightstand, then sat on the bed next to Daisy and skimmed his hand along her bare shin. She smiled at him. "Hey, is it going to be weird at the office now that we've slept together?"

"No, I don't think so."

"I promise I won't act any different," she said. "I know you're still the boss at the office and I won't bring what we do in our personal life into the office or... Cooper?"

"Yeah?"

"What are you doing?"

He slid his hand further under his shirt, caressing her smooth thigh. "I'm wondering if you're wearing anything under my shirt."

She tossed her phone to the side. "Maybe you should check for yourself."

"Maybe I should." He leaned down and pressed a kiss against her knee. The sweet scent of her arousal filled the air and he purred happily. His mate was no longer afraid of him and he couldn't be fucking happier.

He trailed kisses down her shin before moving to the end of the bed. His cock was fully erect now and Daisy stared at it with a hungry look of need that sent fresh desire through his body. Before he could give in to his urge to fuck her hard and fast, he wrapped his hands around her calves and tugged.

She let her legs fall open and he kissed the inside of her calf before settling on his stomach between her open legs. She tried to close her legs, but they pressed uselessly against his broad shoulders.

"Cooper, what, um, what are you doing?"

He kissed her knee again. "Checking to see what my mate wears under my shirt."

He kissed her inner thigh and then made a long, slow lick up her soft skin. She moaned, but her hands clutched at his head and the look she gave him was shy and uncertain. "Are you going to, um…you know."

He licked her other thigh, enjoying the soft sound of her moan, the heady scent of her arousal. "Eat your pussy?"

Her legs jerked and the scent of her arousal thickened. Her pussy was wet. It was wet and waiting for him. He rubbed his erection against the bed as he reached for the hem of her shirt. "I am, sweet mate. I've wanted to taste you for months. Will you let me?"

"Yes," she said so quickly that he had to hide his smile. "Yes, I will."

"Good mate." He kissed her thigh then tugged on the shirt. "Take this off."

She pulled it over her head, her motions and wriggling on the bed, bringing her beautiful perfect pussy even closer to his mouth. He licked her inner thigh before letting his fangs drop. He pressed them in the crease between her thigh and her pussy, dragging them lightly down her soft skin. He purred when she cried out, her fingers sliding into his hair to hold tight.

He lifted his head and purred again to her before pressing a kiss against the soft patch of auburn curls at the top of her pussy. "So pretty, my mate."

"Thank you." Her voice was breathless, and it wasn't his imagination that her hands were trying to push him lower.

He kissed her hip bone. She moaned, her body moving restlessly. "Cooper, don't tease."

He couldn't resist her plea. Besides, he would have plenty of time to tease and torment. Right now, he needed to taste the sweetness he'd been dying to taste for months.

"Yes, my mate," he said before dipping his head between her thighs. He licked her wet pussy lips, his cock becoming almost painfully hard at her taste. Purring and growling, he licked her lips clean of her sweet cream. Her clit was swollen and peeking out from between her lips. He purred again before licking her clit with the tip of his tongue.

She cried out, her hips arching and her hands pulling hard on his hair. Growling happily at his mate's response, he parted her pussy lips with his thumbs and licked her clit with slow brushes of his tongue.

He sucked it lightly, pressing his hands against Daisy's hip bones to hold her steady as he used his lips and tongue to bring her closer to the brink. She begged nonsensical words breathlessly, any shyness she'd felt had long disappeared. He pressed his hands against her inner thighs, spreading her legs wide so he could feast on her. Her hands tightened in his hair and she ground her pussy against his mouth, crying out when he slipped his finger inside her narrow entrance.

She clenched around him and he moaned against her pussy before sucking on her clit again. When he scraped his fangs gently across her clit, she screamed in pleasure, her hips bucking up and her thighs clamping around his head. Fresh wetness flooded his mouth. He pried her legs apart, lifting his head to take a breath of air as she moaned and shuddered her way through her orgasm. Her pussy squeezed tight around his finger and he pressed light kisses against her inner thigh and her pussy. He avoided her clit, knowing it would be too sensitive, and kissed her inner thigh again before untangling her hands from his hair.

He sat up, smiling at his mate as she laid on her back, her legs spread wide, her nipples hard and inviting him to suck. His cock leaked a steady stream of precum, and he was aching to be back inside of her. He wanted to fuck her, wanted to fill her with his come and put his cub in her belly.

Fresh excitement rushed through him. He kneeled between her open legs before pressing his cock against her entrance. She smiled invitingly at him and he slid into her, purring loudly as her tight pussy swallowed every inch of his cock. She was so warm and wet and taking her bare was his number one fantasy come to life.

He propped himself on his hands above her and thrust in and out of her perfect pussy, trying to be slow and gentle with his beautiful mate. He would give her his seed and she would bear him a cub.

Cooper, stop!

He didn't want to stop. His lion didn't want him to stop. He wanted to fuck his mate until she carried his cub. She wanted that too.

You don't know that! Stop!

With a low grunt, he stopped. Fuck, what was he doing? He started to pull out, blinking at Daisy when her slender legs wrapped around his hips and she grabbed his arms. "Don't stop."

"Daisy," he groaned, "I need to put on a condom."

He supposed he could pull out before he came but he knew himself. Knew that he wouldn't, knew that he would come inside his mate and damn the consequences. No, it was better to put on the condom now while he still had a small semblance of control.

"Don't stop," she repeated before squeezing her pussy around his dick.

He muttered a curse, the cords in his neck standing out as he fought the urge to bury himself deep inside of her. "Baby, I'm not wearing a condom."

"I'm clean," she panted. "I promise."

He groaned out another curse. "I am too."

"Then don't stop."

She lifted her head from the pillow and kissed his sternum. Their size difference made the missionary position awkward. She was so short the top of her head just brushed his collarbone, but he couldn't bring himself to switch positions. He liked having her beneath him with her slender but strong thighs wrapped around his hips, and her soft hands roaming his back.

Her warm tongue brushed across his flat nipple and he

groaned, thrusting deep at the sensation. She made a soft giggle. "Someone likes that."

When she sucked on his nipple, he cried out with pleasure, his body shuddering as she teased the sensitive nub. She kissed his chest again and he moved faster, his body moving in a steady rhythm in and out of hers. The heat and wetness of her pussy sent him into a frenzy of need and want.

Her nails dug into his back. "Harder, honey."

He growled and thrust harder, pumping himself in and out, burying his dick deep inside her willing body as his orgasm grew closer and closer. She ran her hands up and down his back, moaned his name, and met each of his thrusts.

With a loud roar and one final hard thrust, he climaxed into her, his hot seed filling up her pussy, his entire body shaking as his release washed over him. He pumped in and out, growling and purring and shuddering, until her pussy had taken every last drop of his come.

He pulled out and collapsed on his back next to her, gasping in oxygen, trying to slow his heart rate as his lion roared in triumph. Daisy leaned over him and swept his hair back from his face. "You okay?"

"Good," he panted. "Really good."

She smiled at him and kissed his chest before resting her head on it. Her fingers roamed over the fresh scar on his shoulder, tracing it lightly. He held her tight, stroking her long auburn hair as his lion purred to their mate.

"God, I love your purring," she said. "It needs to be made into an app to help people relax."

He laughed and she lifted her head to study him again. "I'm on the pill."

Dismay flooded his body and his lion's purring cut out abruptly. She rubbed his chest almost soothingly as he tried to smile at her. "Okay, that's good."

A small smile played at her lips. "You're a terrible liar. I know you want to," she paused, "put your cub in my belly."

He blushed and looked away. She traced her fingers over his chest. "That's what you want, isn't it, Cooper? Me pregnant with your baby."

"Do you want children?" he asked.

What would he do if she didn't? He wanted kids and so did his lion. If Daisy didn't want them...

"I do," she said.

He knew he had a look of relief on his face, but he couldn't hide it.

"Maybe not this year," she said with a small smile. "But sooner than later. How many kids do you want?"

"At least two," he said. "You?"

"I always thought three would be nice."

"I'm good with three," he said.

"But what about four?" she asked with a soft smile. "I'd like a big family."

"If you want four kids, we'll have four," he said.

She laughed. "It's kind of weird that we're talking about how many kids we'll have when I don't know anything about you."

"You know plenty about me," he said.

"Oh yeah? Let's see... I know you used to be in the military, Grayson is your best friend, you're a great boss, and you're really, really, *really* amazing at sex."

"What else do you need to know?" he said with a grin.

She traced the tattoos on his chest. "I don't know. I mean... I don't know your middle name, if you have siblings, if you're close to your parents, if you prefer cake or pie, or if you've been married before."

He kissed her forehead. "James, one younger brother, yes

although they live out of state, pie, *always* pie, and no I've never been married before."

"Any serious relationships?" she said.

"Two. One when I was in my early twenties, and another a few years ago."

"Can I ask why they didn't work or is that being too nosy?" she asked.

"It's not being nosy," he said. "The first one didn't work because I joined the military, and the distance thing made the relationship fizzle out. The second one, she had some anxiety issues and the career I've chosen can sometimes be dangerous. It was hard on her. She worried about me to the point where it was physically taxing on her. Eventually her anxiety and her stress were stronger than her love for me and we went our separate ways."

"I'm very sorry," she said.

"I was too, but it's for the best. I love my job and even though I loved Marla, I couldn't give this up. We're still friends on Facebook. She's married to a finance guy who works an office job, and they have two cubs. She seems very happy."

"Did your lion think of her as his mate?" Daisy said.

"He loved her, but he hadn't yet gotten to the mate point with her."

"How long did you date?"

"Almost three years."

She traced his tattoos again with the tip of her finger. "But we've known each other for only three months and he already thinks I'm his mate?"

"Yes." He wanted to try and explain, to try and make it sound less fucking weird, but he stayed quiet. There wasn't anything he really could say. It *was* fucking weird that not only was his lion instantly in love with Daisy, but he believed her to be his mate too.

Just your lion?

He stared at the ceiling, trailing his fingers over Daisy's soft skin. No, not just his lion. He'd known too from the moment he saw Daisy that she was his mate.

"Is Marla a human?"

"No. Bobcat shifter," he said.

"Have you ever slept with a human before me?"

"Yes. But you're the smallest human I've slept with," he said. "Your turn now."

She made a figure eight on his chest with her fingers. "Rachel, no siblings, my parents died in a car accident when I was seven and I grew up in foster care, pie for me too, and nope, never married before. Only one serious relationship and you already know how that turned out."

He cupped her face and made her look at him. "You grew up in foster care?"

"I did. My therapist said that's probably why I want a big family. My lack of family as a kid, you know?"

"You didn't have any other family who could take you?" he said.

My parents were only children and both of their parents had already passed. My mom's best friend was my godmother. She was given custody of me, but she didn't want the responsibility of raising a kid, so she gave me up to the system."

"Are you fucking kidding me? She just gave you up?" Cooper stared at her.

"Yes. But to be fair, I was kind of an emotional wreck. I was crying a lot and being super clingy with her."

"You were a kid and your parents just died," Cooper said. "Jesus fucking Christ, of course you were crying and upset."

"Monique said it was for the best. She said I needed to pretend I wasn't sad and put on a happy smile, and a nice family would adopt me who would take better care of me than she could. She didn't have a lot of money and I would have been a real financial burden. She thought we'd both be happier if I went to a nice family who had money instead of living with her and being poor."

"Oh my fucking God," Cooper said. "She's a goddamn monster."

Daisy frowned at him. "She wasn't. It wasn't her fault that I never got adopted like she thought I would. There were a couple of families interested in me, but I was still grieving for my parents and didn't make a very good first impression. That isn't Monique's fault. Besides, she would send me cards a few times a year with five or ten dollars in it, and she took me out for dinner every year on my birthday."

"Jesus Christ," Cooper said.

"It was nice of her to do that," Daisy said. "She didn't have to, and the ten or fifteen dollars I got every year was like winning the lottery for me. One time she sent me a twenty-dollar bill and it was right before the scholastic book fair at school. For the first time since my parents died, I could buy books just like the other kids. It was a really great day and I have her to thank for that."

Cooper's stomach felt like it'd been bathed in acid. "Daisy, honey, she wasn't a good person. Your mom and dad expected her to look after you, to raise you and keep you safe. To give you a happy life."

Daisy just shrugged. "Life doesn't always work out the way it's supposed to for a person. She didn't have to stay in contact with me or give me money. She took me to a real restaurant for my birthday, not just McDonalds or Burger

King. During dinner, she would tell me stories about my mom and her when they were younger."

He tried to keep his face neutral. How bad was Daisy's childhood that this woman doing the bare minimum for her had seemed special?

"Do you still talk to her?" He hoped so. He wanted to meet the woman who had abandoned his mate as a helpless child so he could tell her exactly what special kind of asshole she really was.

"No, she stopped, uh, communicating with me when I was ten," Daisy said.

"Of course, she did." He made a low growl of irritation.

"It was my fault," Daisy said.

"How the fuck could it be your fault? You were a kid." He could hear the annoyance in his voice, and he tried to rein it in. The last thing he wanted was Daisy thinking he was pissed at her.

"I didn't like the foster home I was in. It was... well, it wasn't great. I asked Monique to let me live with her." Daisy rubbed at the scar on her arm. "It didn't go well. I started crying and getting emotional, and it really upset Monique. She said it wasn't fair of me to put her on the spot like that and that she still wasn't in a position where she could financially provide for me."

Daisy grimaced. "God this is embarrassing. I probably shouldn't tell you anymore because I don't come off very well in the story."

He cupped her face again and pressed a kiss against her mouth. "Tell me, baby."

She sighed and rubbed at the scar again. "I basically begged her to let me live with her. I promised that I wouldn't ask her for money ever, and that I would be really careful with my clothes, so she didn't have to buy me new ones."

Her face turned a soft red. "I said I would only eat one meal a day. I even lifted up my shirt right there in the middle of the restaurant to show her how skinny I was in an attempt to convince her I wouldn't eat much."

Her fingers rubbed ceaselessly over the scar. "When she kept saying no, I started crying hard. Everyone was staring at us and it was a total scene. Monique took me out of the restaurant, drove me back to my foster home, and I never heard from her again. I looked her up on Facebook a few years ago. She's married now and has a couple of kids. She looks happy."

"Fuck her," Cooper said. "She abandoned you twice as a child."

"Well, I did cry a lot in the restaurant," Daisy said. "We're talking snot dripping and loud braying sobs."

"So what," Cooper said. "You were a *child*, Daisy."

"I was ten and old enough to know better, but I was so tired of being afraid and -"

She stopped abruptly and sat up, pasting a smile on her face. "Enough about my sad sack childhood. What do you want to do today?"

"Why were you afraid?" he said.

She stared at the scar on her arm. "Because my foster home, it wasn't…"

She swallowed hard and the scent of her fear drifted to him. He leaned in and kissed her shoulder. "It's all right, baby. You can tell me. I won't let anyone hurt you, ever again."

She took a shuddering breath. "There was -"

His cell phone buzzed on the nightstand and Daisy glanced at it. "You should get that."

"I don't need to. What were you going to say?" He took her hand, linking their fingers, but it was too late. He could already see from the look on her face that she wouldn't tell him. Whatever moment was happening had passed. If he tried to pry further, it would only make things worse.

He pressed another kiss against her shoulder before grabbing his phone. He read the text. "It's Gray. I guess Shay talked to Ryan this morning. He wants to come over. I'm pretty sure he thinks I'm on the cusp of madness again."

"Again," she said softly. "How close were you to going mad, Cooper?"

He didn't want to answer but she squeezed his hand and persisted. "How close, honey?"

"Close," he said. "My lion was – is – obsessed with you. Not being with you was difficult."

She didn't reply, and he cursed himself in his head. He was going to scare her away if he kept this up. "But he's more chill about you now so, you know… I'm not a crazy weirdo or anything."

Fuck. He was a complete idiot.

She laughed, and relief flooded through him when she pressed a kiss against his mouth. "God, you're cute, Cooper Brooks." A cheeky look crossed her face. "And I know that's a lie. Your lion is one hundred percent into me."

He grinned at her as his cell phone buzzed again. "Yeah, well, he's not the only one."

"Is it Boone? It's Boone, isn't it?" she said.

He growled playfully at her and she laughed again before taking his phone from his hand. She swiped to the camera and leaned against him, resting her head in the curve of his neck and aiming the screen at their faces. "Smile, Cooper."

Instead of smiling, he turned his head and kissed her temple as she took the picture. He studied the picture when she handed his phone back to him. Daisy's face beamed with happiness and her smile was gorgeous.

"Send that to Grayson," she said. "That should help convince him you're fine, right?"

He sent the picture off without typing anything before tossing his phone on the nightstand and pulling Daisy into his lap. He nuzzled her throat and then marked it with a few swipes of his face. "Yes."

She stroked his thick hair. "What do you want to do today?"

"Whatever you want," he said.

She thought for a few minutes. "There's a park with some pretty walking trails not too far from the office."

"I know which one you mean," he said.

"We could go for a walk, maybe stop for coffee after?" she said.

"Sure."

She grinned at him and he could smell her excitement. "I know it's silly, but I'm really looking forward to this. So often when I'm out in public I'm afraid, but now I don't have to be. I smell like you and even better, you're with me. Shifters won't come near me. I can be normal, Cooper. I don't have to be afraid."

He kissed her slender throat. "You don't ever have to be afraid again, baby. I promise."

CHAPTER 20

"It's not a good idea, Daisy."

"It is," she said.

Cooper paced back and forth in the kitchen. His pupils narrowed into slits and Daisy waited as he spoke to his lion.

His pupils rounded and he shook his head. "It's a terrible idea."

"I know your lion wants you to do it."

"I don't care what he wants," Cooper said.

"Yes, you do."

Cooper growled in frustration. "We can do this later. It doesn't have to be tonight. Can't we just watch a movie or something? I'll make you popcorn. Do you like popcorn?"

She smiled at him. "I like popcorn. And if you want to watch a movie, we'll watch one. But after you shift for me."

She knew why he didn't want to. He was worried it would frighten her too much.

"Baby," he said, "have you ever seen a lion in real life?"

"Well, not up close, but I've been to the zoo and seen them there."

He groaned and rubbed at the back of his neck. "It's not

the same. My lion is big, okay? He's going to want to touch you, to rub up against you and mark you. And I won't have as much control over him. I can't guarantee that I can stop him from marking you once I'm in my lion form."

"I'm okay if he touches me."

He made another noise of frustration. "You don't know that. Look, I get why you think you need to do this, but it can wait."

"Don't shifters have to shift to their cat form on a regular basis to be happy and content? I read that somewhere, I'm sure of it," Daisy said.

"Yes," he said, "but I can shift when I'm alone."

"Cooper, I understand why you don't want to shift, but I think it's better to do it sooner than later," she said. "I'm not afraid of you anymore, I swear."

"Me in my human form is a lot different than when I'm in my lion form," he said. His gaze dropped to the scar on her arm. "There are claws and teeth, remember?"

"I remember," she said. She couldn't say this to him, but ironically, she was more afraid of a shifter when they were only half-shifted. Which was ridiculous but childhood trauma wasn't exactly something that could be normalized.

"Next weekend," he said. "I'll shift for you next weekend."

"I'd really like you to shift right now." She knew she was pushing him and part of her hated herself for doing that to him, but she needed to know. If she was wrong and she was terrified of him in his shifter form, it was better to know now. Even a week later, it would be harder on both her and Cooper to end the relationship.

Relationship? You only started having sex with him last night and already you're calling it a relationship?

She ignored her inner voice. What was happening

between her and Cooper was unconventional and inner Daisy really wanted her to be freaked out by it, but she wasn't. Couldn't be. Not when being with Cooper felt perfect.

"Daisy…" Cooper said.

"It'll be okay, honey. Please trust me," she said.

His pupils turned to slits for a few seconds before he sighed and yanked his t-shirt over his head. He unbuckled his belt and unbuttoned his jeans, pushing them and his briefs down his legs. She giggled when he hopped on one leg and then the other to remove his socks, but he didn't smile. His face was tense, and he stared solemnly at her as he stood naked in the kitchen.

"My lion will never hurt you, baby. Remember that, okay?"

"I know," she said.

He closed his eyes and she watched in fascination as his big body rippled and shook. He arched his back, lifting his face to the sky as bones cracked and muscles stretched, and hard flesh turned to fur. It took less than thirty seconds for him to fully shift and she stared in silence at the lion standing in the kitchen.

He was big. Much bigger than the lions she'd seen at the zoo. Or maybe it only felt that way because he was standing less than two feet away from her. She studied his eyes and wide nose, and the heavy brown mane before her gaze dropped to his paws. His claws weren't out but she knew they'd be long and thick and razor sharp.

Before she felt even a trickle of fear, a familiar purring filled the kitchen. She lifted her gaze back to the lion's face – back to *Cooper's* face – and smiled at him. "Hello, Cooper."

He purred again and took a step toward her and then another, his tail waving in the air behind him. He stopped in front of her and she reached out and brushed her hand along his mane.

The lion's purring grew louder. She staggered back against the wall when he butted his head across her hip. A very human-like look of embarrassment crossed the lion's face.

"It's okay," she said as she straightened. "I'm not hurt."

He purred again and she braced herself against the wall when he rubbed his head across her abdomen. She buried her hands in his thick mane and scratched. He made an adorable trilling sound before rubbing his big body along hers a few times. She scratched down his spine, delighted at how soft his fur was.

He made a low roar and turned to headbutt her hip again. He stared up at her and knowing instinctively what he wanted, she moved to a chair and sat. He immediately crowded up against her, they were face to face now and she tried not to flinch when he rubbed his face across hers. She wiped the hair from her mouth and laughed when the lion purred and rubbed his cheek across her forehead, nearly knocking her from the chair.

"Whoa, a little gentler, big guy," she said before scratching his neck. He purred and trilled, rubbing his face all over her face and her neck for nearly five minutes before settling on his haunches in front of her. She scratched his cheeks and then his forehead, liking the way it made him purr.

"You're very handsome," she said before petting the top of his head.

He chuffed happily and licked the scar on her arm. His tongue was scratchy, and he chuffed again when she winced. "That's sweet but it feels like sandpaper."

He purred and rubbed his face against hers again before

moving back and shifting to his human form. She smiled at Cooper when he stared uncertainly at her. "Are you all right, my mate?"

"Yes." She stood and stepped into his arms. "I wasn't afraid."

"Sorry, he marked you so much," Cooper said. "He's been wanting to do that for months."

"I didn't mind," she said.

"He liked it when you called him handsome."

She laughed and kissed his naked chest. "He's very handsome. And big. Really big."

"Why weren't you afraid?" he asked bluntly.

"Because he's a part of you and I'm not afraid of you," she said. "I'll never be afraid of you or your lion again."

"You look happy," Megan said.

Daisy propped her phone on the table. "Do I?"

"Yes. Happier than I've ever seen you before. I'm not surprised considering you've spent the last two days banging your boss's brains out and you finally know what amazing sex is. Does this mean you and Cooper are officially a couple now?"

"I think so," Daisy said. "We haven't really talked about that."

"Of course you haven't. You're too busy having great sex," Megan said with a laugh. She dipped out of the screen view for a few seconds and returned with a protein bar and a sports drink. She tore open the wrapper on the protein bar. "But considering he's been referring to you as his mate for weeks, I think it's safe to assume you're in a relationship. So, how's your fear around other shifters?"

"Still there, but maybe not as bad?" Daisy said. "We went out yesterday for a walk in the park and I wasn't afraid at all. But I think if I didn't smell like Cooper or have him with me, I would still be at least a little afraid."

"Well, it's a fuck of a lot better than it used to be so I'm happy for you, babe," Megan said. She bit off a piece of protein bar and chewed and swallowed. "You tell him why you're so afraid of shifters yet?"

"No."

"You should," Megan said.

"I know. It's just hard to talk about it. You and my therapist are the only ones I've ever told what happened and both times I ended up a shivering, crying wreck after. I don't want him to think I'm weak, even though I am, and he knows that already."

Megan stared sympathetically at her. "One, you're not weak, and two, what you went through was horrific. Never apologize for being emotional about it. So, where is this hot boss of yours. I'd like to meet him."

"He's in the shower."

"What the hell are you doing talking to me then? Get in there with him and have hot shower sex, girl."

"He didn't invite me to shower with him," Daisy said doubtfully.

"Trust me, you don't need an invitation," Megan said.

"Maybe he wants some alone time," Daisy said. "We've basically spent every minute together since Friday night."

"So what? It's only Sunday afternoon, that isn't even forty-eight hours yet. He absolutely won't mind if you join him."

Daisy glanced at the doorway of the kitchen before lowering her voice. "We haven't had sex today. That's weird, right? Like, shouldn't he want to have sex with me every day? What if he's getting bored with me or what if I'm really terrible at it and he doesn't want to tell me?"

"Or maybe he's worried that your crumpet is sore," Megan said.

"Oh my God, Megan," Daisy said with an embarrassed laugh.

"What? Shifters have big dicks and you're little, and it's been a while since you had sex. Don't tell me you're not sore."

"A little," Daisy admitted. "But not so much that I don't want to have sex."

"Well then get your cute butt into that shower."

"What if it isn't that? What if he really is bored with me or I suck at sex?"

"Only one way to find out," Megan said. "Ask him."

"I can't. I'm not brave like you," Daisy said.

Megan leaned forward and stared directly into her camera. "Daisy, honey, you're one of the bravest people I know."

Daisy blinked at her. "What? No, I'm not. I'm weak and afraid and -"

"You're not," Megan said. "For the last sixteen years, you've gone out into a world filled with shifters every single fucking day even though you're terrified of them. That is incredibly brave, my love."

"It didn't feel brave," Daisy said.

Megan smiled at her. "I know. But you'll have to trust me that it was. Now, go find your man and be that bad brave self I know you are."

"I love you, Megan."

"I love you too, Daisy." Megan blew her a kiss and ended the call.

Daisy headed upstairs and walked into Cooper's

bedroom. The bathroom door was halfway open, and she could hear the shower going and see steam drifting out.

"Be brave," she muttered to herself before stripping off Cooper's t-shirt and stepping into the bathroom. She could see Cooper standing directly under the hot spray through the frosted glass. Desire blossomed in her belly. She stared at his naked body. God, he was so good looking and the way he made her feel when he touched her and kissed her and... fucked her was all she could think about lately.

Her pussy was growing wet, her nipples hardening, and she was a little embarrassed by how easily she was turned on by him. Was this even normal?

Cooper lifted his head and inhaled deeply before turning to stare at her through the shower door. She stood where she was, uncertain about her plan to join him, worried that he really did want some alone time or was trying to figure out how to tell her gracefully that she sucked in bed.

He slid open the shower door in a silent invitation. Her pulse hammering away, she stepped into the shower.

"Hello, little mate." His voice was a low growl and when he purred to her, her insecurities washed away.

"Hi there. I wondered if you needed your back washed," she said.

He grinned and pulled her into his wet embrace before turning so that the water sprayed onto her. "Have I told you how fucking sexy you are?"

She blushed as his hands cupped her breasts and kneaded gently. "You're sexy too."

She could feel his erection pushing against her hip. She reached down and wrapped her fingers around his hard length. He groaned when she stroked him back and forth, his purring competing with the sound of the water.

"Does that feel good, honey?" she said.

"Yeah." He purred to her again, his hips pumping against her.

She ran her thumb across the tip of him before stroking the thick vein that ran along the underside with her fingertips. He groaned again and his hips jerked wildly. She squeezed and released before peering around his large body. There was a small built in shower bench at the other end and she released Cooper, sliding around his body as he growled his displeasure.

"No growling," she said.

He leaned down and kissed the back of her shoulder. "I want my mate to keep touching me."

"Your mate wants something else," she said.

She sat down on the bench, leaned forward, and licked the head of his cock. His reaction was almost comical. His hips shot forward and his big hands slapped hard against the wall and the glass door. She would have giggled if it wasn't for the fierce look of need on his face.

"Daisy," he moaned, "do that again. Right now."

His one hand was already cupping the back of her head, already lightly pushing to urge her forward.

She smiled up at him. "Whatever my mate wants."

He purred, the purr turning to a strangled sounding groan when she kissed the head of his cock before sliding her mouth over it. She sucked firmly on just the head before licking the slit. She could taste him on her tongue, and she licked her lips at the wild and salty taste of him.

"Fuck," he moaned. "Fuck, Daisy, don't stop."

She slid her mouth over his cock again, holding the base of him in her hand as she took as much of him as she could before sucking hard. He cried out, his hand tightening on her head, his other one bracing against the shower wall.

She varied the suction while she stroked the base of his cock, teasing her tongue along the shaft and rubbing her fingers through the golden coloured hair at the base of his dick. She cupped his heavy balls in her hand, stroking them with the lightest of touch as he moaned and rocked his hips back and forth.

She stared up at him and opened her mouth wider, silently encouraging him to fuck her mouth.

"Fuck, you're so beautiful," he said before sliding his dick in and out of her mouth. "That's my good mate. Suck harder, baby."

He smoothed her wet hair back from her face, holding it in a loose ponytail as he watched her suck his cock. "Your little mouth looks perfect around my dick."

The heated look in his eyes, the words he said, made her own need unbearable. Still sucking on his cock, she reached between her legs and rubbed at her clit. But it wasn't enough for her. She needed his cock in her aching, empty pussy.

She pulled off of him with a loud pop, ignoring his groan of dismay, and stood. "Sit down, honey."

She tried to get him to sit on the shower bench, scowling at him when he didn't move. "Cooper, I want to ride you."

"I don't think we should have sex," he said.

Shit, he did think she sucked at sex. The urge to flee the shower, to grab her clothes and run away from the humiliation she was feeling was overwhelming.

Be brave, Daisy.

She took a deep breath. "Cooper, if I- if I'm not doing something right when it comes to sex, or if you're getting bored with me, please tell me. I'm open to feedback on things I might be doing wrong, and I'm willing to try new positions or -"

"What?" He cupped her face. "Baby, no. You're amazing at sex. I can't get enough of you. But I'm worried that you're sore or that I'm overwhelming you with my, uh, sexual appetite."

She giggled. "Sexual appetite?"

He grinned in that way that made her ridiculously hot for him. "It's more polite than saying I want to be in your pussy pretty much twenty-four/seven."

She pressed a kiss against his chest. "I'm not overwhelmed and, honestly, I can't get enough of you either. I'm a little tender but not sore, and I really want to have hot shower sex. I've never had sex in a shower before."

He smiled down at her before sliding past her and sitting on the bench. She refrained from clapping her hands with glee but couldn't hide the eagerness as she climbed into his lap.

"Are you wet enough for me?" he said.

"Yes, I... oh, oh that's so nice," she moaned when he slipped his hand between them and rubbed at her clit.

"My little mate is very wet. Did she like sucking on my cock?" His voice had lowered into a sexy rasp that sent fresh wetness dripping out of her pussy.

"Yes," she said. "Very much."

"Good mate." He wrapped one big arm around her waist and lifted her. She held his cock and guided it into her, moaning happily when he slid into her with very little resistance.

The hot water from the showerhead sprayed down her back as Cooper gripped her hips and smiled at her. "Hang on tight, my mate."

She grabbed his shoulders, crying out when he thrust into her with hard and shallow strokes. She bounced on his lap and moaned when he bent his head and kissed between her breasts before sucking on her nipples. She wrapped her arms around his shoulders and rocked against him, the hot coil of pleasure in her belly growing steadily tighter.

Cooper slipped his hand between them and rubbed her clit. He nipped at her throat with his fangs and she screamed his name before coming in a hard rush that took her breath away. He held her tight against him, pumping in and out of her, growling and purring until with one final hard thrust, he came deep inside of her.

He groaned her name and gathered her even closer, stroking her back and shuddering against her until the water started to cool. She eased off of him and shut the water off. Without speaking, they toweled dry and then climbed into bed. She cuddled into him, tangling her limbs with his and resting her cheek on his chest as he rubbed her back with those long and lazy strokes she'd come to love.

"I love you." His voice was low but perfectly understandable.

She rolled onto her stomach and rested her arms on his chest, propping her head on them as she studied him.

"You don't have to say it back," he said. "I know it's early in the relationship and I know I've probably freaked you the fuck out, but -"

"I love you too," she said.

He jerked against her, his eyes widening. "Daisy, I – you don't have to say it if you don't mean it. Being in a relationship is enough to keep me from going mad. You don't have to say you love me."

"I mean it," she said. "I wouldn't say it if I didn't."

He purred so loudly that she put her hands over her ears. "Whoa, turn it down a decibel, honey."

He kissed her before lowering the sound of his purring and she smiled happily at him. "I love you."

"I love you too." He smoothed her damp hair back from her face. "Move in with me permanently?"

"Only if you promise to give me sex whenever I want it," she said teasingly. "No more denying me your awesome dick."

"I wouldn't dream of it, my mate," he said.

They smiled happily at each other and he played with a lock of her hair. "Will you tell me why you're afraid of shifters?"

The smile dropped from her face. "I can't – I mean, I don't want to."

"I know," he said. "And I know it'll be hard for you, but I think it's important that you tell me."

CHAPTER 21

Daisy rested her cheek on Cooper's chest, listening to the steady thump of his heartbeat. "Will you purr?"

He purred and she closed her eyes and concentrated on her breathing. It was almost five minutes before she said, "The first foster home I went to was nice. It was a younger couple, and it was just me and one other foster kid. They treated us well and did lots of little extra things for us that they didn't have to do. I stayed there for a year and a half before I was moved to a different one."

"Why did they move you?"

"My foster parents were moving out of the country. Darryl worked in the oil industry and he got a job overseas."

He stroked her back as that old familiar fear bit at her insides. "My second foster home wasn't so great. Jerry and Maureen were older, and they had this big farmhouse on the outskirts of town. It had seven bedrooms and they took in a lot more foster kids than my first home. When I lived there, they only had four foster kids, but Josh said Maureen told him that in the past, they'd had up to six foster kids at once.

"Who's Josh?" Cooper asked.

Sorrow infused her body and she blinked back the hot tears that were already starting to form. "My best friend. He was one of the other foster kids living there. He was my age and so funny and smart. He was small and skinny, and he got bullied a lot at school because of it."

"Did your foster parents do anything about it?" Cooper said.

"No. They were…uninterested in us. They took in foster kids for the money and that's really about it. They clothed us and fed us and made sure we went to school every day, but that was it. They were very cold people."

"I'm sorry." Cooper continued to rub her back. "Were they shifters?"

"They were humans. But they took in shifters as foster kids. The two other foster kids were shifters."

Fear shuddered its way through her and Cooper immediately purred, pulling her even closer before kissing her forehead. "It's all right, baby."

"Their names were Brian and Angela. They were siblings and tiger shifters. Brian was twelve and Angela was ten. They'd lived with Jerry and Maureen for about six months before I arrived. I was there two months before they took in Josh."

She lapsed into silence. She didn't want to tell Cooper anything else. Her memories of Josh were coated in happiness and pain. The combination made her stomach hurt and her head ache, and she wanted to cry for how short his life had been. How very unfair the world could be and often was.

"I know this is difficult, my mate. I'm proud of you," Cooper said.

He didn't say anything else, but his words comforted her. It was hard to talk about, but she realized that she wanted him to know. Not only because she wanted him to understand her fear, but also because of Josh. A lost little boy remembered by no one but her. Josh deserved to be remembered.

"Josh and I became friends almost instantly. We were in the same grade at school and we liked the same things. Brian and Angela were," she grimaced, "what people would call rough around the edges. I don't know the details of their lives before they went into foster care, but I do know that their dad killed their mom in front of them before taking his own life."

"Jesus," Cooper said.

"Before Josh got there, Brian and Angela mostly ignored me. They liked video games and I liked to read, and they weren't interested in being my friend. But when Josh arrived, they…"

"What?" Cooper said.

"They hated him almost immediately. For no reason." She sat up, wrapping her arms around her knees in an attempt to self comfort.

Cooper sat up too and put his arm around her. She leaned against his solid warmth. "At first, they just made fun of him for how smart he was, for the glasses he wore, for being small. I felt so bad for him, Cooper. He was bullied at school and he was bullied at home, and he never caught a break. He told Maureen that Brian and Angela were being mean to him, but she didn't care. She told them to be nicer to Josh and that was about it. Maureen didn't work, but she and Jerry were gone most nights and weekends. They were part of a poker league that had games almost every night. We were left alone a lot."

"Did Josh talk to his social worker?" Cooper said.

"Yeah. I talked to mine too. But they were both over-worked and they had a lot of kids in their care and Josh… it was easy for him to slip through the cracks, you know? Being teased by a couple of kids in his foster home was a drop in the bucket for the social workers. Especially when they had other kids who were setting their foster homes on fire, or stealing, or doing drugs."

She stared at the scar on her arm. "After a while, their teasing escalated. They started being physical with him, pushing him off the couch or kitchen chairs. One time, Angela slammed Josh's hand in his bedroom door and broke two of his fingers."

"Fuck," Cooper said. "What did your foster parents do?"

"We didn't tell them. Angela and Brian threatened us. They said if we told the truth about what happened, they would," she swallowed thickly, "slice us open with their claws."

Cooper made a low sound of anger and she glanced up at him. "That was the first time they threatened us with their shifter abilities. Josh told Maureen and Jerry that it was an accident and they believed him. Honestly, even if we had told them the truth, they wouldn't have done anything about it."

She rubbed at her scar. "After the finger breaking incident, Brian and Angela started using their shifter abilities to scare Josh. It terrified him when their eyes glowed or they would extend their claws. Hell, it terrified both of us. They loved it when we were that scared. It's like they fed off of our terror or something."

"I'm so sorry, my mate," Cooper said.

"It sounds so ridiculous to admit that I'm afraid of shifters because of two *kids*, but -"

"You were only a child yourself," Cooper said. "It's not ridiculous."

She reached up and tugged on the back of his neck until he bent his head and she could kiss him. "I love you."

"I love you too." He rested his forehead against hers and purred. After a few minutes, he lifted his head. "Better?"

"Yes," she said. "A week before my tenth birthday, Brian and Angela murdered Josh."

"Holy fuck." Cooper's voice was weak with surprise. "They killed him?"

"Yes. It was an accident, they didn't mean to kill him – at least, I don't think they did – but Angela sliced open his throat with her claws and he bled to death in front of me."

"My mate." Cooper pulled her into his lap. "I am so sorry."

"We were in Josh's room," she said dully. "It was Saturday. Maureen and Jerry were gone. They'd been gone most of the day. Josh and I were playing *Risk*. Brian and Angela came in and Angela knocked over the board. Josh was – he was mad. We'd been playing for hours and they just wrecked our game like it was no big deal.

She took Cooper's hand. "Josh shoved Angela. She wasn't expecting it – neither of us ever fought back – and she fell and hit the back of her head on the bookshelf. She wasn't really hurt, she wasn't even bleeding, but she was… angry. And Brian was too."

She started to cry. Cooper kissed her forehead and then her cheeks. "I'm sorry, my mate."

"Brian grabbed Josh and threw him on the floor. He pinned him down and Angela half-shifted. They were both hissing and yowling at him. Josh was crying and I was crying, and I tried to help him, I swear. When Angela's nails turned to claws, I tried to pull her off of him, but she was bigger than me. She punched me in the stomach and then she clawed my arm."

Cooper lifted her arm and pressed a kiss against the scar that ran down her arm.

"I was bleeding from my arm, and I was scared. Then Josh started screaming. Angela kept swiping one claw in the air in front of Josh's throat. She was hissing at him and growling and telling him she was gonna cut his throat."

She licked her dry lips, the tears flowing freely down her cheeks. "I don't know exactly what happened. Everything happened so fast. I don't know if Josh moved his head at the wrong time or if Angela's claws were longer than she thought. I don't know, but I... Josh stopped screaming and made this horrible gurgling sound and Angela – the look on her face. You could see she was in shock."

She wiped at the tears on her face, then took the tissue that Cooper grabbed from the box on the nightstand. "Brian let go of Josh and he and Angela kind of backed away. I started screaming and crying when I saw Josh. There was so much blood, Cooper. It was pouring out of his throat and I didn't know what to do. Josh was grabbing at his throat and I... I grabbed his pajama shirt from the bed. I pressed it against his throat, but it was too late. He died. He died staring up at me and he... and I..."

She burst into tears, the sobs ripping out of her chest with brutal intensity. Cooper held her tight, rocking his big body back and forth as she buried her face in his chest and sobbed. He purred to her and rubbed her back until the sobs slowed, and the pain and the terror inside her had eased a little.

"I'm sorry," she whispered into his chest.

"Baby, no. You have nothing to apologize for." He kissed the top of her head and handed her more tissue. "Don't say you're sorry. What you've gone through is horrible and traumatic. You have every right to be this upset."

She wiped at her face and leaned against him. "Maureen and Jerry came home a few hours later. I was still sitting in his room and holding Josh. They both freaked out and then they..."

"They what?" Cooper said.

"They covered it up. Or tried to."

"What?" Cooper's body stiffened and she could hear the shock in his voice. "What do you mean they covered it up?"

"After Angela and Brian told them what happened, Maureen sat me down and told me that I needed to keep my mouth shut about what really happened. She said they were telling the police Josh cut his own throat because he was being bullied at school."

"You are fucking kidding me," Cooper said.

"I didn't want to lie. I said I would tell the police the truth, and then Jerry…"

"What did that motherfucker do to you?" Cooper was growling now, his body a hard and rigid board beneath hers, and the anger practically seeping out of his pores.

"He told me if I didn't tell the police that Josh killed himself, they would tell the police I killed him."

"That fucking cunt," Cooper said. "I'm going to kill him."

"He's already dead," she said. Cooper jerked beneath her. "Jerry said the police would believe him and Maureen over me because I was just a stupid little kid. He said that no one would take my word over theirs. He said he'd leave me alone with Angela and Brian if I told the truth. That terrified me. I didn't want to die like Josh did."

"Fuck," Cooper said. "I'm sorry, baby. I shouldn't… I'm angry but I'm not trying to upset you or make this about my reaction."

"It's okay," she said. "I don't mind."

She really didn't. Hearing Cooper's anger, seeing his disbelief and his horror, weirdly made her feel a little better. Like she wasn't crazy for thinking that Jerry and Maureen were monsters.

"I was terrified so I did what they told me to do. I told the police that I was in my room when I heard Angela screaming.

Angela told them she came into Josh's room just as he cut his throat with a knife from the kitchen."

"Jesus fucking Christ," Cooper said.

"The police didn't question me that much. At least not that day. I spent the week switching between numb disbelief and terror. I could barely sleep or eat, and I couldn't be in the same room with Brian and Angela. My birthday was the following weekend and that's when I asked Monique if I could live with her. It's why I freaked out so much, why I cried so hard, and begged her to let me stay with her. I was so afraid of Angela and Brian. I was paralyzed with fear."

"Of course you were," he said before stroking her hair. "Baby, anyone would have been terrified in your position."

"After Monique brought me back, I couldn't leave my room. I literally couldn't do it. I would freeze up with terror and start to cry when I tried. I peed my pants." She stared at him with trembling shame. "I couldn't leave to go to the bathroom, so I peed my pants."

"It's all right, my mate." Cooper kissed her forehead and stroked her hair. "It's all right."

"The next day, Jerry took Angela and Brian out of the house and that was the only way I could leave my room. I showered and used the bathroom, but I still couldn't eat. I kept seeing Josh's face, kept seeing his look of surprise as the blood ran out between his fingers. I still wasn't sleeping well, and I was... well, I think I was going crazy."

"What happened then?" Cooper said when she didn't speak for a few minutes.

"Later that day, my social worker dropped in. She would do that sometimes. All the social workers did – just randomly drop in to check on one of their kids. When she saw me, she immediately removed me from the house. Maureen and Jerry tried to stop her. They said that I had the flu and that's why I looked so bad, but she didn't believe them."

"Thank fucking God," Cooper said.

"She took me to McDonalds," Daisy said. "She bought me an ice cream cone, and we sat in her car in the parking lot. She talked about Josh. She said she knew that I missed him and was grieving, and she would look into therapy for me. She told me that sometimes people, even little kids, have something called depression and that even if I thought Josh dying was my fault, it wasn't."

She rubbed at the scar. "I sat in her car watching my ice cream melt all over my hand and I... I lost it, Cooper. I knew I had to tell the truth. I wish I could say it was because I wanted justice for Josh, but, honestly, I was really scared that Angela would do the same thing to me. I didn't want to die like that. I didn't want to die afraid and peeing my pants like Josh did. I felt horrible about that for a really long time but my therapist, she... well, she helped me work through that part of the trauma."

"I'm glad, baby." Cooper kissed the top of her head.

"I told my social worker what really happened to Josh and," Daisy swallowed hard as fresh tears leaked down her cheeks, "she believed me. She took me to a friend of hers who was a police officer and I told him what happened. My social worker had me placed in a temporary emergency foster home. They removed Angela and Brian from the home, and the police questioned Maureen and Jerry. They denied everything, but Angela and Brian were just little kids too, you know? It didn't take long before Angela confessed to the police. Maureen and Jerry were charged with something... I'm not sure what, and I don't know what happened to Angela and Brian."

She slumped against Cooper, closing her eyes as he held

her tight and rocked her again. "I Googled Maureen and Jerry about five years ago. They were both dead. They died in prison actually. Maureen from cancer and Jerry from a fight with another inmate."

"Good," Cooper said. "They deserved to die."

"I don't know where Angela and Brian are now. I didn't remember their last name so I couldn't Google them, and when I tried to get in touch with my old social worker to ask her, the agency said she'd retired and moved to Costa Rica. They wouldn't give me her contact information."

"Where did you go after Maureen and Jerry's?" Cooper said.

"I moved from foster home to foster home until I turned eighteen," Daisy said. "My social worker made sure I went to human only foster homes, but it was too late. The damage was done. I was terrified of shifters and it made it impossible for me to find an adoptive home. No one wanted to deal with my fear and my trauma. I took the job at your firm because my therapist said it might help me with my fear. An immersion type thing, you know?"

He rested his forehead against hers. "Thank you for telling me what happened, Daisy." He wiped the tears from her cheeks with his thumbs. "I'm so proud of you for how brave you are, my mate."

"I'm not brave," she said. "I'm weak and afraid and -"

"You're not." He cupped her face and stared solemnly at her. "You found justice for your friend, and you've managed to live your life despite your fear. I don't know that I would have the strength to go out every day and face my worst fear. You are so very brave, little mate."

"I don't feel brave," she whispered.

He pressed a kiss against her mouth. "You will someday, my mate. I promise."

CHAPTER 22

"Cooper? I have the file… oh, sorry, I didn't realize you were in a meeting with Wes." Daisy stopped in the doorway of his office.

"No problem," Cooper said. "Is that the Salder file?"

"Yes." Daisy set it on his desk along with a steaming hot cup of coffee. "I figured your other coffee would be cold by now." She grinned at him before picking up his old half-empty cup of coffee.

"Thank you, my mate," Cooper said.

"You're welcome."

She headed toward the door and Cooper took a quick glance at Wes before saying, "Is Lusa still dropping you off at Anna's place for tutoring tonight?"

"She is. You're good with picking me up?" she said.

"Yes."

"Great. Thank you."

His gaze dropped to her perfect ass when she turned and left his office. She shut his door and he glanced at Wes. "Sorry."

"No problem." Wes took a sip of his coffee. "Things seems to be going well with your mate."

A little surprised – Wes rarely spoke about anything personal when at work – Cooper said, "Yeah. It's been great, actually."

"I'm happy for you, Cooper."

"Thanks, Wes." He sipped at his fresh coffee. Daisy was a thoughtful and generous mate and in the two weeks since she had shared with him her traumatic past, it felt like they'd grown closer with each passing day. Everything was perfect between them and while Daisy kept teasingly warning him that they were in the honeymoon phase and sooner or later he'd be annoyed by something she did, he seriously doubted it. Had he and his lion ever been this happy before? He didn't think so.

He leaned back in his chair. "So, you heard that Boone's grandmother is in the hospital, yeah?"

Wes nodded. "He texted me earlier. She fell and broke her hip, he said."

"I guess she's doing all right, but you know how he feels about her. He's taking a few days off to stay at the hospital with her. I figured I'd put Chase or Gray with you tonight, but I forgot that Gray took the day off, and Chase has some concert he's going to tonight."

Cooper glanced at his laptop screen. "I don't have any other free guys to go on the stakeout with you until Boone gets back. Unless you've changed your mind about me going with you?"

A small grin crossed Wes's face. "I don't think that's wise, Coop. Pretty sure you won't be able to keep your cool around him."

"He shouldn't have gone after my mate," Cooper said.

"Technically, it's our client he was going after," Wes said.

"Stop being the voice of reason, Wes."

Wes laughed and took another sip of coffee. "I can do the stakeout by myself."

"Oh yeah? You gonna do a stakeout on your bicycle?" Cooper said.

That earned him another laugh from Wes. Cooper grinned at him. "Take a few days off, Wes. You and Boone have been looking for this Xander guy every day for the last two weeks."

"It's a big neighbourhood," Wes said. "But I have a good feeling about the area I'm checking out tonight."

"It'll still be there when Boone gets back. Xander hasn't made any attempt to contact Anna since that night at the burger joint. Maybe being chased by you was enough to scare him off."

"Maybe," Wes said.

"But you don't think so."

"No."

Cooper scrubbed his hand through his hair. "Honestly, I don't think so either and the sooner we find this asshole, the better I'll feel about my mate tutoring Anna. But I'm okay with you taking a few days off."

"I'd rather keep looking for him," Wes said. "Besides, I've got the car thing for tonight figured out."

"You hire Eleanor to drive you over there?"

Wes nodded. "I did."

"She gonna do the stakeout with you?"

He was only teasing, but a flush covered Wes's cheeks. "Well, she's not going to be a part of the stakeout in that she'll be in any danger. I need to use her car so I can blend in. The guy knows what I look like so it's not like I can stand on a street corner and watch for him. Right?"

He sounded weird and defensive. Cooper held his hands

up. "Hey, I'm not arguing. Expense whatever the cost is to have Eleanor waiting around to drive you back home."

Wes shook his head. "You're not paying the extra cost accrued because I don't drive."

Cooper waved his protests off. "Don't worry about it. Hand in the receipt from Eleanor for reimbursement."

"Cooper, I don't feel right about -"

"We're a team, Wes," Cooper said. "We support each other, right? So shut the fuck up already and hand in the car service receipts for the nights that Eleanor joins you on the stakeout."

"Okay, boss," Wes said with a small smile. "Thanks."

"Like I said, we're a team."

CHRIST, THIS HAD BEEN A MISTAKE. WHY THE FUCK DID HE think he could sit with Eleanor in her car all goddamn evening?

Wes stared out the window as Eleanor drove toward Rose Valley. Like usual, he was sitting in the back seat. Eleanor had mentioned more than once that he was welcome to sit in the front with her, but he'd never taken her up on the offer.

It was safer to sit in the back seat. From the back seat, he couldn't do something stupid like rest his hand on Eleanor's smooth thigh. Couldn't lean over and nuzzle her silky hair, maybe lick a line from the bottom of her slender throat up to her earlobe.

His nostrils flared and he stared grimly at his lap, willing his goddamn erection to go away. Why the fuck did he torture himself like this? There were a dozen reasons why he couldn't sleep with Eleanor, least of all the fact that he was probably old enough to be her goddamn father. His lust for her was inappropriate and if Eleanor could read his thoughts about her, she'd be disgusted.

Bullshit, his inner voice said. *She wants you. Don't try and pretend she doesn't. You can smell her lust for you.*

The pressure of his erect dick turned painful. Eleanor lusting after him was both exhilarating and terrifying. It was also dangerous. It eroded his already badly weakened resolve not to seduce her.

Fuck. He needed to find a new driver. One who didn't smell like strawberries or have high firm tits that would fit perfectly in his hands.

His lion purred loudly at the thought of touching Eleanor's tits but didn't say anything. Not unusual. His lion rarely spoke to him before the accident and it had practically turned into a damn mute since the accident. The landscape outside the window flew by in a blur – Eleanor was a fast driver – but he didn't really see it.

Four years. That's how long it'd been since he'd lost focus for a crucial ten seconds and a man died as the result. That old and familiar guilt rolled through him. His erection was gone, and nausea churned through his stomach.

His lion had retreated so far inward that Wes could barely feel their connection.

It's all right, Wes said. *It wasn't your fault.*

His lion didn't respond. Wes could feel him curling up into a tight ball, barricading himself against Wes's comfort. The beast shouldered the same feelings of guilt that Wes did and refused to accept any type of solace over it.

"You okay?"

Eleanor was staring at him in the rear-view mirror. Part of him wanted to tell her to keep her eyes on the road, but the thought that it would make him sound even more like a father made him cringe.

"You look like you're going to throw up," Eleanor said.

"Maybe it's the way you take corners," he said.

She wrinkled her nose at him but didn't laugh like he hoped she would. He fucking loved her laugh.

"Seriously, though, are you feeling okay?"

"Are you okay?" he said. Partly to avoid the question, but also because she hadn't been filling the interior of the car with her usual chatter.

"I'm fine," she said.

"You're not."

She slowed to a stop at a light and twisted in the seat to stare at him. "Shit, can you smell that I'm lying? Is that a thing that shifters can do? Oh my God, that's so cool. If I could smell a liar than maybe that asshole last night wouldn't have -"

She stopped abruptly, her face turning pink. A tidal wave of jealousy crashed over him and his lion uncurled and sat up. It made a low growl as Eleanor turned away and gripped the steering wheel.

He couldn't smell that she was lying, but he'd spent enough time with her, had obsessed enough over her, that he could read all of her moods as easily as he could read his own. "What did he do?"

He could smell her surprise. Hell, he was surprised too. He'd been using Eleanor as a driver for over a year and never once made any attempt at personal talk. It was too... dangerous.

The light turned green and Eleanor stepped on the gas. The car zoomed forward, his stomach lurching a little at the speed, and she darted in and out of lanes until she found one that was relatively clear.

He wouldn't ask her again, he told himself. It wasn't any of his business, and besides, he didn't care if Eleanor was dating someone. She *should* be dating. She was young and gorgeous and –

"He ditched me at the restaurant," Eleanor said suddenly. "He said he needed to use the restroom and then he never came back. Who even does that nowadays? Like, holy shit, guy, if you aren't having a good time, either man up and tell me, or do what normal people do and have a friend send you a fake 'I need you' text."

She turned left and then glanced at him. "Have you ever ditched a woman at a restaurant?"

"No," he said.

"Of course you haven't," she said. "I don't even know why I asked. You're a gentleman and you have some damn manners. Why are guys my age such," she waved her hand in a vague circle, "immature idiots?"

He didn't reply. She didn't look surprised by his lack of response. He supposed after over a year of driving him, she was used to his silence.

"Anyway, I'm feeling sorry for myself because I thought the date was going well. But," she took the exit for Rose Valley, "I'm pretty sure I talked too much because I always talk too much. My friend, Janelle, says I need to talk less when I first meet a guy. She says I'd have better luck if I kept my mouth shut for more than thirty seconds. But I figure they might as well see the real me right away. You know? If they don't like how much I talk when they first meet me, then we know the relationship is never gonna work out, right?"

"Right," he said.

The robotic voice of her GPS told her to take her next right and Eleanor switched lanes, flicking on her turn signal. "Janelle says it makes me look selfish. Like all I want to do is talk about myself. She makes a good point. People who talk a lot do come across as self-involved. I went on the date last night determined to talk less and I tried, but the guy was so freaking dull. He wasn't saying much, and it started to feel awkward as shit, so I did what I do best. I talked."

The GPS announced the destination was ahead on the left. Eleanor pulled into an empty spot on the quiet street between a red SUV and a silver Corolla and put the car into park. She killed the engine as Wes studied the street.

It was lined with apartment buildings, with a small park with playground equipment at the end of the street. The setting sun and the chill in the air meant the park was empty. Two men were walking down the street and Wes eyed them carefully. Neither was Xander, and he relaxed against the seat as Eleanor squinted out the window.

"I don't see any bars or pubs," she said. "Are you visiting a friend who lives here?"

"I'm on the job," Wes said.

"Oh." Eleanor waited a few minutes before saying, "So... you said you would need me until midnight."

"Yes."

She tapped her fingers against the steering wheel. "And the job requires you to sit in my car?"

He nodded and stared at the apartment building across the street. A couple was stepping out of the building into the growing darkness. He took a closer look at the man before leaning back again.

"Oh my God." He could smell Eleanor's excitement as she turned to face him. "You're on a stakeout!"

"I'm a security consultant, not a police officer," he said.

"Yeah, but you're on a stakeout. Admit it."

"Yes," he said.

She clapped her hands and unclicked her seatbelt. "Holy shit, this is so friggin' cool."

He didn't say anything, and she scanned the street. "Who are we looking for? Give me a description."

"*We're* not looking for anyone," he said.

"Oh, c'mon," she said. "You can't expect me to just sit here and not help. I'll be bored silly."

"I told you to bring a book," he said.

"I did." She picked up a book from the front seat and showed it to him before letting it drop onto the seat again. "But this is way cooler. C'mon, Wes, let me help."

He couldn't resist her enthusiasm and it would be helpful to have another set of eyes looking for Xander. He unlocked his phone and found the picture of Xander before handing his phone to her. Their fingers brushed and his lion purred. Wes couldn't blame him. His heart was thumping, and heat was building in his groin from just that brief touch.

She studied the picture carefully. He ignored the urge to reach out and sweep back the lock of dark hair that had escaped the clip and was brushing against her cheek.

"He's thinner now. Also, he's grown a beard and dyed his hair dark brown," Wes said.

"Okay." She took another look at the picture before handing his phone back to him. "Is he dangerous?"

"He could be."

"What did he do?"

"He's stalking a young girl. Believes she is his mate even though she's only sixteen and he's twenty-two."

"Gross," Eleanor said. "So, he's a shifter?"

"Yes. A cheetah shifter." He hesitated. "Most male shifters do not prey on young girls. We understand what is appropriate and don't want a child for a mate."

"Oh, I know," she said. "He's a sicko but that doesn't mean all shifters are. I mean, I don't know a lot of shifters, but the ones I've met all have age appropriate partners. Like,

I know you probably wouldn't even consider dating someone in their twenties. Would you?"

Her cheeks were pink, and he could smell the nervous energy drifting from her soft skin.

"I wouldn't," he said.

Now he could smell her disappointment, but she nodded and smiled at him. "Right. Okay, well, I'll take the left side of the street if you want to take the right. Sound good?"

"Sure," he said.

She turned and settled in her seat, her gaze on the street, as silence descended. He'd upset her, he didn't need to have a shifter's sense of smell to know that, but it was better for both of them if she thought he would never be interested in her.

CHAPTER 23

"In television, they make stakeouts seem much more exciting than they actually are," Eleanor said. She stretched before moving her neck from side to side. She'd put her hair up in a messy bun about half an hour ago and Wes studied the nape of her neck. She had a vertical line of small daisy tattoos starting at her hairline that disappeared beneath the collar of her shirt. He wondered, not for the first time, how far down that line of daisies went. What he wouldn't fucking give to find out.

He looked away before he got another erection. For the last couple of hours he'd managed to do his fucking job and concentrate on looking for Xander rather than picturing Eleanor naked and in his bed. But his blood sugar level was getting low and his lion was restless, and Eleanor was a distraction he was finding more and more difficult to ignore.

"I've been trying really hard not to talk your ear off," Eleanor said, "but it's a herculean effort for me. How do private detectives and cops not die of sheer boredom?"

She glanced at him in the rear-view mirror. He shrugged and looked out the window. The street was empty, and he tried to concentrate on studying the doors of each apartment building rather than wondering if Eleanor's nipples were the same shade of pink as her lips.

"I'm starving. I should have eaten dinner. Did you eat dinner?" Eleanor turned in her seat to face him.

"No," he said. He'd had Eleanor pick him up at work and he'd meant to grab something from the café down the street beforehand but ran out of time. Something his growling stomach was complaining about now.

"I'd give my left boob for a piece of beef jerky right about now," Eleanor said. Her face brightened. "Hold on."

She leaned across the seat and popped the glovebox open, rummaging around until she squealed in happiness. She sat up, a look of glee on her face and a granola bar in her hand. "Well, it's not beef jerky, but it'll stop us from passing out, right?"

She ripped open the packaging and carefully broke the bar in two before holding out one half to him.

"I'm good," he said.

She cocked her head at him. "I heard your stomach growling, Wes. Take it."

He took it. She smiled happily and bit into her own half as he bit off a piece of his.

"Oh Jesus," she said, "this is terrible."

He swallowed the bite he'd taken with difficulty as Eleanor chewed ferociously before swallowing. "My God, I've never had anything this hard in my mouth before."

"That's what she said," Wes said.

Eleanor stared at him before laughing. "Did you just make a joke?"

His lion purred to her and Wes swallowed down the sound. Which wasn't so easy when there was a chunk of stale granola bar stuck in his throat.

As if she'd read his mind, Eleanor produced a water bottle from the knapsack that was her purse and held it out. "I've only got one water left, but we can share, right?"

He opened the bottle and took a drink. He handed it back to her and she drank before wiping her mouth. "Daisy told me you were a lion shifter."

He looked out the window again. "I am."

"That's cool. I figured you were a lion or tiger because you're so big. It's kind of weird that you have dark hair though, right?"

"Why is it weird?" He scanned a man who stepped out of an apartment building in front of the car, but he was a redhead and too short to be Xander.

"Well, because lions have gold fur and green eyes, so you'd think you would have blond hair and green eyes. Like your boss. He has blond hair. Although his eyes are blue... hey, when he's in his lion form, do they stay blue?"

"Lions don't have green eyes. When did you see Cooper?" The only green on his lion was its sudden jealousy.

"A couple weeks back. I was having dinner with Daisy and he was at the pub too. So, why aren't you blond?"

He took a quick look at her, but she'd turned back around and was studying her side of the street diligently. "Our shifter side is not responsible for our hair and eye colour. They're determined by our human genes."

"Oh," she said. "Yeah, that makes sense." She glanced at him in the rear-view mirror. "I prefer dark hair anyway."

He didn't say anything, but his lion purred happily, and he couldn't help but feel a little pleased himself. Which was stupid because nothing could happen between him and Eleanor.

"What, uh, do you prefer for hair colour?" Eleanor said.

He could smell her arousal for him again and hating himself, he said, "Blonde. I like tall blondes with blue eyes."

Her lust dropped away like it'd taken a swan dive off a cliff. He had the immediate urge to take back what he said, to confess his lie just so he could smell her need for him again. Instead, he clenched his jaw and stared out the window.

"Yeah," Eleanor said. "Most guys prefer the blondes over us brunettes. I dated a guy who asked me to wear a blonde wig when we were…"

She cleared her throat. "Anyway, it was kind of fun the first couple of times but by the sixth time, I was starting to get suspicious that he was pretending I was someone else."

She laughed but it had a ragged hurt note to it that made his lion purr to her again. "Of course, he *was* banging a blonde woman on the side, so… you know, suspicion confirmed."

He wanted to kill the guy. He wanted to hunt him down and tear his throat out for making Eleanor feel less than the perfect dark haired, dark eyed beauty she was.

"Did you love him?" He really needed to knock it off with the personal questions.

She shook her head. "No. I cared for him a lot, but it wasn't love. Which made it easier to burn all the shit he left at my place. Pro tip – don't try and burn a cheap synthetic wig. Your apartment will stink like burnt plastic for days and your landlord will be suuuper pissed at you."

He laughed, and her arousal for him filled the interior of the car again.

"Oh my God, you laughed. I don't think I've ever heard you laugh before. You have a great laugh." The look on her face was one of pure delight.

"Thanks." He stared out the window, reminding himself that he was here to do a job, not make small talk with

Eleanor. It was better if he didn't know anything about her. Better if he –

"Wes? I think I see him."

He was immediately on high alert. He stared in the direction that Eleanor was pointing. There was a man walking toward a large brick apartment building on the other side of the street. Wes opened his door a crack and sniffed the air. The faint scent of cheetah drifted to him and his lion snarled with satisfaction. It was Xander. He'd shaved his beard into a goatee, but it was him.

"Stay here," he said to Eleanor. "I'll be right back."

He stepped out of the car and closed the door. He waited until Xander was walking on the sidewalk leading up to the building before he crossed the street. When Xander stepped inside the building, Wes jogged toward it.

Xander knew what he looked like which meant Wes needed to be careful that he didn't see him and take off. But he wanted an apartment number so they could tell the cops exactly where the asshole was.

He looked through the glass door of the building. Xander opened the door marked 'stairs' and started up the stairs. Wes tried the front door, not surprised that it was locked.

He smelled Eleanor's scent a couple of seconds before she said, "What's the plan here?"

"The plan was for you to stay in the car," he said.

"You might need my help."

"I don't need... is that a knife?" He stared at the small pocketknife she was holding in her right hand. The blade was only a few inches long and looked about as dangerous as a plastic spoon.

"Yes."

"Why do you have a knife?"

"For protection," she said. "I'm a woman who drives strangers around for a living. I'm gonna carry a knife."

"That's not going to do shit," he said. "You should carry mace or bear spray."

"Yeah, but this also has a corkscrew so I can open a bottle of wine."

"While you're driving?"

"No, not while I'm driving…look, what's the plan?" she said in exasperation as she closed the knife and tucked it back into her pocket.

"The plan is for you to go back to the car," he said.

"Not gonna happen." She tried the door. "Shoot, it's locked. Hold on."

He watched in disbelief as she pressed one of the buzzers for the apartments.

"Hello?" The voice that came out of the speaker was tinny and bored sounding.

"Oh, hey, um, I'm in apartment 415, and I, like, totally locked myself out of the building," Eleanor said in a high-pitched singsong voice that was completely different from her usual. "Do you think you could, like, do me a huge favour and buzz me in? I would be, like, so grateful."

"Yeah, sure, whatever."

The door buzzed and Eleanor whipped it open before giving him a look of delight. "Did you like the way I disguised my voice?"

"You didn't need to disguise your voice," he said. "The guy didn't know who you were."

"Man, you are no fun at all," she said. "I thought being a spy would require disguises and shit like that."

"I'm not a spy and neither are you," he said. "Go back to the car, please."

"No way," Eleanor said and slipped inside the apartment

276

building before he could stop her.

"Eleanor!" He followed her inside. He wanted to take her by the arm and march her back to the car, but he didn't have the time. Besides, he was terribly afraid if he touched her, he would kiss her. Maybe even push her up against the wall and finally have a good feel of those amazing tits before he slid his hand into her jeans and touched her pussy until she was wet enough to take his cock.

"Wes? Earth to Wes." Eleanor snapped her fingers in front of his face. "Hey, are we doing this or not?"

"We're not doing anything. Go back to the car, Eleanor."

"Unless you're planning on carrying me out of here kicking and screaming, I'm helping you," Eleanor said.

He growled in frustration and Eleanor's eyes widened. "Did you just growl?"

"Yes." He stalked toward the stairwell door and Eleanor trailed after him.

"That is so cool. Growl again, would you?"

"No." He opened the door and checked the stairs before climbing them two at a time, Eleanor right behind him.

He sniffed the air at the first floor landing before taking the next set of stairs. At the second floor landing, Eleanor, puffing lightly, said, "Man, I gotta increase my cardio if I'm going to get into the spy business."

"We are not spies and you're not getting into the business," he said. It would be a cold day in hell before he let Eleanor do anything remotely dangerous.

"This Xander guy knows what you look like, right?" Eleanor said.

"Yes," Wes said.

"Maybe I should go first in case we run into him on the stairs. He won't recognize me, and I can distract him while you tackle him."

"No," he said. "Stay behind me. And why would I tackle him?"

"Aren't you going to do a citizen's arrest or something?"

"No. I'm going to find out what apartment he lives in so I can give the information to the police who will then arrest him."

"But I should still go first because if he sees you, he's gonna run, right? And you'll never catch him, not when you're -"

He glared at her. "I might be older than you, but I'm not quite ready for the goddamn nursing home yet."

"Whoa," she held her hands up, "somebody's projecting. I wasn't gonna say you were old. I was gonna say when you're a lion shifter and he's a cheetah shifter. Daisy told me about how he outran you at the restaurant because cheetah shifters are super fast."

His lion grumbled like a small cub, pissed off that Eleanor knew he had failed at his job earlier. "How close are you and Daisy?"

"We're friends," Eleanor said. "Why?"

He climbed the third set of stairs. He stopped abruptly on the last step and tried not to groan when Eleanor bumped into him and her tits pressed against his back. Was she trying to kill him?

He sniffed the air again and moved to the landing, smelling in the direction of the fourth set of stairs before turning and reaching for the door to the third floor. He opened it and eased his head out to glance up and down the hallway before inhaling.

He stepped into the hallway and Eleanor crowded up behind him. "How do you know he's on this floor?" she whispered.

"I can smell cheetah in the hallway," he said.

"But do you know it's his scent?" she said. "There could be other cheetahs living in the building, right?"

"Yes, but the scent is fresh, and he just went up the stairway so it's likely him."

"Right. Good point." She looked up and down the hall, studying the doors that lined it. "Which apartment is his?"

"I don't know." He walked down the hallway, inhaling deeply as Eleanor trailed after him.

"Can't you tell by the scent?" she said.

"It's fading here," he said as he stopped halfway down the hall, "which means he probably went into one of the apartments past this point, but I can't tell specifically which apartment he might have -"

They both froze when an apartment door at the end of the hallway opened.

Shit. The hallway was well lit and straight with no convenient corners to hide around. If it was Xander coming out of the apartment, they were too far from the stairwell door to get there before Xander saw him. And if he saw him, they were fucked. His only chance to find this guy and he'd fucking blown it. Cooper was gonna kill him.

As the person started to step out of the apartment, Eleanor grabbed his arm and whipped him around to face her. He had a few seconds to see the combination of fear and excitement on her face before she gripped his head and pulled it down toward her. Her lips pressed against his and at the first feel of their softness, his shock turned to pure lust.

He forgot he was on the job, forgot that Xander might recognize him and run. He pushed Eleanor up against the wall. She made a soft *oof* when her head smacked against the wall. He swallowed the sound before sliding one hand into her silky hair and holding her head still. He licked the seam of her lips, growling "open" when they didn't part.

She opened her mouth. He angled his lips over hers and slid his tongue into her mouth. His free hand gripped her ass and he pulled her up snug against his erection. He purred to her as he pushed his thigh between her smooth ones.

He nipped at her bottom lip and purred again in encouragement when Eleanor ground her pussy against his thigh. Her arousal was thick and intoxicating and he wanted to breathe in the scent of it for the rest of his life.

He rubbed his thigh against her crotch, smiling when she moaned and clutched at the front of his jacket. He kissed her neck and then marked her, two hard swipes of his stubble across her soft skin.

She gasped, and he eased the sting by licking and kissing the red marks before licking his way to her ear. He sucked on the lobe and chuckled when she whimpered and rocked harder against his thigh.

"Does that feel good, little butterfly?" he breathed into her ear.

"Yes," she moaned.

"It's not enough though, is it? Your greedy pussy wants my dick."

Her cheek heated up against his, but she nodded. He let go of her ass to stroke her hip and then traced his fingers over her ribcage toward those perfect tits. "First, you're going to show me how pretty your tits are, then I'll give you my cock."

"Excuse me!"

The woman's pissed off voice made them both jerk in surprise. Wes pulled away from Eleanor. He was hellishly aware of the way the front of his jeans were tented as he stared at the slender elderly woman standing next to the elevator.

He could tell by her scent that she was a tiger shifter. He

guessed her age to be somewhere around ninety. She stared at them in disgust before she pointed her cane at Wes. "In my day, lion shifter, a woman didn't take kindly to being mauled in a public space. You're lucky I'm not calling the police on you with the way you had your tongue shoved down that young lady's throat."

"Oh, uh, I wanted him to, um, do that," Eleanor said.

She was trying to be helpful, but Wes groaned when the tiger shifter turned her rheumy gaze to Eleanor. "Well, ain't that sweet. Do you normally do your whoring around in apartment hallways with a man twice your age, then?"

"No, ma'am," Eleanor said gravely. "I usually do my whoring in private like the good Lord intended."

The old tiger shifter's mouth twitched, and a look of amusement crossed her face. She thumped her way past them, stopping briefly to whack Wes on the shin with her cane. "This is a nice building and I intend to keep it that way. Keep it in your pants when you're in the hallway. You hear me?"

"Yes, ma'am," Wes said.

He waited until she'd gone into her apartment before staring at Eleanor. "Why did you kiss me?"

Her face turned bright red. She straightened her shirt and smoothed down her hair. "Why do you think? To keep Xander from seeing you and running. Was it him coming out of the apartment?"

He had no fucking idea if it'd been Xander or not. He'd been too consumed by her, by her taste and her scent and the sound of her moaning. His dick was hardening again, and he muttered a curse under his breath before looking away from her.

"I don't know."

"What? How do you not know?"

"How do *you* not know?" he said.

"Maybe because I was a little distracted by your tongue in my mouth," she said.

"You were the one who kissed me," he said.

The redness in her face was spreading down her throat and into her chest. She cleared her throat. "Well, I know it was a guy and I think it was Xander, but I'm not sure. He went out that exit," she pointed to the exit at the far end of the hallway, "but I didn't get a good look at his face. Looked like his body size, but it was a different jacket."

"Fuck," Wes said.

"He could have changed his jacket," she said.

"Maybe." He rubbed at the back of his neck.

"What do we do now?"

He scanned the hallway. "Set up a stakeout outside of the building again until I know for certain he's here."

"Or," Eleanor said, "we could break into the apartment and see if there's anything in it that points to it being his place."

"That's illegal, Eleanor."

"Oh please," Eleanor walked down the hallway to the last apartment, "like you've never done anything illegal before."

She tried the doorknob as he joined her. "Locked. You'll have to pick it open."

"I am not breaking and entering," Wes said. He tried not to stare at her swollen mouth, tried not to remember how it had sounded when she moaned, or how close he'd been to touching her tits.

Fuck, he needed to get his head in the goddamn game.

"We'll be like two minutes, tops," Eleanor said. "All we need to do is look for pictures or identification and then we can leave. If it isn't his place, we keep doing the stakeout. But if it is… we call the police and bada bing, bada boom, you got your man."

She raised her hand in a high-five, dropping it after a few seconds when Wes didn't smack it. "C'mon, Wes. You know I'm right."

"Do you want to go to jail, Eleanor? Because that's what will happen if we get caught."

"We're not going to get caught. Two minutes, that's all we need."

He sighed. She made a good point and if he had to sit for another few hours in the car with Eleanor after knowing how her lips tasted, he'd go fucking crazy. Eleanor made a soft squeal of delight when he pulled a small leather pouch from the inside pocket of his jacket and opened it. It held a tension wrench and a hook pick and Eleanor clapped her hands quietly.

"I knew you'd picked a lock before."

He scowled at her before crouching and staring at the lock. It was a simple enough lock, a type he'd picked hundreds of times before. Of course, he hadn't had Eleanor crouched beside him, her firm thigh brushing his, the intoxicating scent of her lust still lingering on her.

His hands shaking, he inserted the tension wrench into the lock and then used the hook pick to try and lift the pins inside the lock one by one. He muttered another curse, sweat sliding down his back when it didn't work.

He tried again and failed a second time, glaring at Eleanor when she said, "You're not very good at this."

"You're not helping, Eleanor," he said.

When he failed a third time, his lion made a low roar of anger. He was embarrassed by Wes's ineptitude.

You're not the only one who's fucking embarrassed, Wes snarled at him.

"Here, give it to me," Eleanor said. She plucked the wrench and the hook from his hand and elbowed him out of the way. He watched in utter disbelief as she slid the wrench in and then the hook and a few seconds later, the lock clicked open.

She handed him the tools with a look of triumph.

"How do you know how to pick a lock?" Wes said.

"It's called the internet, Wes," Eleanor said.

They stood and she used the hem of her t-shirt to cover her hand before opening the door. They stepped inside the apartment and Wes closed the door.

"Hello?" Eleanor called. "Anyone home? It's your local *Pampered Chef* representative calling. Can I interest you in a deluxe cooking blender with a dual-sided cleaning brush, strainer bag, and boil-over guard?"

She shrugged when Wes stared at her. "I used to be a *Pampered Chef* representative. Hey, believe me when I say don't ever get sucked into an MLM. They will try and bleed you dry."

"Helloooo?" she called again. "Anyone home?"

When there was no reply, she glanced at him. "Where do we look first?"

"You stay right here," he said. "I'll look – Eleanor!"

She'd already walked down the short hall and disappeared. He followed her down the hall. It opened up into a small living room connected to a tiny kitchen.

"Well, it doesn't look like a crazy stalker's apartment," Eleanor said.

"How would a crazy stalker's apartment look?" Wes said.

Eleanor waved her hand in the direction of one of the walls. "Pictures of poor Anna covering the wall with stuff written like, 'she will be mine' and 'I love her' written in his blood or something."

"You watch too much television."

"Or this isn't his apartment," Eleanor said. She headed

toward the kitchen as Wes stopped at the small desk tucked against the wall in the living room. There was a laptop and a tablet sitting on it and he ran his finger over the tablet screen.

Expecting the lock screen, he blinked in surprise when the tablet flickered into life and showed the main screen. He glanced at Eleanor – she was standing in front of the fridge and staring at a couple of mini polaroids stuck to it – and then opened the message app.

Like most iPad's, the message app was connected to a cell phone and he read the conversation that was open in the message app. If this was Xander, he had left to pick up someone with the nickname "BooBunny" from their job.

"Wes?"

"Yeah?"

"This is Xander's place. He's in these pictures."

"Okay, good." He started toward Eleanor, frowning at how pale she was. "What's wrong?"

"I know this girl."

"What? What girl?"

"The girl in the photos with him." Eleanor pointed with a shaking hand to the polaroids. "I know her. Her name is Tabitha and she -"

"Works as a housekeeper for David Landon. Fuck." He stared at the pictures. They were selfie shots of Tabitha and Xander. Someone had used a glitter pen to write "BooBunny" under Tabitha's face and "BooBear" under Xander's.

"I read his phone messages on his iPad," Wes said. "He's on his way to pick up Tabitha from work right now."

Eleanor gripped his arm, her fingers icy cold. "Doesn't Daisy tutor Anna on Thursday nights?"

"Yes." Wes yanked his cell phone from his pocket.

"Who are you calling?" Eleanor said.

"Cooper."

CHAPTER 24

Cooper snatched his keys from the side table and ran out of the house. His lion was snarling and growling, its obvious fear heightening Cooper's fear. He yanked open the truck door and slid behind the wheel, jamming his key into the ignition.

He reached to put the truck in gear. His hands were shaking and the adrenaline rushing through him made him jittery and sick to his stomach. He sat back and took a few deep breaths.

Our mate is in danger, his lion growled.

"I know. I fucking know," Cooper said. "But we can't save our mate if we get in a fucking car accident. Give me two fucking minutes."

His lion growled in anger but retreated. Cooper blew his breath out in a harsh rush before trying Daisy's cell number again. Like before, there was no answer and his fear cranked up another notch. His cell phone buzzed, and hope blossomed in his chest only to die quickly when he glanced at the screen. He answered it on speaker as he backed out of the driveway.

"Hey."

"Wes called and told me what he found. Where are you?" Grayson's voice was worried.

"On my way to Landon's place."

"Cooper, don't -"

"She is my mate, Grayson!" He could hear the panic in his voice.

"I know, buddy. It'll be okay. Did you try Daisy's number?"

"Yeah. She's not answering."

"She might turn it to silent while she's tutoring."

"Maybe." He took a left off his street.

"Listen, I'm on my way, but Ryan and I are across the fucking city. It'll take us at least an hour to get there with traffic. Wes said he called the police and they're sending a unit to Landon's place. If Xander is there, don't go into the house. Wait for the police and -"

"No," Cooper said.

"Cooper, you can't go in there on your own. It's too dangerous. Wait for the police."

"Like you waited when your mate was in danger?"

He could hear Grayson sighing. "Fuck. Promise me you'll wait for Wes at the very least. He's on his way over there."

"I promised her she'd never have to be afraid again, Grayson." The words stuck in Cooper's throat. "I promised her, and now there's a shifter who might hurt her or kill her and it's all my fucking fault."

"It isn't your fault."

"It is! If I hadn't taken Landon as a client, if I hadn't let Daisy keep tutoring Anna -"

"Daisy is a grown woman and you can't tell her what to do, Coop," Grayson said. "This isn't your fault. Besides, maybe Xander isn't doing anything but picking up the house-keeper. He could be playing the long con, right? And if so, then Daisy is perfectly safe. We know where Xander lives, the police will arrest him, and this'll be over."

"He's not just picking up the housekeeper," Cooper said.

"You don't know that for certain," Gray said.

"Landon isn't home tonight. He's at some fucking charity function which means Daisy and Anna are there alone."

There was a heavy silence before Grayson said, "Well, fuck."

"If this asshole hurts my mate, I will tear him apart," Cooper said. "I love her, Gray. I love her and I can't live without her."

"I know. She'll be all right."

"I have to go. I need to call Lusa." He hung up without waiting for a reply and pulled up Lusa's number from his contacts.

She answered on the second ring. "Hey, Coop, what's up?"

"I need your help."

"ANNA, I'M SO PROUD OF YOU. YOU ANSWERED EVERY question correctly." Daisy set the notebook on the small desk in her bedroom and swiveled in the chair to face Anna.

The teenager was stretched out on her bed and staring at her phone. She sat up, grinning at Daisy. "Yesterday my teacher said she was impressed with my improvement."

"I'm not surprised. You're doing great."

"Great enough to take an ice cream break?" Anna said.

Daisy laughed. "Sure."

Anna slid off the bed and the two of them headed downstairs to the kitchen. "We've got mint chocolate chip, rocky road, pecan praline, and vanilla," Anna said. "We just stocked up."

"That's a lot of ice cream for just you and your dad," Daisy said with a laugh.

Tabitha looked up from where she was sitting at the island with her phone in her hand. "They both have an ice cream addiction. But it works out well for me because I'm also an ice cream addict."

Anna grabbed bowls from the cupboard. "How come you're still here, Tabs?"

"I took my car in for an oil change this morning so my BooBear is picking me up. He's running a little late."

"BooBear." Anna snorted and rolled her eyes.

Tabitha grinned at her. "It's an adorable nickname and it suits him. He calls me BooBunny."

"Okay, *BooBunny*," Anna said. "You want some ice cream while you wait?"

"Nah," Tabitha said. "He should be here -" her phone buzzed and she glanced at the screen. "And here he is. Bye, ladies."

"Bye, Tabs." Anna grabbed the ice cream scoop. "Don't forget to set the alarm."

"You bet." Tabitha blew her a kiss and walked out of the kitchen.

"What kind do you want?" Anna held the scoop over the containers of ice cream.

"Mint chocolate chip, please."

"Two scoops or three?"

"Two is good." She sat down at the island and watched as Anna put two generous scoops into a bowl. She handed it to Daisy, took two scoops of the rocky road for herself and put the ice cream away before sitting down next to her.

"I like your scarf, by the way." Anna eyed the long and

narrow scarf wrapped around Daisy's throat. "It matches your hair."

"Thank you," Daisy said.

"Did you crochet it yourself?" Anna picked up one end and studied it.

"No, my mate did."

Anna laughed. "Seriously? The tattooed lion dude crochets?"

"How do you know I'm talking about Cooper?" Daisy said.

"Because I have eyes? I was there when he put his arm around you at the office, remember?"

Daisy grinned. "We weren't actually dating then."

"Shifters are, like, ridiculously possessive, right?" Anna said with a roll of her eyes. "It's freaking annoying."

Cooper's possessiveness didn't actually bother Daisy all that much. She supposed it was a combination of being in love with him and her need to feel wanted and loved by someone. She understood Anna's feelings about it though. Cooper might be possessive, but he wasn't controlling, unlike Anna's former boyfriend Xander who had gone beyond possessive to controlling.

"How are things going with Scott?" Daisy said.

Anna shrugged. "Still doing the friend thing. I'm not sure I'm ready to date again or - hey, you're back." She stared in surprise at Tabitha.

Tabitha sat down next to her. "Mick needed to use the bathroom."

"Mick? Don't you mean *BooBear?*" Anna said.

Tabitha laughed and grabbed the spoon from Anna's hand. She ate the ice cream and then licked the spoon in an overexaggerated manner before handing it back to Anna.

"Gross, Tabs." Anna made a face and slid off the stool. "Did you reset the alarm when you came back in?"

"You know it," Tabitha said. "We're safe as bugs in a rug in here."

Anna tossed the spoon in the sink and grabbed another one. "Hey, what are you doing tomorrow night? Dad has another charity thing and Brittany's party got cancelled because her mom caught her smoking weed in the back yard last night. You wanna hang out after you're done work? We can order in sushi and play some *Call of Duty*."

"Sure," Tabitha said. "Mick's working so my night is free."

Daisy spooned some more ice cream into her mouth before pulling her phone out of her pocket. She would text Cooper quickly, just to say hello and remind him to pick up milk on his way to pick her up. Before she could call him, there was motion at the kitchen door. She glanced up when the man walked into the kitchen, her stomach dropping. He had shaved his beard into a goatee, but she recognized him easily enough.

The man Tabitha was dating was Xander.

Horror filled her body, and her fingers went numb as her phone fell to the island counter.

Tabitha smiled at Xander as he joined her at the island. She slid her arm around his waist. "Hey, honey. I want you to meet Anna and Daisy. Anna is David's daughter and Daisy is her tutor. Anna and Daisy, this is Mick. He's... Daisy, what's wrong?"

The spoon fell from Daisy's fingers to join her cell phone. Anna turned at the sound, and Daisy nearly fell off her stool when she shrieked and backed away.

Tabitha flinched and stared at her. "Anna? What's wrong?"

Daisy jumped off the stool. Her legs were weak and trembling and familiar fear was enveloping her body, stealing her breath and making it impossible to think clearly. She stumbled over to Anna, putting her arm around the girl's thin shoulders.

Anna's body was trembling like a live wire and when she wrapped her arms around Daisy's waist, she could feel the icy coldness of Anna's hands through her t-shirt.

"Daisy," Anna whispered.

"What's wrong?" Tabitha stood, glancing at Xander when he curled his hand around her arm. "What?"

"Tabs," Anna said in a quiet and terrified voice. "Get away from him. That's Xander."

"What?" Tabitha frowned. "Anna, honey, this isn't Xander. This is Mick, my boyfriend. He's a lynx shifter, not a cheetah shifter."

"It's Xander," Daisy said. "He lied to you."

Tabitha stared at Xander. "BooBear? Tell them you're not Xander."

He didn't answer. He was looking at Anna and he purred loudly. "It's so good to see you again, sweetie."

Tabitha's eyes widened. "You fucking asshole!" She tried to yank her arm free, punching him in the chest when he didn't let go. "Let go of me!"

He growled at her. Both Daisy and Anna cried out when he grabbed the back of Tabitha's neck and squeezed so hard, she screamed.

"Shut the fuck up, you stupid little whore," he snarled before shaking her.

Crying, Tabitha tried to wrench free and he growled again before slamming her up against the island. "Stop fucking moving."

He bared his fangs at Tabitha and raised his hand to show

her his claws. "Move again and I will slice your fucking throat open. I swear it. Are you going to be a good girl and hold still?"

Her face red and biting her bottom lip compulsively, Tabitha nodded.

Xander sighed and then smiled at Anna. "Have you missed me, my love?"

Anna's shaking increased and Daisy could see tears sliding down her cheeks. Her own terror was threatening to swallow her whole and she couldn't stop staring at Xander's fingers. His nails were still long with deadly sharp claws and she closed her eyes as a vision of Josh's slit throat went through her mind. For a minute, she was so scared, she thought she might wet her pants.

You're braver than you think, my mate.

Cooper's voice was so vivid, she could almost believe he was standing next to her. He wasn't, she knew that, but she was still somehow comforted. Her fear eased to the point where she no longer felt frozen and her lungs started working again.

She took a deep breath and opened her eyes. "It'll be okay, honey," she said to Anna.

Be brave, my mate.

"You need to leave," she said to Xander. "Right now."

He ignored her, staring intently at Anna. "Have you missed me? You're all I've thought about. I love you so much, sweetheart."

"I don't love you," Anna said. "I hate you. I want you to leave."

"Don't fucking say that!" Xander shouted.

Tabitha cringed and Anna squeezed Daisy's waist until it felt like her ribs might crack.

"I love you. I gave up everything for you," Xander said.

"And you just fucking walked away like what we had didn't matter. Do you know how much you hurt me?"

"I'm sorry," Anna said. "I didn't mean to do that."

Xander smiled at her and the madness in it sent chills down Daisy's spine. "I know, sweetheart. It was your parents. They put those ideas in your head, told you I wasn't right for you. But they're wrong. You know that, right?"

Anna glanced at Daisy before nodding. "Yeah, okay."

"We are meant to be together. You are my mate."

"I can't believe you lied to me," Tabitha said. "You are such a -"

"Shut the fuck up!" Xander roared before he slammed Tabitha's head against the island.

"Tabitha!" Anna screamed.

Tabitha's eyes rolled up in her head and she crumpled to the floor like a broken toy. Anna tried to dart toward her. Daisy held her still, shaking her head. "Don't go near him, honey."

"You killed her," Anna sobbed. "You son of a bitch. You killed her."

Daisy's phone buzzed and the familiar chime of Cooper's ring filled the kitchen. She edged toward the island and Xander shook his head before pointing one claw-tipped finger at her. "Don't you even fucking think about answering it."

She froze where she was, eyeing his claws as he smiled at the crying Anna. "Don't cry, sweetheart."

"You killed her," Anna said as Daisy's phone stopped ringing. "You killed Tabs."

"She's fine," he said dismissively. "She's only uncon-scious. C'mon, sweetie, we need to go."

"I'm not going anywhere with you," Anna said.

He growled at her. "Don't you talk back to me. You are going with me and that's it."

"I won't," Anna said.

Cooper called her cell phone again. Daisy could have cried with relief. Cooper knew something was wrong. He had to. He wouldn't call her twice in a row like this when she was tutoring. He was probably on his way over right now. She just needed to keep Xander distracted for a little while.

If you're wrong, you're dead and Anna is kidnapped by a maniac.

She wasn't wrong. She couldn't be wrong.

Xander glared at her ringing phone and rubbed at his temples like his head hurt. He paced back and forth in front of the doorway. "This is supposed to be fucking easy. Why are you making this so hard?"

Daisy eyed the knife block that was sitting on the counter. It was a few feet away but if she was quick –

"Don't even think about it." Xander stopped pacing and stared at her. "I am very fucking fast. I will gut you before you even get close to the knives."

"My mate is a lion," Daisy said.

"You think I don't know that? You goddamn reek of him," Xander said.

"If you kill me, he'll hunt you down. There won't be anywhere you can go that he won't find you," Daisy said.

"Well, it's a good job I'm not gonna kill you then, huh?" Xander said. "Anna, it is time to go."

"I told you I'm not going with you," Anna said.

"You will or I'll kill Tabitha," Xander said.

Anna paled and Daisy squeezed her shoulders. "She needs to pack some stuff."

"She doesn't. I'll buy her new shit," Xander said.

Daisy shook her head. "You have to let your mate take some personal stuff with her. You can't expect her to leave everything behind."

"Daisy, what are you doing?" Anna said.

Daisy stared at Xander. "Fifteen minutes for her to pack up some clothes and personal items isn't going to make a difference. Her dad won't be home for hours and my mate isn't picking me for another hour."

Xander stared at Anna, and Daisy made her voice soft. "Fifteen minutes, Xander. Don't you want your mate to be happy?"

"Fine," Xander said. "She can pack up some shit."

"Great." Daisy took Anna's hand. "We'll go up to Anna's room, pack her stuff, and be right back."

Xander snorted. "Do you think I'm fucking stupid? We all go to Anna's room together."

"Daisy?" Anna whispered.

Daisy squeezed her hand. "C'mon, honey. Let's get your stuff packed so you can leave with your mate."

CHAPTER 25

Cooper's lion roared in anger when it saw the car in the driveway. Fear combined with relief that Xander was still there clawed its way up the back of Cooper's throat as he shut off the truck.

Of course, there was the possibility that it wasn't Xander's car, but he knew in his gut that it was.

Our mate! Protect our mate!

His lion tried to surge forward and take control. Cooper battled him back with every ounce of his willpower.

Let me free!

"Not yet," he said as he called Lusa's cell phone. "You can't get into the house without me. Just wait."

"You at Landon's place?" Lusa's voice was crisp and all business and Cooper felt a surge of affection for his IT person.

"Yes. Were you able to log in remotely to the office server?"

"Of course I was," Lusa said. "I don't run a chickenshit operation on our servers, boss. I'm ready to go when you are. But maybe you should wait for the police?"

"No," Cooper said. "My mate is in danger, Lusa."

"I know, but -"

"I'm not waiting," Cooper said. "Who knows how fucking long it will take them to get here. Disable the security system."

Faintly, he could hear Lusa typing and then she said, "Done."

"Thanks. I gotta go."

"Coop, wait. The doors will still be locked, and Landon had thick deadbolts put on every door. You won't be able to break them down."

"I'll break in through a window," Cooper said.

"Landon had security film put over the glass, new window locks, and wireless window alarms that aren't attached to the main security system put on all the first floor windows."

"Fuck," Cooper said.

"It was my goddamn idea," Lusa said. "Sorry, boss. But Landon's got French doors off his bedroom balcony, left side of the house. When I was setting up the system, he had no plans to secure those doors with additional locks or alarms. The lock will be easy to pick."

Cooper opened the glove box and grabbed a small leather pouch. He slid out of the truck, closing the door gently before jogging toward the left side of the house. He opened the gate to the wooden privacy fence and eased into the yard as Lusa said, "If you can climb to the top of the property fence, you could potentially reach the bottom bars of the balcony."

He stared up at the bottom of the balcony and then the top of the fence before muttering under his breath, "Are you fucking kidding me?"

"You can make the leap," Lusa said. "I know it's far, but

you're a goddamn lion. You've got this. Or you could do the smart thing and wait for the police."

"Daisy needs me."

She sighed. "Be careful, Coop."

He ended the call and stuck the phone and the leather pouch into his pockets before grabbing the top of the six-foot privacy fence and boosting himself up. Balancing one foot on a fence post and the other on the narrow top edge of the fence, he glanced at the quiet and dark neighbour's house on the other side of the fence before looking at the balcony. He could see easily in the dark and he studied the iron-wrought rails and cement floor. It was at least a twenty-foot leap to the balcony and without a running start, the odds of him making it were –

We can make it, his lion snarled. *Our mate needs us!*

Adrenaline sparked through his veins and his lion surged forward, his strength and his adrenaline dumping into Cooper's system as well. His muscles bunching, he leaped for the balcony and caught the bars, grunting when his shins banged painfully against the cement base. He hauled himself up and over the railing, landing with a soft thud on the floor. He stayed low and peered through the glass doors. Landon's bedroom was dark and while he had a view of the door, it was shut, preventing him from seeing into the hallway.

Praying that Landon hadn't decided to upgrade the security system on the doors, he took the tension wrench and pick hook from the leather pouch and picked open the lock. Holding his breath, his blood pounding and his lion growling continuously, he turned the handle and pulled. It opened and when no alarm blared, he released his breath and stepped into the room.

His blood froze and his lion snarled with anger and fear

when he heard the roar of the cheetah followed by his mate's scream.

"Hurry the fuck up!" Xander snarled at them.

When Anna flinched and dropped the clothes she was holding, Daisy bent and scooped them up, placing them in the small suitcase on the bed. "I don't think you have all of your toiletries, Anna. Let's check the bathroom again and -"

"No!" Xander growled. "She has enough of her shit. Let's go, Anna."

Anna closed the suitcase and Daisy zipped it shut as slowly as she dared. She tried to think of another excuse to delay as Xander paced restlessly in front of the door.

"Let's double check that you have everything you need." She started to unzip the suitcase, crying out when Xander roared so loudly that her ears rang. Anna started to cry, and Daisy pulled her closer, stroking Anna's hair with a trembling hand.

"It'll be okay, honey. Don't cry."

She wished she sounded like she believed it. Wished she didn't sound like she was on the verge of crying herself. Her fear was creeping back in, slow and insidious like a dark bruise blossoming on skin.

You didn't really think I was gone, did you? You're going to die today. Xander is going to take Anna but first, he'll slit your throat and you'll bleed out like Josh did.

Her limbs were freezing up and her surety that Cooper would save them was starting to fade. Black spots swam in her vision. She'd been holding her breath for so long she was starting to feel dizzy. She tried to relax her body, tried to force air in and out of her lungs, but it was impossible. She was going to die and -

Be brave, my mate.

Cooper's voice in her head was steady and calm. She released her breath in a harsh rush and sucked in another one as Xander stalked toward them.

"You've got enough of your goddamn shit, I said!"

Anna flinched against her. Daisy tightened her grip on the young girl's trembling body as Xander spat a curse and ran his hand through his hair.

"I don't mean to yell at you, sweetie. Okay? But you have to do what I say. A good mate does as she's told, right?"

"Right," Anna whispered.

"Okay, good." Xander caressed her hair before smiling at her. "It's time to go, my love. Leave your phone on the bed."

"I need my phone," Anna said.

"I'll buy you a new one," Xander said. "Let's go, Anna."

Anna tossed her phone on the bed and reached for the suitcase.

"I'll carry it downstairs for you," Daisy said and grabbed it before Anna could pick it up. Holding it in her right hand, she followed Anna out into the hallway. As they walked toward the stairs, Xander right behind them, Daisy glanced at Anna's pale face before tightening her grip on the suitcase.

Cooper wasn't here and as much as she wanted to believe he would be outside waiting for Xander, she couldn't count on it. And if Xander left with Anna, they'd never find her again. She couldn't let that happen. She *wouldn't* let that happen.

Her body beginning to shake from a combination of adrenaline and fear, she pulled Anna's suitcase in front of her and whipped around. She charged at Xander, using the suitcase like a battering ram against his midsection as she plowed into him.

"Anna, run!" she screamed as Xander tripped over his feet and fell backward. Her momentum carried her down with him and she landed on him with a hard thud.

"Run!" she screamed again. "Anna, go, goddammit!"

Anna ran for the stairs as Xander roared in anger and tossed Daisy off of him like she was a sack of flour. He scrambled into a standing position. Daisy popped to her feet, jumping onto his back and wrapping her arms around his neck.

Hissing and snarling, he staggered back and slammed her into the wall. Pain radiated through her body and she cried out as he slammed her up against the wall again. Her head smashed into the wall with enough force to dent the drywall. Her head went woozy and her ears rang. She lost her grip, slithering down the wall and staring wide-eyed at Xander as she wavered on the edge of unconsciousness. He whirled to face her, his body swelling and a golden beard growing on his face.

"You fucking bitch!" he snarled, his eyes glowing with hellish light. "I am going to rip your fucking face off and -"

He grunted with surprise, staggering forward when Anna jumped onto his back. She raked her nails across his forehead, and he roared with pain as blood appeared in thin lines across his flesh.

"Stay away from her!" Anna shrieked.

She tried to gouge at his eyes. Xander roared again before reaching around and grabbing Anna's hair. He pulled her off his body as she screamed in pain. He shook her roughly and threw her against the wall. She fell to the floor, landing face down with a horrible meaty thud and her thin body went limp.

"Anna? Sweetie?" Xander flipped her over. "Open your eyes, Anna. Open them!"

When she didn't move, he screamed, a high-pitched wail that was half human and half animal before turning to face Daisy.

"You did this!" he screamed at her. "You made me hurt my mate!"

He roared in anger and Daisy screamed as he lifted her to her feet. He wrapped his hand around her throat and squeezed, cutting off her air supply, as he raised his other hand. The nails were sharp claws and she stared in terror at them.

"I'm gonna tear you open," he growled. "I'm gonna rip open your stomach and feast on your guts you stupid, little -"

The low growl made him freeze. His face paled and the terrible, bruising pressure around Daisy's throat eased as Xander turned his head to stare at the massive lion standing in the hallway.

He released Daisy, a low whine slipping from his throat. The lion growled again and Xander took a step back from Daisy. "I didn't mean to hurt her. I didn't -"

Cooper took a step toward him and Xander howled piercingly before shifting. He turned and took off down the hallway. Coughing and gasping in air, Daisy watched through watery eyes as Cooper crouched and then leaped. The cheetah shifter was moving incredibly quick, but the hallway wasn't long enough for him to escape Cooper's attack. She felt more than heard the thud when he landed on Xander's back.

She closed her eyes, the sick feeling in her stomach deepening when Xander's howling and snarling cut out and Cooper roared in triumph. The sudden silence in the hallway was broken only by her ragged breathing.

The lion's head brushed against her shoulder, and his

warm breath washed over her face. Keeping her eyes closed, she reached out and buried her fingers in his heavy mane as tears leaked down her cheeks.

The lion purred and his head bumped against hers before he backed away and she lost her grip on his mane.

"My mate."

Cooper's voice was quiet and low. Her eyelids fluttered open and she stared up at him.

"Cooper," she rasped, forcing the words past her throbbing throat. "My mate."

His face twisted. She gasped when he leaned down and lifted her to her feet. He hugged her hard, picking her up until her feet dangled. She buried her face in his throat, kissing his warm skin as he purred to her.

"Are you all right, my mate?" he said.

"Yes. Is he dead?" She couldn't look down the hallway, didn't want to see his mangled body.

"He's alive," Cooper said.

She jerked in surprise and stared up at him. He brushed his mouth against hers as the wail of sirens filled the air. "For now. If we stop the bleeding. If we don't…"

He shrugged in obvious disinterest as Daisy gasped, "Anna!"

She wiggled out of Cooper's grip, relief flooding through her when she turned and saw Anna sitting up. Her hair was matted with blood, but she managed a small trembling smile. "I'm okay."

"Don't try and stand," Cooper said. "Stay still until we can get paramedics here."

Anna nodded and then said, "Dude, you might want to get some clothes on. If my dad comes home and sees you standing naked in the hallway, he's totally gonna fire you."

Daisy started to laugh. It hurt her throat and her head, but she couldn't stop. Anna joined in, the laughter spilling out of her slender body until she was holding her belly and groaning. "Stop making me laugh. Oh God, it hurts to laugh. It shouldn't hurt to laugh."

Still giggling, Daisy turned to Cooper. He was staring down at her and the love in his eyes made her heart knock against her ribcage. Her giggles died out and she cupped his face, rubbing her thumb along his cheekbone. "Thank you, my mate."

He swallowed hard. His eyes were rimmed in red and his voice was husky when he said, "I love you, Daisy."

"I love you too, Cooper."

EPILOGUE

"Daisy? I'm back." Cooper shut the front door and took off his boots.

"I'm in the bedroom," she called.

He walked upstairs, the scent of clean laundry mixing with the scent of his mate. Daisy was sitting cross-legged on his bed – no, *their* bed – surrounded by a pile of clean laundry. She folded one of his t-shirts as he sat on the bed beside her and picked up a shirt to fold.

"Do you care if I do your laundry?" she said as she folded a pair of socks and added them to the pile of folded ones. "I had some to do and figured I'd do yours too."

"No, I really appreciate it. Thank you." He grinned at her and she laughed.

"What?"

"This is very… domestic of you," he said.

She shrugged. "I like doing laundry. I find it relaxing."

"Well, don't feel like you have to do my laundry ever, but I appreciate that you did."

She leaned forward and kissed him. "Should I have mentioned that I'm a bit on the boring side? Spending my

Saturday afternoon doing laundry is not a rare occurrence for me."

"Considering I was working on a Saturday afternoon, I can't judge," Cooper said.

"How did it go?"

"Fine. I knew the police would have more questions, so I wasn't surprised when they asked me to come in. Things were a little chaotic on Thursday night."

"Yeah," Daisy said. Cooper studied the faint bruising on her throat. His lion was still pissed off that Cooper hadn't allowed him to kill Xander, but he would get over it. His lion's bloodlust for the cheetah who had hurt his mate had been high, but it didn't justify killing Xander. The cheetah shifter had been running from him and killing a man trying to flee wasn't Cooper's style.

"How do you feel, my mate?" he said.

"Exactly the same way I feel every time you ask me that question. Which, by the way, I think we're up to about seventy-eight times now."

He laughed and handed her the folded shirt to add to the pile before grabbing a pair of shorts. "It hasn't been that many times. It hasn't even been forty-eight hours and I'm worried you're having nightmares or -"

"I'm not. I'm," she paused in thought, "good. I mean, I'm not great or anything, but considering what happened and that my worse fear almost came true, I'm surprisingly good. Does that make sense?"

"Yes," he said. "You were so brave, baby." He purred to her and a soft smile crossed her face.

"You helped me to be brave. Just knowing that you think I'm brave made me feel that way even when I was terrified," she said. "I talked to Anna this morning. Tabitha left the hospital this morning. She's doing okay. She lives alone and doesn't have any family in the city, so David hired a private nurse to live with her until her concussion symptoms end. Oh, and Anna's mom arrived late last night. She really wants to meet both of us this week. I said we would love to have dinner."

"Sure." Cooper folded the last pair of shorts as Daisy slid off the bed and carried her clothes to the second dresser he'd brought in from the spare guest room. As she put them away, he piled his clothes at the end of the bed and grabbed his crochet from the bag on the floor next to the bed.

He started a new granny square as Daisy hung a couple of dresses in the closet. "Are you sure you don't mind sharing your closet? I can keep using the spare room closet."

"No," he said. "This is your room now too."

"You're so sweet." She hung a pair of dress pants next to the dresses and glanced at the square he was working on. "That's looking good."

"Thanks. Ten more to go and then I can start putting it together. Wes's birthday is next month so I need to get the damn thing done."

"Hey, do you think Wes and Eleanor were acting weird at Landon's?"

He paused with his crochet hook stuck in the granny square. "What do you mean?"

"I don't know. They both just seemed weird. I mean, I didn't see Eleanor for very long before you made me go to the hospital, but something seemed off about her. Did Wes seem all right?"

"Honestly, everything was so chaotic, I didn't notice anything." It wasn't exactly a lie. He hadn't noticed if Wes was off, but it had nothing to do with the general chaos and everything to do with Daisy. He'd been almost frantic to get her to the hospital, to make sure she was truly all right. Wes could have been walking around naked and singing opera for all he would have noticed.

Daisy grabbed his pile of t-shirts from the bed.

"I can put those away," Cooper said.

"I don't mind." She opened the drawer and placed them neatly inside before returning and picking up the stack of his boxer briefs. "I think I'll text Eleanor and see if she wants to have dinner this week. Just to check on her."

"Whatever you want, my mate." He'd split the yarn and he scowled and pulled out the stitch before grabbing the loop with the hook again.

"Cooper?"

"Hmm?" Christ, he'd split the yarn again. If he kept this up, he'd never be finished Wes's blanket in time.

"Cooper, look at me."

He glanced up, his stomach dropping when he saw the small velvet box in Daisy's hand. Shit, why had he hidden it in his fucking underwear drawer? It was such a goddamn cliché.

Daisy's cheeks were red, and he could smell her excitement and her nervousness.

"Is this what I think it is?"

He thought briefly of lying and his lion growled at him.

We do not lie to our mate!

He set his crochet on his lap. "Yes."

She carried the box to the bed and sat down beside him, staring intently at him as she held the box in a tight fist. "When did you buy this?"

He tugged at the ball of yarn. "Uh, what does it matter?"

"When, Cooper?"

"Two weeks after you started working at the office."

Her jaw dropped and she stared first at the box and then at him. "You're kidding me?"

"No," he said. "I know how that makes me sound, but I... my lion made me do it."

"It was only your lion who wanted to buy me an engagement ring?"

"Shit," he said. "No, it wasn't only my goddamn lion."

To his immense relief, a smile broke out on Daisy's face. "I can't believe you bought an engagement ring two weeks after meeting me. Wait," a horrified look crossed her face, "it is for me, right?"

He bellowed laughter before dropping his crochet over the side of the bed and hauling her into his lap. "Of course it's for you. Who else would it be for?"

"Well, I realized I was being pretty assumptive. When were you planning on asking me to marry you?" Daisy said.

He shrugged. "In six months or so."

"Six months?" She looked a little annoyed.

"Three months?"

"Three," she said. "You're gonna wait three months to ask your mate to marry you? That seems... rude."

He laughed and purred to her. "How about a week. I'll take you out for a romantic dinner, we can go for a moonlit walk on the beach after dinner, and I'll get down on one knee, quote a few romantic poems and then ask you to marry me."

"That does sound very romantic." She toyed with the box in her hand. "Or... you could straight up ask me right now and then we could spend the rest of the afternoon having hot and dirty sex."

He grinned and took the box from her, popping it open so she could see the ring. "Will you marry me, Daisy?"

"Yes, Cooper, I will," she said with a soft and sexy smile.

He slid the ring onto her finger, snapped the box shut and tossed it on the floor. "Now, about that hot and dirty sex..."

DARK OF NIGHT EXCERPT

SHADOW SECURITY SERIES, BOOK THREE

Eleanor hung her damp towel on the hook. She smoothed her t-shirt, tugged self-consciously at her shorts, and ran her hand through her wet hair.

Stop stalling and just go out there already.

She stared at her chest. It was obvious she wasn't wearing a bra, but she'd be damned if she put one on to go to bed. She had to wear the torture device all day, she wasn't wearing it all night too. Besides, the look of unease bordering on panic that crossed Wes's face when the motel clerk confessed the room booking error, made it more than clear that he wouldn't exactly be seducing her tonight. Hell, she'd be lucky if he didn't decide to sleep in the car.

She balled up her dirty clothes, tucked them under her arm, and opened the bathroom door. Wes was sitting at the small table, staring at his phone, and he didn't look up as she stuffed her clothes into the side pocket of her small suitcase.

She sat cross-legged on the bed, plucking her t-shirt from her chest. "Bathroom's all yours."

"Thanks." Without looking at her, Wes grabbed his toiletry bag and clean clothes from his suitcase and disappeared into the bathroom.

She shoved her pillow behind her back and leaned against the headboard. Her stomach growled loudly. She was regretting her decision to skip eating in favour of sleep. Especially since she was certain she wouldn't get much sleep, not with Wes lying in the bed next to her.

The shower turned on and she immediately had a vision of a naked Wes in the shower. Not that she knew what a naked Wes looked like, but she could imagine it. Could imagine it in lust rattling detail, as a matter of fact.

She studied the bathroom door. What would Wes do if she popped into the bathroom and offered to wash his back for him?

So, now you want to be arrested for sexual harassment?

Wes wanted her. There was no way a man could kiss a woman like he'd kissed her, no way a man could say the dirty delicious stuff he'd said to her, if he didn't want to have sex with her. He just needed the tiniest push in that direction.

Eleanor, no. You're acting desperate and gross. Wes has made it clear he's not going to sleep with you.

The reminder that Wes had rejected her rather soundly, killed her lust. Starving and feeling sorry for herself, she slid off the bed and rooted through her purse for some money. She couldn't sit here and listen to Wes in the shower, knowing she'd never see him naked. She wasn't into that kind of mental torture. She'd grab them some food from the vending machine. It was better than nothing.

Holding the cash and the door cardkey, she stuck her feet into her sandals and left the room. The vending machine was near the office and she walked past the other first floor rooms, the warm wind blowing her wet hair back from her face.

She studied the contents of the vending machine before buying a couple of sodas, two packages of those crackers and fake cheese abominations, and a couple of chocolate bars for dessert.

Juggling the drinks, the food, the cardkey, and her change, Eleanor walked back to their room. She stood in front of the door, trying to decide the best way to get the cardkey to the lock without dropping everything.

The door suddenly whipped open and she squeaked in surprise, stumbling back when a wild-eyed and dripping wet Wes shouted, "Eleanor!"

"What?" she said. The sodas were starting to slip, and she squeaked again when Wes grabbed her arms and pulled her into the room, slamming the door behind her. The food and drinks tumbled to the floor and she stared at him in confusion. "What's wrong?"

"You can't just leave the room like that, Eleanor." Wes's voice was weird. Higher than normal, like it was on the verge of cracking. "Where were you?"

"Getting us some dinner." She pointed to the food on the floor. "Why are you freaking…"

Her voice died in her throat and her irritation that the soda would probably be too fizzy disappeared.

"Wes," she said.

He ran a hand through his wet hair, pacing with short jerky strides back and forth in front of her. "You can't leave the room without telling me. Do you understand? It's late and dark, and who the fuck knows what type of people are lurking around this place."

"Wes," she said.

"You could have been kidnapped," he said. "Did you

think about that possibility? Did you even take your mace with you?"

"Wes," she said.

"I gave you that mace for a reason, Eleanor. You're supposed to carry it with you at all times, not just when you feel like it or when it's convenient for you. Even if you're -"

"WES!"

"What?" He stopped pacing, annoyance on his face, and hands on his hips. "What, Eleanor?"

"You're naked."

"Dark of Night" will be available in 2021

ABOUT THE AUTHOR

Ramona Gray is a Canadian romance author. She currently lives in Alberta with her awesome husband and her super cute dog. She's addicted to home improvement shows, good coffee, and reading and writing about the steamier moments in life.

For more information about Ramona, check out her website at

www.ramonagray.ca

facebook.com/RamonaGrayBooks

twitter.com/RamonaGrayBooks

instagram.com/ramonagrayauthor

amazon.com/Ramona-Gray/e/B00OD26SAM

bookbub.com/profile/ramona-gray

The Welder

The Electrician

The Landscaper

The Firefighter

The Cop

The Paramedic

Working Men Series Bundles

Working Men Series Books One to Three

Working Men Series Books Four to Six

Working Men Series Books Seven to Nine

Other World Series

The Vampire's Kiss (Book One)

The Vampire's Love (Book Two)

The Shifter's Mate (Book Three)

Rescued By The Wolf (Book Four)

Claiming Quinn (Book Five)

Choosing Rose (Book Six)

Elena Unbound (Book Seven)

Other World Series Box Sets

Other World Series Books One to Three

Other World Series Books Four to Six